LITTLE VOICE LOST

DI RITA GUPTA MURDER MYSTERY

BOOK 3

SAM CARTER

CHAPTER 1

Nelly Crosby would always remember the moment she stopped living. She breathed, walked, mumbled, but her life stopped that second, on that fateful day.

It was a nice day, as it happened. The summer sun played hide and seek with clouds, and the views over the cliffs out to the sea were gorgeous. The dog, Pike, was barking, probably asking Matt to come out and play.

Matt should be at school, but he had a tummy ache in the morning, and then vomited once. He didn't want to go, and Nelly had relented, seeing he wasn't feeling great. The boy was still in bed and Nelly went upstairs to check on him. He was drowsy, with his eyes closed. She passed a hand over his head, and took his temperature. He wasn't hot. He wasn't sick. He was just tired from the vomiting that morning.

"Why don't you get up darling?" Nelly coaxed. "I've made some fresh apple juice."

Matt yawned, and then turned around, still wanting to sleep. Nelly patted his shoulder, and kissed the back of his head. Maybe he just needed a good rest.

Nelly went back downstairs, and into the garden. She threw the ball at Pike, who ran after it, chasing. From inside, Nelly heard the phone ring. She was hanging out clothes on the line, so she tried to ignore it. But it kept ringing. Sighing, she went inside, and answered.

From the patio door, she could see the open land behind her garden, which turned into dense woods. That stretched out like a bumpy green carpet all the way to the sandy shores of the bay. Seagulls drew question marks in the blue sky, their lonely cries carried over in the wind.

Nelly answered the phone. It was Angie, her neighbour three doors down. Nelly could hear Angie's one month old son crying.

"He's not settling," Angie said. "I've given him Calpol, but he's still grumpy. Not feeding either."

Angie was alone at home, like Nelly. Unlike Nelly, whose husband was at work, Angie was a single mother. She had a six-year-old girl as well.

"Do you want me to come over?" Nelly asked, looking out the window. She saw the ball in the air, and then Pike, running after it.

"Do you mind? I'm not sure what's going on with him."

Angie thought quickly. She didn't want to leave Matt alone for long. He was capable enough, bless him, but he was still a little boy. It was mid-morning. She was only going three doors down. Theirs was a safe, quiet neighbourhood. Not much happened around here, and she would be back soon.

"I've got Matt, but I'll pop around quickly."

"Thanks, Nel."

Nelly went upstairs. Matt was still in bed. She knelt down and spoke to him softly.

"I'm going next door to Angie's," she said. "Will you be okay?"

Matt didn't respond. Nelly made sure he was alright, and decided to let him sleep.

Nelly hurried down the road to Angie's. Angie opened the door, and from her flushed face, Nelly could see she was troubled. She followed Angie inside, and took little Tommy from her lap. The baby did have a high fever, and only settled when on Angie's lap. As soon as he was put down in his cot, he screamed.

"I've changed him, fed, Calpol, the whole lot. What should I do?"

Nelly held little Tommy for a while, but he didn't settle in her arms. "I think you should take him to the doctors."

"I called but there's no appointment."

"Then you might have to take him to the hospital. Given he's only a year old, I don't think you'll be waiting long."

Nelly looked at Angie hopefully. "Can I leave Lucy with you?"

"Yes, sure."

"Ok. Let me get her ready." Angie went upstairs to Lucy's room, taking baby Tommy with her. Nelly went outside and lit a cigarette. When Angie came down, she helped her out with the baby. Angie walked to the bus stop, and Nelly went back to her house with Lucy.

"Where's Matt?" Lucy asked, when they were inside.

"He's sleeping, why don't you play in the garden, and I'll see if I can bring him downstairs."

Nelly noticed the patio door was open, and she couldn't remember if she had shut it or not. It didn't matter, as Matt was upstairs. She went up the stairs, and into his room. The door was open, and the bed was empty. Nelly didn't panic.

She went into the bathroom, and opened the door. The bathroom was also empty. Nelly stared at it, and with the first jolt of panic stabbing inside her, she moved the bath curtains. The bath was also empty. She went into the master bedroom, and then checked the smaller guest bedroom. Both were empty.

"Matt!" She called out. She knelt on the carpet and looked under her bed. There was an old suitcase, but no child. Nelly ran into the smaller bedroom and had a look under the bed again. Nothing there either.

She ran into every room upstairs, checking the airing cupboard as well. The windows were shut. There was no sign of Matt. Her heart rate had gone nuclear, and she couldn't breathe. She ran down the stairs, and checked the downstairs bathroom. She had definitely locked the front door when she went out, she remembered that even through her panic. She had used her keys to get in.

She checked the kitchen, and every nook and cranny on the ground floor.

She rushed out into the garden, and grabbed Lucy by the shoulders. The girl stopped, and looked up at her, scared.

"Was Matt out here? Have you seen him?"

"No, I haven't."

Gasping, and an emptiness spreading across the chest, Nelly checked the garden shed. The dog was in the shed, sniffing around. "Where's Matt?" Nelly wailed, and the dog looked up at her curiously.

She rushed out, and checked the narrow side entrance. The gate was locked. There was no sign of Matt anywhere.

She ran around the small garden. It was an average forty feet long stretch, with a two-metre-long fence at the back.

"Matt?" She cried out. "Matt?" Her words were lost in the wind from the sea.

Could he have gone out the front? But she had locked the door.

Her rational mind tried to tell her Matt could've climbed the fence. There was an apple tree in one corner. Nelly went to the tree, and heaved herself up. The lower branch didn't get anywhere near the top.

"Matt?" She screamed again, her voice now hoarse. She looked around the garden one more time. She checked in the shed, pulling out the garden tools, moving the lawnmower in desperation.

She stood in the middle of the garden, tears now streaming down her eyes.

"Matt?" She screamed. Only the seagulls answered, their forlorn cries distant, an echo of her despair.

Nelly told Lucy to stay indoors, and she locked the patio door, and the front door. Then she ran around the block, and to the path that skirted the rear of the terrace. The land was open here, falling out to the woods beyond her. Her last hope was that Matt had climbed over the fence, and fallen to the other side.

She ran up and down the path, but there was no sign of Matt. She ran towards the woods, each breath like fire in her lungs. She held her hands as she surveyed the wide, wild trees and gorse. How would Matt run here, and get lost?

She screamed his name once again, then her knees buckled. She kept herself upright somehow, and ran back to the house. Lucy was inside, now wide eyed with fear. With ice cold fingers, Nelly grabbed her phone from the kitchen counter, and dialled for the police

CHAPTER 2

Detective Inspector Rita Gupta sipped her glass of wine, and stared back at her dinner companion, Jack Banford.

"So, what did you think of my dad?" She asked, lightly. She was now back in touch with her long-estranged father, Jay. That was fortunate, as her mother was long dead. Rita had no siblings, no other family, apart from Jay and his second wife, Anna, and their son, Aaron.

Jack took his time to answer. His dark brown eyes glinted, and his handsome square jawed face moved as he chewed on a crisp.

"I like him. He's trying hard to make up for the lost years. He feels bad about it."

Rita knew that as well. Jay had cooked every night, even hoovered the flat. She couldn't ask for more.

"What happened at the end makes me feel even worse, in that case," Rita sighed.

"That wasn't your fault."

"No? A mad man wanting my life ends up taking it out on my dad. After I reunite with him all these years later. If I wasn't here, would that happen to him?"

Rita and Jay had got into a lot of trouble recently, when a crazed psychopath got too close for comfort.

"Baptism by fire?" Jack raised his eyebrows, eyes dancing with mischief. "Only joking. He won't hold that against you. It could've happened anytime, anywhere. It's just bad luck, that's all. And besides, it got you closer, didn't it?"

Rita wasn't sure if violently traumatic times got people closer together, even if they came out of it alive. She worried that Jay might get scared of ever coming back to Scarborough. She wouldn't forgive herself if that happened. Jack reached out and touched her hand. His fingers were warm, but he slowly withdrew his hand. He had noticed the concerned expression on her face.

"He doesn't mind. If you ask me, he was glad he was there. That meant a great deal to him."

Rita sighed, and nodded. "Yes, I guess that makes sense."

They drove home after dinner. Jack dropped Rita off to her flat on North Marine Road, on the south side of Scarborough Bay. He came out of the car and walked her to the door. Rita felt his presence, and the familiar conflict reared its head. Getting romantically entangled with Jack right now was not on her agenda. But she couldn't deny they were attracted to each other.

Jack had been her first boyfriend, and after two decades they had met again, by accident. Second chances do happen in life, Rita had realised. What she chose to do with it was another matter entirely. She could only go where her heart took her, and currently, the road ahead was shrouded in mist. She was happy to wait and bide her time.

She put the key in the lock and turned. Jack's face was half hidden in the shadows. Rita didn't want the silence to drag on. Jack had never made it clear exactly what he wanted, apart from friendship. But she had seen the look in his eyes. She knew he was also playing for time, and they were both playing it safe.

"Goodnight then," Rita said lightly. "Thanks for dinner."

"You're welcome." He sighed. "Catch at you at work sometime, I guess."

"Yes." Rita saw Jack in the station often enough, when he came to defend or prosecute a client. Jack was a partner in Scarborough's biggest law firm. He had stayed in this small sea side town, and done well for himself.

He stepped back, and suddenly she felt a mad, insane urge to grab him, feel his strong arms around her. A hunger to feel his lips, touch him, overcame her. Her hands became fists at her side. She was glad it was dark.

Jack walked back to his car, and the moment lingered, then passed. Rita waved at him as he put the window down to say goodbye. Then she went inside, shut the door, and leaned against it, her head sinking over her chest.

She put the lights on, and went around her flat, checking the rooms. She wasn't paranoid, but what happened a few weeks ago had put her on edge. She locked her bedroom door when she slept.

She had bad dreams about the man coming after her father. But it was the only place she could call home. And she couldn't deny the location was lovely. Perched on a hill, overlooking the harbour and sea. She always had this dream of living in a house by the sea, and fate had thrown her a surprise. Most of her life, she didn't have much going for her. She was glad she grabbed the opportunity to live here when it came her way.

Rita was shutting the kitchen windows when her eyes fell on the radio she'd left on the counter. A red dot was flashing on the top. She wasn't on duty, but she'd forgotten to leave the radio at work today. She flicked the radio on, and then turned the black knob on the top to get the right frequency. A male voice squawked from the speaker.

"All units alert. Missing eight-year-old IC1 child, four feet six, blond hair, last seen wearing a grey top and blue jeans. Repeat, all units alert."

Rita frowned and picked up the phone to ring the North Yorkshire Police switchboard. She was put through to Inspector Steven Bennett, the duty uniforms officer.

"We've been looking for the lad all day, guv," Steve said. He was a veteran of the NYP, and he sounded tired. "The family lives in Osgodby, by Clayton Bay."

"That's outside Scarborough, right?" Rita had a vague memory of visiting Clayton Bay when she was a teenager. It was quieter than Scarborough, from what she remembered, if she had the place right.

"Yes, it's about twenty miles down south on the A165 from here. The lad lives with his parents on a street just off Osgodby Lane. I've been to see the parents. They're stressed obviously. The neighbours are helping."

"When was it reported?"

"Around 11 am today. We sent two units down, and now all our units are in the area. The Coastguard's been alerted, and a helicopter swept the beach. No sign of the boy as yet. The neighbours are asking around, with the uniforms."

“Have you told them to keep the news out of social media?” Rita was already thinking of journalists camped outside the parents home. Hopefully, they would find the boy soon. By tomorrow it would all blow over. But if not…

“I have, but you know what people are like in this day and age. I wouldn’t be surprised if one of the neighbours has shared already.”

“Keep searching, I guess. Do you have enough units? I can always ask the D Sup to release more from Leeds and York.”

“If you wouldn’t mind, please guv, that would be great.”

Rita hung up, realising she didn’t particularly want to speak to Nicole Perkins, the venomous, pint-sized harridan who was her boss. But she had no choice. She sighed, and pulled out her phone. Nicole answered on the seventh ring, when Rita was about to hang up.

“This better be good, DI Gupta,” Nicole said before she said hello. Her voice was short, clipped, and impatient.

“Sorry to bother you, ma’am. A nine-year-old boy is missing from Osgodby. Our uniformed units have reached capacity. I want permission to ask for more units from York and Leeds.”

Nicole was silent for a few seconds. Rita could imagine her levers clicking, wondering if Rita was trying to get one over her. To say Nicole was paranoid was putting it mildly.

“Very well,” she sighed at the end. “Call them up and give my name as clearance. And I want a full report first thing tomorrow morning.”

“Copy that, ma’am.”

CHAPTER 3

Rita got up before the alarm at six am the next morning. Sleep had been disturbed, and she had a persistent dream about a brother she never had. He was a little eight-year-old boy, and she saw her mother trying to pull the boy towards her, but he kept biting her hand, and running away. Rita tossed and turned, but the dream kept coming back. With it, the endless pain of her mother's loss, and what she had discovered when she found Clara's body.

In the end, she had given up trying to sleep. When the nightmares sunk claws into her flesh, the only way to get rid of them was to get up and get out. It was five in the morning, and the sun was still a shy, pink presence over the sea, far away. She changed into her running gear, and dragged herself out, even though her body protested.

It was always the same. The first two minutes felt like twenty. But she got to the slope that went down to the beach, and slowly, it got easier. She tried to keep her mind a blank, and the knots inside her loosened. Someone had told her once running, cycling, or any physical activity became a form of meditation. She believed that now. She didn't have time to meditate – or so she told herself. But running worked for her. The physical stress took away her mental stress. It became therapeutic.

She stopped on the rocks overlooking the beach, panting. The tide was still out, the sea grey, the waves receded from the beach. A man was walking with his dog. The horizon was still pink at the rims, and the vast dome of the sky was lighting up in shades of gold and blue. The bare ribbed cliffs surrounded the sea like the hands of a skeleton. The waters were silent and watchful, the waves gentle.

It was close to six am by the time she got back. She checked her radio and phone - still no word on the missing boy. No body sighted – that would be a tragedy, but at least it was news. The lack of any finding was not good.

As Rita showered, she tried to think of the last time a child had vanished from Scarborough. She couldn't remember. It would've stayed on her mind, because a missing child would be national news, if the child hadn't been found after three to four days.

Rita was at her desk by seven thirty. She still took public transport, a habit from her life in London. In Scarborough, she had replaced the underground with the bus.

She picked up a coffee and yogurt from the canteen, although her eyes did fall on the bacon baps. Bacon tasted nicer up here and she had to force herself to look away. At her desk, she opened her laptop and focused on the case. Uniforms had taken interviews and put up basic information about the family.

Matt Crosby lived with his parents, Nelly and Stuart. Nelly was a housewife and Stuart worked in the cement factory nearby. Stuart was a middle manager, overseeing the work of a team. Neither parent had a police record. Matt was the only child in the family. He was doing well at school, there were no concerns academically or socially. He wasn't bullied, and didn't miss days.

Stuart was Matt's step dad. Matt's real father lived in York, and Nelly had supplied his details. His name was Mark Aldridge, and he worked as a security guard at York University. Mark wasn't aware of what had happened. Rita checked Mark's name on the national police and crime database and found nothing. She entered the names of all three parents on the Home Office Large Major Enquiry System, or HOLMES, as it was better known, the supercomputer that hosted the information of all criminals worldwide.

None of the three parents turned up on any of the databases. Nelly had mentioned that Mark lived with his girlfriend, and visited them every fortnight to spend time with Matt. Matt had also gone to York to spend weekends with his father.

Rita checked the reports from the duty Uniforms team, and the Coastguards. Two uniforms teams had swelled to four, and that's all Scarborough had. The Coastguards had helped on the streets as well, until Rita had called for more support. But that didn't arrive till late last night. Two more uniformed teams had joined from York. The search pretty much died out in the evening, but Rita knew they would be out in force today.

The Coastguard helicopter had looked out ten miles to sea, in the hope of finding a body. They used ultrasound maps and infra-red, to see if there was a heat spark anywhere in the water. Rita knew it was extremely difficult for a little boy's body to give out much heat, but it was still worth a try. Her heart constricted when she thought of the little boy being swept out to sea. She also knew it was almost impossible for him to end up by the sea by himself. The house he lived in wasn't that close to the beach. There were woods, and a big dual carriageway in between.

She was about to pull up a map of Osgodby Lane, when the door opened, and DC Maggie Long entered with DC Rizwan Ahmed.

"Now then, guv," Maggie grinned at her. Rizwan said hello, and the two sat down at their desks.

"Alright, what did you two think about the missing boy, Matt Crosby?"

Maggie shook her head. "Can't believe it, guv. Nowt like that's ever happened around here. Not in my time anyway."

Maggie looked at Rizwan, who agreed. Rita asked them, "What's Osgodby like? There's a nice beach there, right? Went there once as a child, I think."

"Yes, Clayton Bay," Maggie said. "It's gorgeous. My parents drive down there sometimes to go for a walk when the tide's down."

Rizwan said, "There's a lot of caravan parks around there as well. It's a nice coastline. There's a bird watcher's paradise at the Bempton Cliffs. The coast stretched down south all the way to Hull and the Humber River."

"Thanks for the geography lesson," Rita grinned. "Now that you mention it, I remember going to the Bempton Cliffs on a school trip. I think so, anyway. Long time ago."

"Aye, I did that too," Rizwan said.

The door opened and the Detective Sergeant, Richard Staveley walked in. He was a short, podgy man with a pot belly, and an excellent detective. He greeted everyone and sat down at his desk.

"Did I miss much? Any sign of the missing boy?"

"Nope, none so far," Rita said. "The D Sup let me authorise more uniform units from York last night. Hopefully we find something today." She looked back at the two constables.

"Was Scene of Crime down there yesterday?"

"Shola didn't have time, she was at a robbery crime scene. She will go down there today. The boy vanished from his house, right?" Shola Adebayo was the head of Scene of Crime in Scarborough and Whitby.

"Yes, that's right." Rita folded her hands, placed her elbows on the desk, and rested her chin on her hands.

"He was in his room upstairs, asleep. That's when his mother last saw him. It was about ten am. The garden has a fence at the rear, but it can be climbed easily. Less than two metres height. Mother went to the neighbour's house, three doors down. She locked the front door. When she came back the boy was gone. Ergo, he could only have left through the back fence. There was no sign of struggle."

Richard said, "What sort of struggle would there be? He's a little boy. If someone had climbed over the fence, and knocked him out with a blow to the head?"

"There was a dog," Maggie said. "Not a big dog, but it would have made a fuss. Tried to bite the intruder."

Rizwan added, "The dog could be silenced with food, or some other treat."

Rita looked at the report on her screen. "When the mother came back, the dog was in the shed. But when she left, the dog was playing with the ball in the garden. I think someone opened the shed door to put the dog in there."

She rose and went to the white board. She took a black marker pen and started a timeline. She wrote ten am and then circled it. After a gap, she wrote 10.30-10.40 am and then circled that as well.

"The mother, Nelly, came back at around 10.30. Matt was gone. Which means if Matt was abducted, then the intruder had half an hour to climb the back fence, take Matt, and then climb back over and run away with the boy." She raised her eyebrows. "Not enough time."

Richard shook his head. "I've got a ten-year-old boy. This wouldn't be easy. Far too many chances of things going wrong. The boy would fight, although Matt is eight and he couldn't exactly fight off a grown man. If we assume it's a man. I think it has to be, otherwise, how will they get over the fence, jump down, and run away with Matt?"

Rita said, "Assuming again, that they did run away. What if they had a car waiting on the other side of the fence? There's nothing there but open meadows, which then become woodlands."

Rizwan said, "A car makes more sense as a getaway vehicle. I wonder if there was a driver, in that case. Makes life a lot easier, right?"

"Good point. A driver would be useful, unless Matt was knocked out or unconscious."

Rita pursed her lips together. "Nelly returns and looks all over, she also checks the back, and the meadows, according to her statement. No sign of Matt. None of the neighbours saw anything. No one left from the front door. There was no car in the drive. If any of the neighbours happened to look out the back., might they have seen the abductor? Or Matt?"

Rizwan said, "But so far, no witnesses."

Rita shook her head slowly. "The abductor planned this. Maybe he got lucky with Nelly going to see the baby at her neighbour's house, but he knew Nelly would be alone at home at that time. And most of the households would have at least one parent, if not both. It was a school day, and Matt didn't go as he wasn't feeling great that morning."

"He kept the house under surveillance," Richard said.

Rita pointed a finger at him. "Excellent point. The neighbours might have seen a new car, or someone walking up and down over the last few days. Let's make sure we ask during the door to door."

Maggie was hunched over her laptop, and she raised her head.

"There's a path that skirts around the back of the houses, before the meadows open up. That's the path Nelly ran down, looking for Matt. A car could easily turn off the road, and park right behind the house. No one would see it. Osgodby Lane is a quiet place, no one would pay attention to a car joining the road from that path."

Maggie turned the laptop around so the others could see. Rita peered at the screen, at the row of terraced houses, and the cars on the road. It was a live map image, and there wasn't anyone on the street. The waters of Cayton Bay glinted at the back. The residential streets joined a main road that went down to a roundabout, from where the bigger A165 swept down south to the remainder of the coastal towns and villages.

A memory flashed across Rita's mind. Driving down a coastal road, the summer sun spilling inside the car, radio on loud, and singing along with her mother. Clara took them on drives on Sunday, and they found a beach where they sat down to have a picnic. The sun beams pierced through her heart, leaving her forlorn again. She would always miss her mother, and miss the years Clara couldn't live.

She forced her mind back to the present. "Eastfield seems like a bigger village," Rita said, pointing to the cluster of houses behind Osgodby.

"Yes, it's larger," Richard said. "And it's got Seamer next to it, with the railway station. These three villages cluster together in the south. Are you thinking of where the abductor might have lived? If he was local, I mean?"

"Exactly," Rita nodded. "He has to be local to carry out surveillance on the family. Is there any CCTV around there?"

"Unfortunately, no," Rizwan said. "That's the first thing I looked at." He grinned at Maggie whose mouth dropped open.

"Shut your face," Maggie said. "I told you there was no CCTV, after I checked with Traffic upstairs."

"Good to see you're learning," Rizwan grinned, pleased at the outburst. Maggie rolled her eyes and pulled the laptop back to herself.

"No CCTV," Rita said. "But there will be cameras on the main road, and on the A165, definitely."

"There's also the A64 which goes in the other direction," Richard said, pointing at the map on the wall. He went up to it, and put his finger on the long A road that snaked its way inland, to the east of North Yorkshire. "The A64 goes right through Eastfield and to York. That's also a potential escape route for the abductor."

"Or up north towards Whitby," Maggie said.

Rita was looking at the map on the wall, chewing her bottom lip. "If I was him, I would avoid the bigger roads. They have cameras. The smaller country roads don't and there's hundreds around here." She went to the map, and her forefinger zig zagged across some of the numerous lanes that covered the countryside like loops of spaghetti.

"In which case," Richard said, his voice darker now, "We have no hope of finding where he could be."

“Maybe, or maybe not. He had to take a turning somewhere. But we need to find the getaway car first.” Rita rubbed her hands together. “Too many ifs and buts, and not enough evidence. Let’s get cracking, shall we? Who do we have at the family home?”

Maggie said. “The parents, and the FLO, Lucy Kirby, is already there.”

“Good,” Rita said. The Family Liaison Officer or FLO was an indispensable support to the family in these situations.

“Richard and I will head down there. You two get all the CCTV footage from the main road, of cars turning into their street, and leaving, yesterday morning.”

“And hopefully,” She added, “Matt will turn up at some point today, in any case.” Even as she said the words, Rita knew they sounded hollow. Missing children, if found, were reunited with their parents within a few hours. Matt was gone overnight, and with every passing second, the chances of finding him grew slimmer.

“Let’s go,” Rita sighed, heading for the door.

CHAPTER 4

The Crosby's lived in Seaview Avenue, a street of detached bungalows and single-family homes off the winding Osgodby Lane. Richard parked the car outside number 68, behind the squad car. Rita was relieved to see the absence of media vans, and reporters. If word had spread, it still hadn't knocked on the radar of some local reporter. She knew it was only a matter of time.

Richard said hello to the uniformed sergeant who got out of his car to meet them.

"The FLO's in there with the family," The man said. His name badge had the word Carlisle printed on it.

"Any news from the neighbours?" Rita asked.

"We did a door to door in the morning. Nowt to report as yet," Carlisle said. "There's a neighbour's social media group, and I've sent your DC's a link to it just now. They can join it."

Rita nodded her thanks, and they went inside. Lucy, the FLO, opened the door. She showed them into the living room.

Nelly was sat on the couch, staring out the window. She wore a loose pink baggy top, and jogging bottoms. She looked up at them and her dead, cold eyes flickering to life slowly as Rita and Richard entered the room.

It was a cosy living room, TV in one corner, bookshelves in the alcoves, with family photos in front of the books. A thick pile light grey carpet covered the floor. The smell of cigarette smoke was strong, and although the windows were open, Rita realised Nelly had given up going outside to smoke. Matt wasn't here, and she probably didn't care.

"Who are yer? Have you heard about Matt?" Nelly sat up straighter. She looked at them with a wild expression. Rita knew that look. She had dealt with a case like this once. Nelly was swinging from despair to hope like a drowning woman clutching at a straw.

"Not yet," Rita said. "But we are looking, and we will not leave any stone unturned. You have my word on that." She showed Nelly her warrant card. "I'm DI Rita Gupta, and this is Sergeant Richard Staveley."

Rita sat next to Nelly, facing her. A smell of stale sweat and cigarette smoke came from the woman. Dark bags sagged under her eyes, they seemed to drag her face down, down turning her lips.

"Why are you here? Shouldn't you be out looking for Matty?" Nelly's voice was high pitched, with a tinge of panic.

"I need to ask you a few questions. I know this is difficult for you, but your help will be invaluable to find your son."

The door opened, and a man came in. He was thin and sallow, his bony shoulders hunched in, with a large head that looked disproportional to the rest of his body. He had a light stubble on his cheeks, and the look on his face was a mix of fear and anxiety. He wasn't a good-looking man. His lips were thin, like his jaws, and his cheeks were sunken.

His dark eyes swivelled from Rita to Richard, then to Nelly. Rita noted Nelly averted her eyes when the man looked at her. The man came inside the room, and stood in the middle, staring at them.

Rita said, "You must be Stuart Crosby, Matt's step-father?"

"Aye. Who wants to know, like?" Stuart shoved his hands inside his pockets, and stared at Rita.

Rita introduced herself for the second time. "We were just asking your wife to describe in her own words what happened."

"Christ Almighty," Stuart huffed, and rocked on his heels. "Haven't you heard it enough times already?" He glanced at Nelly, who was staring at the floor.

"Yes, but we still need to hear it from Nelly. In fact, we can start with you. Where were you yesterday when Matt disappeared?"

"I was at work." Stuart took his hands out of his pockets and shoved them back in again.

"Why don't you sit down?" Richard asked. He shifted on the sofa, which was opposite the sofa where Rita and Nelly were sat. Stuart sat down. His feet moved, and so did his hands. His nervousness was a contrast to Nelly's quiet despair.

"When did you go to work?" Rita asked.

"I leave at seven in the morning, and get to the factory for around half seven. I'm home by around five."

"You work at the Parsons Cement Factory outside Eastfield, is that correct?"

"Yes."

"And you stayed at work the whole day yesterday?"

Stuart shook his head. "We had to meet a client in Shipton. A farmer who's building a new shed for his cattle. I went there with a colleague."

Rita glanced at Richard, as she didn't know where Shipton was. Richard shrugged.

"Where is Shipton?"

Stuart said, "It's a village north of Scarborough. Takes about an hour from here."

"When did you leave the factory, and then return?"

"I used the company car." Stuart frowned, trying to remember. "I left around ten, and was back by twelve."

"And when did you hear from Nelly?"

Rita glanced at Nelly, who was now looking at Stuart. Husband and wife shared a silent communication.

"It was around half eleven," Stuart said softly. "At first I couldn't hear what she was saying, she was crying so much. Then I realised. I came straight home. It was about mid-day. I looked around the back, and we drove around. The neighbours came around to help. The police also arrived."

Stuart's head sank down on his chest. His hand cradled his forehead, and he remained like that.

"Thank you," Rita said. She turned to Nelly. "Now, please tell me what happened."

Nelly recounted the events, her words hesitant, voice thick with sorrow.

Rita waited till she had finished. "Has Matt ever run away before?"

The question seemed to shock Nelly. Her eyes widened, and her jaw went lax. "No. Why would he?"

Stuart stirred, but Rita ignored him. She kept her eyes on Nelly. "No reason. I'm just asking."

"No. He was happy, he didn't have any problems."

"And everything was fine at school? As far as you know?"

"Yes, it was all good." Nelly frowned at Rita. "What're you trying to say?"

Before Rita could answer, Stuart snapped. "There was nothing wrong with Matt. He was happy here, and thriving. We don't like what you're trying to suggest."

Rita stared at him for a while. "These are just routine questions, that's all. We have to cover all bases as you can imagine." She paused and cleared her throat, letting the tension in the room die down.

"When did you last see Matt?" Rita asked Stuart.

"The night before. He was going to sleep, and I tucked him in." His jaws clamped, and his nostrils quivered, then turned red. "I didn't know that was the last time I'd see him."

"It won't be," Richard said. "We will find your son. Please remain positive, however hard it might be." He glanced at Rita and she nodded.

Richard asked Stuart. "How was your relationship with Matt?"

Rita watched as Stuart appeared confused, then angry. "Why the hell are you asking these questions? First you ask Nelly if Matt used to run away, now this crap." Stuart's face became red, his thin, sunken cheeks getting more sucked in. A snarl appeared on his lips.

"I know what you lot are like. You want to make us look guilty, don't you? As if we had something to do with…with this."

Richard raised a hand to placate him. "Mr Crosby, you're barking up the wrong tree here. All I want to know is that if you and Matt had a happy and normal relationship."

"Of course we bloody did!" Stuart shouted the words out, and stood up. He stumbled backwards, and narrowly avoided landing on the TV. He leaned against the bay windows, and folded his arms across his chest.

Rita nudged Richard, and he understood. Rita observed Stuart carefully. She didn't blame him for suffering with emotional overload. She knew that parents could act irrationally in these situations. What she found interesting was the lack of empathy between husband and wife. They had looked at each other once, sat far away, and seemed distant.

"To think you're sat here making accusations," Stuart shook his head.

"Mr Crosby," Rita said quietly. Stuart glared at her.

Rita kept her voice low. "No one is blaming you. Please don't blame yourself, either." Rita looked at Nelly. "You didn't do anything wrong. In a quiet neighbourhood like yours, something like this doesn't normally happen."

Tears burst from Nelly's eyes then, and she lowered her head, weeping. "I didn't leave him for that long. I really didn't."

Rita reached out and touched her arm. Nelly held her head and wept. “It’s not your fault,” Rita said. She couldn’t imagine the heartbreak Nelly was going through.

Rita glanced at Stuart. He was ashen faced, all the rage had seeped out of him like air seeping out of a burst car tyre.

“Apart from the two of you, who else had contact with Matt?” Rita asked Stuart. Stuart looked at Rita like she had two heads. Then he shook his head, and the scales seem to fall from his eyes.

“I…well, he saw his own dad a few times, obviously. His name is Mark.”

“When was the last time Matt saw Mark?”

Stuart looked at Nelly, who had dried her eyes but a new, troubled look darkened her face.

“I called him yesterday. He came over. And…” She looked away, seemingly lost for words.

“What happened?” Rita pressed.

“He tried to punch me, okay?” Stuart weighed in. “He’s out of control.”

Rita glanced at Nelly, who was now staring down at her hands. “Why did he try to punch you?”

Stuart shrugged, and tried to look evasive, but he couldn’t avoid Rita’s direct stare.

"He…uh…we had an argument. We've never really got on. We were quite emotional and stressed, as you can imagine. He just got angry."

"Angry enough to punch you? That's quite extreme," Richard said.

Nelly intervened. "Stuart asked Mark if he had Matt, and Mark denied it, then got angry. Mark has a quick temper. It got out of hand very quickly."

Rita cut her eyes to Stuart. He shrugged. "He's always been like that. Nelly had to hit him with a broom. He got off me, and ran away."

Rita and Richard exchanged a look. Richard asked, "Where did he go? Was he driving?"

"Yes. He came in his car – a blue Honda. I heard it start up, then he drove off."

"Do you know the car's registration number?"

Stuart glanced at Nelly, whose face was blank. He shook his head. "No, sorry."

Rita looked over to Stuart. "Why did you ask him if he had Matt? He wouldn't have come over if he had taken Matt, correct?"

Stuart spread his hands, drawing his shoulders up like he was complaining. He reminded Rita of a whiny, difficult teenager.

"I just asked a simple question. That's all. All he had to do was say no."

Rita stared at him. She could see how Matt's father would feel insulted. She wondered how often Mark and Stuart had sparred – verbally, at least. Stuart had admitted they didn't get on. Rita let it go for now, but it was an important factor she would return to. She glanced at Nelly.

"So, what's Mark's routine of seeing Matt?"

"He comes on Friday evenings or Saturday morning, and takes Matt away for the weekend. He brings Matt back on Sunday afternoon."

Rita exchanged a glance with Richard. They both knew speaking to Mark was vital.

"We need his number, please, and address," Rita said. She waited while Richard wrote it down. Then she looked at Nelly. "We need to see the back garden, please."

CHAPTER 5

Rita and Richard waited for Nelly and Stuart to leave the room, then they followed. The kitchen area was open plan, with the kitchen counter to the left, and the dining area to the right. Sofas and chairs were arranged around a fireplace with a flat screen TV on the wall.

Nelly stopped, and Rita could tell from her face she didn't want to go outside. Lucy led them through the patio doors, which were open. The June sun was angling in, lighting up a broad patch inside the kitchen area. Two Velux windows in the ceiling let in ample light. A wonderful room in the summer, but this summer was turning into a nightmare for Matt's parents.

Outside, after the patio stones, the grass was well trimmed. There was a shed to the left, with the door closed. Around the grass verge there was a row of plants on either side, and at the end, by the fence, a couple of trees that grew over the fence.

In the right corner, Rita saw the apple tree. It would be easy, she now realised, for a man to scale the tree and jump over the fence. The wooden fence was no taller than six feet, just above Rita's head height of five feet eight.

Any able person could climb that fence, with a little effort. But it would be harder with eight year old Matt on their shoulder, unless Matt was encouraged to climb the tree himself. But Matt was unwell, and sleeping when his mother left him in bed upstairs.

Rita walked out into the sunshine of the garden. She put on her gloves first, and went to the shed. It was small but well arranged, and she could stand inside. It had the usual lawn mower and gardening tools, a folded up table tennis set, and an old golf club bag. The place was warm and smelt of mown grass and old furniture. Rita could imagine the dog getting in here, and the door shutting behind it.

Again, she thought of the scenario. Did Matt let the dog in here? Or did the intruder? But the dog wouldn't obey the intruder, unless it was lured in by a treat.

Rita came out, and joined Richard to look at the top of the fence. None of the wooden posts were damaged, and they would be easy to grab hold of and scale.

"I could sling a child over my back, get on that tree, and get down to other side," Richard remarked. "And I'm a short arse." Richard was five feet six, a good two to three inches shorter than Rita.

Rita smiled at him. "I'm sure you could. Do you think that's what happened?"

Richard grimaced. "I'm not sure. I just know this fence isn't exactly formidable. Shall I get on that tree and have a look?"

"Go for it. Just don't slip and fall."

Richard put his gloves on, and tested a branch of the apple tree. Then he climbed, putting his feet on the sturdy lower branch. He raised his head above the level of the fence.

"What can you see?" Rita asked.

"A grassy clearing, that's the meadows. Then it's the woods. The woods slope down to the roads, I can see the A156 from here. Then it's the sea, in the distance."

Richard got closer to the fence, shaking the trees. He gripped the top of the fence post and looked down.

"Not that big a drop, to be honest. But with a child on my back? I don't know."

Richard hopped down from the tree. They had a look around the rest of the garden, but found nothing of interest. Rita had a look at the side of the property. There was a black wrought iron grill gate, which was locked. She went back inside the house, and saw Nelly sitting on one of the bar stools in the kitchen.

"Who else came to the house to see Matt?" Rita asked.

Nelly answered. "He played with the lads on the street. They're our neighbours, and I can give you their names. They're helping to spread the word, and organising a search party to help you lot."

Richard took out his notebook and wrote the names down. Then he went outside to make some calls.

Rita asked, "Did any other adult have contact with Matt? What about your parents, or Stuart's?"

Stuart had gone out of the room, as he had a call from work, Nelly said. "Yes, my parents saw Matt, obviously. They live in Scarborough, and used to be down often before. Now they're older, and it's getting harder. Stuart's parents aren't that fussed, as Matt's their step grandchild."

In her mind, Rita discarded the grandparents as suspects. To abduct Mark, they needed to be physically able. "What about the parents of the boys he played with?"

"A couple of the mothers came for coffee in the morning. Matt never saw the dads, to be honest. The men folk are mostly at work."

Rita was thinking laterally, her mind humming. "What about school? And on the sports ground?"

Nelly frowned as she thought. "Matt likes football. He knows the coach well, and we took him to practice on Saturday morning. He played twice a week after school, on the school grounds. I'd say he knew the coach quite well."

"Anyone else?"

Nelly frowned. “His form, or class teacher. Oh yes, and the educational psychologist at school. Matt had told the teacher he missed Mark, so they called me in to ask if everything was okay at home. It was, of course. Mark was busy at the time, although I must say he has done his best for Matt. He takes him on holidays, to football matches and so on. Anyway, Matt was perhaps a little sad, so he told his teacher, who called the school psychologist. Mr Warren, his name is, Edward Warren.”

Rita scribbled in her diary. “And the football coach, and form teachers as well please.”

“The coach is Andrew, I can’t remember his last name. He’s got a beard. Tall, black guy. Teacher’s called Charlene. I think Trilby is her last name, can’t be sure. I can call the school and ask if you want.”

“Did any of these people ever visit your house?”

“Yes. Charlene and Mr Warren visited once, to do like a check to see if everything’s ok. That was about a month ago.”

Rita wrote all of this down. “Anyone else? Please don’t leave family members out.”

“My brother and his wife came a couple of times. They live in Bempton. They also have a boy, Paul, who’s two years older than Matt. They got on well together.”

“When did they last see Matt?”

"They came recently, last weekend. They stayed the night."

"Bempton's not far from here, is it? Can I please have your brother's details as well?"

Nelly stared at Rita for a while, then nodded.

There was a knock on the door, and Lucy, the FLO stuck her head in and looked at Rita. "Richard wants you outside, now."

*****

A small crowd had gathered outside the house. Stuart was standing next to Richard and the uniformed officers, who were guarding the front door. Rita scanned the crowd quickly for reporters, but still didn't see any. She exhaled in relief. It was only the neighbours.

Two more uniformed cars had arrived, along with a van. One by one, the officers were alighting from the van, stretching, and sharing coffee from a mug. Rita knew they had done a door to door already yesterday, but they would fan out further afield, checking the meadows and woodlands.

Behind the van, she saw the smaller white vehicle of the canine unit. The trainer officer was on the pavement with his German Shepherd dog, who was muzzled, and sat obediently at his master's feet.

Rita had a soft spot for these dogs. Not only were they highly trained, they were also extremely well behaved. More so than a human being, Rita often thought. She wanted to go over and say hello to the dog, who was called Rexie. But she had to deal with the crowd of neighbours first, who needed guidance.

She got inquisitive glances as she went on the pavement, and stood next to Richard.

"What have you told them?" She whispered.

"Nowt so far. I was waiting for you. This lot have helped the uniforms already yesterday, with the door to door."

"I don't want them trampling over evidence in the backyard, or in the house," Rita whispered again. "Leave them out of the meadows as well. They're better off with knocking on doors."

"I agree, guv."

Stuart was smoking, and glancing at them while he spoke to one of the neighbours. Rita stepped forward, and raised her voice.

"Good morning. My name is DI Rita Gupta of North Yorkshire Police. Thank you for helping us yesterday."

The crowd fell silent, watching her closely.

"We are pursuing various angles of investigation. At this stage, we do not have any sightings of Matt, but that will change going forward. We will share any findings with you. Has anyone posted about Matt on social media?"

Several hands went up. Stuart came up to Rita. "It's the neighbourhood WhatsApp group. They started posting last night. Many of them have also put it on their social media pages."

Rita had expected this, and it was too late to stop it. She knew she or the D Sup, Nicola, had to conduct a press interview without delay, and launch a Crimestoppers appeal.

She raised her voice again. "Has anyone set up a page for Matt?"

The crowd was silent, but several faces looked at each other, then started muttering. Well, that was something, Rita thought.

"We would like to set up a page from the North Yorkshire Police website, and I would like all of you to subscribe to that page. Then you share the link online, as much as you want. That will give us broader coverage."

The murmurs grew louder, and a woman at the front raised her voice. "Have you set this page up already?"

"Yes, we have. Please visit our website. And if you could continue to please help the officers with the door-to-door enquiries, we would be grateful." Rita raised a hand. "At every house, please ask the person's name and phone number and note it down. Then ask them if they have seen Matt, obviously. Do you know what Matt was wearing when he was last seen?"

From the silence, she knew they didn't.

"The officers will provide you with the details. Ask the people you meet if they saw anyone in this area, or in the woodlands behind, that they haven't seen before. Ask them if they saw anyone suspicious around the Crosby house, from the front or the back. Over the last days and weeks, if you saw any new cars, or people, on the street, please tell us immediately."

Rita took out her notebook and read out the names of the two neighbours who visited the Crosby household. Two women came forward.

"Take statements from them," Rita said to Richard. He nodded and got busy. Rita went over to the canine team. Rexie recognised her and wagged her tail, then put her front paws on her chest to say hello. James, his trainer, restrained Rexie, and she sat promptly, looking a little sad.

"It's okay," Rita laughed, "Let her go." James took the muzzle off Rexie, and Rita sat down, stroking the dog's head. Rexie tried to lick her face, and Rita tried her best to avoid that from happening. She stood, and patted Rexie's head. Rexie nudged her legs and looked up at her with a hopeful look in her dark brown eyes.

"I don't have any treats, don't look at me like that," Rita smiled. She often wished she had a dog. But with her work schedule, and living alone, it wasn't possible right now. Rexie didn't bark even once. James put the muzzle back on.

"We're going in, soon," James said. "Any instructions?"

"Wait till I inspect the room once and take some samples. Shola's just arrived, I see." They both looked to where the Nigerian born forensics officer was stepping out of her car. She saw Rita and waved, and they waved back.

"I'll tell the mother to get some clothes out for you," Rita said. She bent down to pat Rexie, who again reared up on her hind legs and put her front paws on Rita's chest.

"I'm sorry," James said. "She only does that to people she likes."

"I like her too," Rita patted Rexie briefly, then went back into the house. She eyed Shola, but she was speaking to her assistant, and getting her gear ready. Soon, the white scene of crime tent would be up in front of the house.

Rita went inside, and asked the FLO to show her Matt's room. Nelly was in the kitchen, and she didn't look back as Rita followed Lucy upstairs.

CHAPTER 6

The landing upstairs was narrow, with three rooms and a bathroom. Rita put on her sterile gloves and shoe covers. She peeked inside the master bedroom. The king size bed was unmade, and it was slept in, but only on one side.

In the second bedroom, Rita saw a double bed, and this was also slept in, with a man's trousers and vest on the bed. This was clearly the guest bedroom as it didn't have a wardrobe or mirror, only a chest of drawers, and an old desk and chair that had seen better days.

Was Stuart sleeping here? The couple didn't say if another man was living with them, so Rita assumed he was. That was interesting, she thought. The couple was going through a calamity, and instead of comforting each other, they were drifting apart. Rita wondered about the family dynamics.

Matt's room was painted with Batman and Robin cartoons on a wall, and a single child's bed by the window. The blind was drawn on the window, and the room was dark. Rita turned the light on. There was a desk and chair in one corner, with a bookshelf above it.

An iPad rested on the table, with a couple of exercise books. There was a schoolbag on the carpet. Rita looked inside the school bag. She found the usual books and a pencil case but nothing else. A collection of stickers and football club clips were stuck on the front of the bag. Matt supported Leeds United.

Rita checked under the bed. There was a roll out clothes drawer, and neatly folded pyjamas, school uniforms and football shorts were kept inside. Rita looked around the rest of the room. On the side wall adjacent to the desk, she saw some scribbles on the wall. It was a child's writing, in small letters, done with a pencil. They were not visible when looking at the desk, Rita had to approach from the right side. She leaned in closer, frowning.

I want to see my daddy.

When will daddy come? Tomorrow.

Beneath the writing, there was a drawing, with the same pencil it seemed. It was a stick drawing of a man with a small figure holding his hand. Father and son.

Rita took photos, her mind whirring. Was Matt unhappy here? Rita knew she needed to speak to the psychologist at Matt's school. That would be her next stop. Nelly had told her about this, but that didn't lessen Rita's suspicions on Nelly. She wasn't hiding anything. Rita took the iPad, and from the bathroom, she took Matt's toothbrush, for DNA samples.

When she went downstairs, Stuart was coming in through the door. He looked at her warily.

"I need to take a mouth swab from you, please," Rita said. "Unless it's been done already." None of her team had told her. She heard someone speaking in the kitchen, and she recognised Richard's voice. A woman, likely Nelly, answered.

"No, not as yet," Stuart said. He went into the open plan kitchen and dining area and Rita followed.

Richard took the mouth swabs for DNA from both Nelly and Stuart. Rita addressed the couple once the swabs were taken.

"I've taken Matt's iPad, and we need a couple of his clothes for the dog to sniff, and for our own forensics. Is it okay if the dog trainer comes in?"

"Yes," Nelly said, tonelessly. Her face was blank, colourless, as if there was no blood left in her body.

"As soon as we hear something, Lucy will let you know," Rita said. She indicated to Richard, and they left.

*****

St Bede's school was about twenty minutes' drive, inland towards Eastfield. The school had a flat, rectangular reception area, with the soft floor playgrounds next to it. Across the playground, the double story structure of the school was visible.

Richard and Rita were shown into the headmaster's office, which was in the main building at the rear, on the upper floor. The headmaster wasn't in his office and his secretary said Mr Colin Athey was in a teacher's meeting. He wouldn't be any more than ten minutes, as he knew Rita was expected.

As they waited, Rita got a call from Jack Banford. She excused herself and went into the corridor. She could see the playgrounds below her, and the road beyond the tall fences of the school.

"I guess you're searching for the missing boy, right?" Jack's warm voice came down the line.

"How did you know about him?"

"The secretaries at work were talking about him. One of them lives in Osgodby. Word has spread, thought you might want to know."

"Thanks, I was expecting that anyway. Just seen the parents, now at the school."

"Osgodby's normally a quiet place. Lots of caravan parks around there. What happened is unusual, but I guess it could happen anywhere." Jack was silent for a beat, then spoke again.

"Janet, the secretary who's lived in Osgodby for most of her life, said that she knows the couple."

"Oh, really?" Rita was intrigued.

"She lives opposite them, two doors down. They moved in three years ago, according to Janet. She did see two men shouting at the front door once. Then one of them got in his car and drove away. A woman was also there – Nelly, the boy's mother."

"I need to speak to Janet," Rita thought quickly. "Did she describe the men she saw?"

"I asked her already." Rita heard a smile in Jack's voice. "Because I knew you would."

"You'll be a detective at this rate, Mr Banford. Looking for a change of career?"

"Depends on what's on offer. I need a good package."

She heard the smile in his voice and couldn't help grinning. "Do you now? Won't be as good as your plum lawyer job. But, you know, sometimes we do things because we love them."

Rita bit her tongue as soon the words left her mouth. Bloody hell, did she just say that?

"Sorry," she said quickly. "What did your secretary Janet say about the men in front of the Crosby house?"

"One of them was Nelly's husband, Stuart. The other man was about five feet ten, slim build, and he wore a blue jacket and jeans. She saw it from her front garden when she was clearing out the leaves."

Jack paused. "Janet said she'd seen the man before, but couldn't be sure."

"He might be Mark Alridge, the boy's biological father. I'm surprised he's not arrived as yet."

"Hmm. The boy disappeared from the back garden, didn't he? Is there a fence?"

"Yes, there is, but it can be climbed. It's not that tall. And there's an apple tree that leans over it. So, anyone could have jumped into the garden. I'm not sure they would have time to abduct Matt though." Briefly, Rita explained her reasoning to Jack.

"But if Richard could climb the tree, a bigger bloke would find it easier. Right?"

"I know, but I'm not sure if that's what happened. It would take too long to go upstairs, bring Matt down, and then go over the fence." She pressed her lips together, thinking. "Or it might not."

"Exactly. Keep an open mind, detective."

"Shut up. Go and free a criminal using your legal crap."

Jack laughed. "Oh, that worked. I'll remember it."

"It's part of PACE," Rita said, referring to the Police and Criminal Evidence Act, the legislation which governed all of police work. "Part seven, section 2b. Didn't you know?"

"Guess I need to look it up." Then he grinned, aware Rita was pulling his leg.

Rita heard footsteps, and looked to her left. A man in a suit and a woman were approaching. She said goodbye to Jack and hung up.

The couple stopped in front of her, and Rita showed them her warrant card. The man was of medium height, with a roundish face, and blond hair. His light blue eyes stared at her.

“I’m Colin Athey, the Principal, and this is Charlene Wright, Matt’s form teacher.”

“Can we go into your office to talk?” Rita asked.

“Of course.”

Richard and Rita sat opposite Mr Athey, and Charlene pulled up a chair to grab a seat next to the principal.

“As you know, we are here to ask about Matthew Crosby, the boy who’ missing since yesterday. He wasn’t at school yesterday as he was unwell. When did you last see him?

Mr Athey looked at Charlene, who cleared her throat. “I see Matt every day, as you can imagine. I teach English, and do two lessons with his form, daily. I saw his parents as well, when they pick him up, but I only speak to them at the parent teachers evening. It was mostly his mother actually, Nelly. I hardly saw the stepfather.”

“Did you ever see his real father? His name is Mark Alridge.”

Charlene shook her head and looked at Mr Athey, who shrugged. “No, we didn’t.”

"What was Matt like?" Rita looked at Charlene directly. The woman blinked.

"He was a lovely child. Quiet and reserved mostly, but he was good academically. He wasn't a big lad, but he liked his football." Charlene smiled. "His dad took him to a Leeds United match, and he loved that. He told me about it the next week. His real dad, I think, not Nelly's husband."

"You saw him yesterday, what did he seem like to you?"

Charlene's face changed, a dark shadow clouding her features. "He was a little sad to be honest. He kept his head down and looking at the floor. I spoke to him during the recess, and he was missing his father, he told me. I took him to the school psychologist, Mr Warren. Or Ed, as we call him. They had a good chat and he felt better after."

Rita nodded. "Yes, Nelly said that he had seen Mr Warren a few times. You and Mr Warren did a home visit, didn't you?"

"Yes, we saw Matt at home. Stuart wasn't there. Mother and son had a perfectly normal relationship. Matt seemed okay at home. But he did want to spend more time with his real dad."

"Mark Alridge, yes." Rita paused. "You mentioned Matt had a good relationship with his mother. What about with the step father, Stuart?"

"That I don't know. I never saw the two together. I don't know if Ed did."

"Did Ed visit the house more than once?"

"Yes, on the second visit I was unwell so I couldn't go. I think Ed also saw Stuart once when he came to pick up Matt from school. I haven't met Stuart."

"And Ed, or Mr Warren, didn't have any concerns with Matt's interactions with Stuart."

Charlene shook his head. "No. We thought Matt was happy at home, but obviously his relationship with his dad was distant, and that bothered him."

"How often did he see his dad?"

"Every other weekend," Charlene said. That was what Nelly had also mentioned, Rita thought.

Charlene said, "Matt did find it hard to make friends. He was a loner at school." She stopped then, and looked at Mr Athey. Rita saw their hesitation, and knew they had reached an important juncture.

"What is it?" She asked.

Mr Athey took over. He licked his lower lip before speaking. "Well, Ed thought Matthew might be on the spectrum."

Rita and Richard looked at each other. Richard asked, "You mean the autism spectrum?"

"Yes," Mr Athey said. "Ed had spent some time with Matthew. He suspected Matthew to be low on the spectrum, or have mild Autism. He wanted to refer Matthew to the health services. We were discussing it, and were about to tell his parents. Sadly, we didn't get the chance."

Mr Athey sighed. "I hope you find the lad. What are the chances, do you think?"

"We are always hopeful of finding a missing child," Rita said. "It's giving up that causes the most damage. The investigation is intense, and a huge number of officers are involved, as you can imagine. We will find him."

Rita glanced at Charlene. "Can we meet Mr Warren please? It seems he knew Matt rather well."

Both teacher and principal nodded. Mr Athey picked up the phone and had a short conversation with Mr Warren.

"He's in his office," Mr Athey said. "He will see you now."

CHAPTER 7

Charlene rose and took Rita and Richard downstairs. Mr Warren's office was down a narrow corridor with several teachers' offices on either side. Charlene knocked a door that bore Mr Warren's name and a muffled voice asked them to enter.

Ed Warren was a slim, nerdy looking man with glasses. His dark hair was thick and curly, and he had a kind face, with attentive, grey eyes that rested on Rita. He had a frank, warm smile, and somehow, Rita felt at ease in his company.

Drawings by children were framed on the wall, along with landscape paintings. The walls were yellow, with flowers on the wallpaper, and the carpet was light grey.

"Please have a seat," Mr Warren said. "And call me Ed, please. Everyone does."

"Thank you." Rita took out her warrant card, but Ed waved it away.

"There's no need. I know who you are. Colin already informed me."

He smiled gently at Rita. It made the corners of his eyes crinkle. Then his eyes lost the brightness.

"I can't believe Matt's gone missing. I only saw him the day before. Are you any closer to finding him?"

Rita saw genuine concern in his eyes. He was leaning forward, his neck muscles taut, eyes fixed on her. She didn't think he was acting.

"Not yet, unfortunately. Can you please tell us more about Matt?"

"He's a wonderful child. Very polite and obedient. I think he missed his father. The separation trauma was deep for him. He was young then, about three years old. His mother said how he became very clingy, and cried more. He was like that for a year, if not more. That's when he started school."

"You were in contact with him then?"

"Yes," Ed nodded. "But not much. For about three years, he was settling in well at school. It's only recently that he's found it difficult." Ed stopped and it seemed he left something unsaid.

"Please carry on."

"He seemed to be more disengaged at school and at home in the last year or so. That's when Charlene brought him back to my attention."

"And what changed in the last year?"

"Well, they moved into their new house. And Stuart moved in with them."

That was news to Rita. She realised that she hadn't explored Nelly and Stuart's relationship in detail.

"So, Matt had not lived with Stuart before?"

"Not as far as I know. They met, but they didn't live in the same house. I'm not sure, and I don't want to say anything, but it's possible Matt felt a little insecure after Stuart moved in with them."

Again, Rita felt an evasiveness in Ed's manner. His earlier warmth was replaced by a guarded look on his face. He licked his lips, and looked away from her scrutiny.

"Is there anything else, Ed?"

He moved his neck slowly, and looked back at her. He was calm, but an uncertainty masked his face.

"Did you have any concerns about Stuart?"

Ed's eyebrows rose. "How do you mean?"

"In his interactions with Matt. The way he settled in with the family." Rita shrugged. "In general."

Ed blinked a couple of times. "I didn't see anything unusual. The first time I met them at their home, Matt was kicking a ball with Stuart in the garden. Matt was into his football. Stuart and Matt seemed to have a normal relationship."

Rita gazed at Ed for a while, and he looked back at her. Rita didn't think he was hiding anything.

"What was their interaction like? Were they close?"

Ed shrugged. "Well, Matt was closer to his mother, but then you expect that. For someone who had known Matt for two years, I'd say Stuart's interaction with him was quite standard."

Richard asked, "And what do you mean by standard?"

"Stuart helped Nelly make him lunch. He encouraged Matt to eat his greens. He asked Matt if he wanted to take him to football."

"And what did Matt say?"

"He wanted to go with Stuart. Like I said, their interaction was normal."

Rita stared at Ed closely. He was being sincere, she could tell. Nothing about him made her wary, so far.

She asked, "Did you ever meet Matt's biological father – Mark Alridge?"

Ed shook his head. "Matt talked about him, of course. He missed having a father figure in his life. He spoke of Mark in an excited voice, about going to football matches with him, and the Leeds United Museum in the club grounds." A smile flickered in the corners of Ed's lips. Then he looked up at them.

"Does Mark know about Matt's disappearance?"

"Nelly has informed him. I think he's on his way here. Do you know when Matt last saw his father?"

Ed didn't know.

Richard spoke up. "Did you have any other concerns regarding Matt?"

"What do you mean?"

"Any physical, or sexual abuse? Did you see any bruise marks on his body anywhere?"

"Not on his visible body," Ed sighed. "By that I mean his arms, legs and face. You have to remember that I'm not allowed to examine him like a doctor does. That's not my remit. And also, either Charlene, or another female teacher was always with me when I conducted the sessions with the Matt. That's the usual protocol. I'm not allowed to do it alone."

Ed shrugged. Rita observed him closely. His manner was relaxed, his neck muscles weren't contracted, there was no forced expression on his face. Rita knew the signs of a liar, and she couldn't see them on Ed. Rita handed him her card, and Richard accepted with thanks.

"Please call us if you remember anything else," Rita said. Ed looked at the card, and then inclined his head.

"Of course I will."

CHAPTER 8

Scarborough Police Station was small, but it was still the main police station in the coast for North Yorkshire Police. As Rita stood at the lectern, facing the darkened room and the amassed officers from five police stations, she knew how much was at stake here. Shortly after her presentation, news of Matt's disappearance would be hit the national newspapers and social media.

Rita pointed at Matt's photo on the screen behind her. She had spoken about the timeline already.

"Matt was wearing a grey top, dark jeans, and white trainers. He had a mole on his left temple which is black, and distinctive. It's a raised mole, and his mother wanted it to be removed as its easily visible. His eye colour is grey green. His hair is light brown. Four feet seven inches tall. You should have the description on your phones by now."

Rita flicked the screen using the remote in her hand. Photos of Nelly, Stuart and Mark Alridge appeared. Rita still hadn't met Mark. She didn't know if Mark had arrived at the crime scene. She had to rush back from the school as Nicole had arranged an Incident Meeting without informing her.

"None of the three parents are known to the CSODS – Child Sex Offender Disclosure Scheme. No PCNs on them either. The grandparents and Nelly's brother Alistair, his wife Rachel, are all clear as well."

On the front row, Rita saw a pint-sized shape move. She knew it was Nicola. The D Sup raised her voice.

"Have you checked Stuart's family?"

"Yes. His parents have never seen Matt. They live in Stirling, in Scotland. Stuart doesn't have any siblings."

Nicola asked, her tone haughty and sharp as usual. "Do you have any suspects?"

Rita ground her teeth together, and paused. Nicola clearly wanted to embarrass her in front of everyone. The police officers here weren't fools. They knew Nicole's question, so soon after the disappearance, made no sense.

"As it happens, we are following up closely at the school, and with the neighbours."

"A man picked up Matt two weekends ago and apparently had an argument with Stuart. We think the man was Mark, Matt's father. He is our next port of call."

Rita spoke to the rest of the room before Nicole could ask her anything else.

“As you know, the first forty-eight hours are the most critical for a missing person. It’s been just over one day that Matt is missing, and every second is now valuable.” She paused. “Have we set up posters at bus stops and train stations?”

“Yes,” A voice said from the middle of the room. Rita recognised it as Inspector Steve Bennett, a veteran uniformed Inspector of NYP. “We’ve also done a door to door in a five-mile radius from the house, with the help of the neighbours and the extra units. No one’s seen Matt.”

“Thank you.” Rita addressed the room again. “Has anyone been approached by members of the press for information? If so – have they offered you money, or a card with a number to call them?”

There was a faint murmur across the room as several heads looked at each other, and then shook in denial.

“Remember that false news can hamper the investigation. All manner of weirdos will start bombarding us with sightings of Matt. Please do not speak to the media, even if they offer you, shall we say, incentives.”

Nicole half turned in her seat and raised her voice again. For a small woman, she had a loud voice.

“And anyone found to leak news to reporters will be suspended immediately.”

Rita asked, “Has the enquiry desk been set up?”

Rizwan, also sat on the front row, answered. "Yes guv. It's at the front desk. Online, there's a link from the main website, and the first photo is now Matt's."

"Good. Any enquiries yet?"

Inspector Bennett answered. "A few sympathisers have dropped in to help, but no one with any concrete information."

"Okay," Rita sighed. "I'm going back to the crime scene. Is Scene of crime there now?"

Maggie answered from the front row. "Yes, guv."

*****

In half an hour, Maggie and Rita were standing at the rear of the Crosby residence. With her back to the fence, Rita looked at the grassland in front of her, where a row of uniformed police men moved slowly, their eyes on the ground. All of them stayed in line, no one broke rank.

The line stretched from the end of the path on Rita's right, where the houses ended, and the path began. The path was wide enough to drive a car down. And there was a road, from where a car could easily trundle down this path. Due to the fences, no one would see the car. And so far, no witnesses had come forward to say they had seen a car on that road, yesterday morning.

Inspector Bennett walked up to Rita. He took off his cap and scratched his head. His bulky uniform jacket made him look bigger than his slim, six feet tall frame.

"Nowt, as yet. The lads have been as far down the fields to where the grass ends and the woods start." He indicated the slowly advancing line of women and men, taking each step in synchrony, their heads lowered, eyes not missing anything.

"They're retracing their steps now, but I'm not holding out much hope."

"Let's get into the woods as soon as we can," Rita said. She had a sinking feeling as well. The sun was warming up the sea in the distance, and it was turning to a brighter blue. White sailboats of clouds drifted slowly in the sky, as if taking time to watch the scene below. Rita shook her head.

"Get the feeling we're barking up the wrong tree here?" She asked, half speaking to herself.

"Aye, I do," Bennett agreed.

"Guv," A voice shouted from behind. It was Maggie. She was on her haunches, with the forensic gait analyst and tyre marks expert, Bob Marsden. Maggie beckoned at Rita, her face excited. Rita hurried over, but when she got to the dirt track, she didn't see anything obvious immediately.

Bob, the bearded Scotsman, glanced up. "Och aye," he said in his Highlands brogue. "He's covered his tracks well, like."

Bob had an instrument which could only be described as a long handle brush. The brush tips were fine like a man's moustache, and no more than a couple of inches long. At the base of the long black handle, there were three tiny red buttons. Bob pressed one, and the brush tips started to quiver. Bob applied the brush to the dirt track very softly, and a layer of dust scattered in the air. He stopped quickly, and then leaned to take a closer look. Rita and Maggie joined him.

"See that there?" Bob pointed to the faintest of ridges on the ground. "Ah ken those are car tyre marks, like. He wisnae gonna leave them there, so he used a broom or summat, to brush them over, to hide his tracks."

Rita inspected the ground, squinting. Sometimes she wished she had glasses. The marks were faint, and damaged by the disguising effect, but she could see a pattern of lines, and potentially, it could be a car.

"Are you sure?" She asked Bob.

"Aye," he affirmed, his grey eyes dull but watchful. "Like ah said, he tried his best to hide 'em. There's more here."

He got up stiffly, and walked over to another section. A white circle had been placed over various spots on the ground. Bob applied his electronic brush again, displacing dirt. Rita saw more patterns on the ground.

She looked behind. They had left the Crosby's home, and were at the next neighbour's back fence.

The white circles stretched along the path, to where it joined the road, up a slight incline.

"And here," Bob said, crouching on the ground again, "There's a wee splash of oil, which he tried his best to cover up as well."

Rita saw a darker, damp patch that was quite diffuse, and unless Bob had pointed it out, she would have missed it.

"Ah ken its oil from a leaky carburettor valve, and nae from the exhaust pipe at the rear. Engine oil is darker, aye?"

"If you say so," Rita murmured. "Only an old engine would leak oil, right?"

"Ah ken so," Bob looked up at her, some respect in his eyes. "He tried his best to hide this, but he didnae succeed entirely."

"You keep saying he," Maggie said. "What if it was a woman?" She looked at Rita and shrugged. "The woman could've been the driver."

Both women looked at Bob enquiringly. He grimaced, and got to his feet, his knees popping.

"You lassies will be the death of me," he complained, holding his back and straightening slowly. "Come this way, then."

Rita had noticed the smaller blue circles, arranged in two clusters outside the Crosby rear fence. Unlike the white circles which denoted the car tyre marks, these were only in one place – opposite the fence.

"These are boot prints. Again, he tried his best to hide this. He must have like a dust pan or summat. The size of the prints show they can only be a man's shoe size – I'd say aboot ten or eleven, give or take."

"So he had some time to hide his tracks," Rita said, straightening from inspecting the shoe marks. Like the tyres prints, she was lucky to see them. If it wasn't for Bob and his gizmo, they'd never know a car had driven up here.

"No' tae much time, like," Bob said. "He didnae do a perfect job. Lucky for us, eh?" Bob grinned, showing his tobacco-stained teeth.

Rita crossed her arms over her chest, and nodded at him. Then she looked at the apple tree whose branches reached over the fence. The sun was warming up her back.

Matt's abductor came here by car. He was a tall ish man. About six feet. He had to be athletic, or he wouldn't be able to climb the fence, and over to the other side. He jumped down, maybe he watched for a while first, before he made any moves. Did he see the dog in the garden? Did he put the dog in the shed, so it wouldn't bark when he came down with Matt?

Rita racked her brain, playing possible scenarios in her head. The apple tree would've hidden the man from the neighbours on either side.

Most importantly – this man wasn't a stranger to this household. The dog didn't bark – that much the uniforms had picked up from the neighbours.

Was it Stuart? But why would he abduct Matt?

Could it be Matt's dad, Mark?

CHAPTER 9

"Penny for your thoughts, guv," Maggie said. Her comment broke Rita's reverie. She had been staring intently at the apple tree rearing up over the fence, lost in her visualisation of a man coming down from it, with a child. She explained her rationale to Maggie, who shrugged.

"If that was me, I'd want a helper. Someone to grab the child on the way down, and help to put him in the car."

"Matt must've been passed out," Rita mused. "If he hadn't been unconscious, or if he was fighting, then he would've made a racket, or fallen to the ground. That's why I think whoever took him knew Matt well, and he wouldn't have fought. If Matt was awake, he went of his own will. He thought it was an adventure. Like a game."

"A treasure hunt," Maggie grinned. "I used to love doing those with my brother. Dad used to take us on them in the fields near our house. He went and hid a couple of Easter eggs in a basket the night before. It was great fun."

"That's why I suspect the father. Mark Alridge. Matt would go with his dad without question, because he liked spending time with him. And he scribbled those words on the wall. *I miss my dad.*"

"And Mark got very defensive when Stuart asked him if he knew where Matt was. They got into a fight. Then he ran out."

Rita nodded. "We need to find Mark, and track his car." She pressed her lips together. "But Matt could also have gone with someone else he knew. For example, one of the school teachers he was close to. Charlene, his form tutor, or Ed Warren, the psychologist. Though I have to say, that would be far-fetched."

"The teachers have alibis. They would have to know that Nelly went out at that specific time, and left Matt on his own."

"You mean someone was watching the house. They saw Nelly leave?"

"That's exactly right," Rita turned to Maggie. "How else would they get Matt alone?"

Maggie nodded, as Bob came up to them, wheezing, his back bent. His knees were bent out laterally, and he had a strange gait. Kind of funny, Rita thought, for a man who was a forensic gait analyst.

"I no' think this man would've been here long, like. He mustae scarpered as soon as he put the wee lad in his car."

“That’s what we think as well,” Rita said. “Did you find anything else?”

“No,” Bob shook his head. “But I might be able to get a good estimate on the car’s age, from the tyre treads. The gait might be harder to analyse. He was a man, no doubt aboot that, like. Tall as well, but no’ taller than that fence, which is nae more than six feet, ah ken.”

“No,” Rita grimaced, “not much in that fence at all.” She looked back at Bob. He was stroking his beard, and holding the black brush in his hand, looking like a wizard, Rita thought.

“What else can you tell us about the car?” She asked. “Any idea of the make?”

“Nae for sure,” Bob grunted. “The tyres wouldnae give us a clue about the car’s make. But if it’s an old vehicle, then that oil spill might tell us about the age of engine.”

Rita heard steps approaching and turned to see Shola. She was in her sterile, white forensic suit, and carried a briefcase in her gloved hand.

“I came to take swabs and samples from here,” Shola said. “I’d shake your hand if you didn’t contaminate me.”

“Too late for that, I’m afraid,” Rita said. “I tarnished you a while back.”

“That you did. You certainly know to make a splash. Scarborough was a quiet place before you turned up.”

"Boring, you mean," Rita grinned. Shola laughed.

"There's nothing boring about you and the D Sup. No love lost there, innnit?"

Shola slipped into her native Yorkshire accent very easily. She was the only black woman that Rita had seen in Scarborough since she arrived. Shola was born and raised here - a native, in other words.

Shola leaned closer. "I heard her comment about suspects in the Incident Room. I mean, what does she think you are, eh? Inspector Clouseau?" Shola was referring to Peter Seller's character in the Pink Panther.

"Excuse me," Rita frowned, as Shola, Maggie and Bob all joined in the laughter. "I'd like to think I'm not an old bumbling French detective."

"Nah, but you're definitely a Southerner," Rita poked at her. "Even if you were born and raised here."

"Well, I'm Northern now, so you better get used to it. Right, are you going to gossip all day, or do some work, Miss Adebole?" Rita raised her eyebrows in a severe manner, but then grinned. Shola rolled her eyes.

"Come on Henry," she called her assistant. Henry was thin and lanky, and he stepped up to his boss. "The queen of crime has landed, obviously."

Shola went to the fence, and Rita followed. Shola put her briefcase on the ground and took out her tablet device. She pointed it at the fence, and examined the surface. The special camera lens in the device worked like a high-powered microscope. Shola was scanning for shoe prints, flecks of blood or sputum, or anything unusual. Henry was taller, so he took the device from her, and examined the top of the fence.

Rita let them get on with it. "Any sign of the father as yet?" She asked Maggie, as they walked down into the fields, to meet the uniformed officers searching there.

"Not yet, no. Rizwan's arrived, and he's at the front, helping with the door to door. Uniforms are aware to let us know as soon as the father arrives."

"It's odd," Rita frowned. "If it was my child, and I was close to them, I would've been here like a shot."

"You think there might be a reason he's not here yet?"

Rita shrugged at Maggie's question. Maggie said, "Well, he's not answered his phone. It's switched off. We've left loads of messages."

"And he's not used that number recently? We can't triangulate the signal?"

"Nope, he's not used it. He must have another phone."

An uneasy feeling was growing inside Rita. Mark was now high up on the suspect's list. He had the motive – he wanted his son back for himself. As for opportunity, all he had to do was drive down here. And means – well, he could definitely climb the fence, and chances are that Matt would come with him.

But it was a little too easy, Rita thought. Far too neat. Mark fit in the role of the aggrieved father nicely, but why would he abduct his son now? Surely he had lots of chances before. He separated from Nelly when Matt was two years old. It was far easier to abduct a toddler than an eight-year-old boy.

A shout from behind distracted her. Shola was waving at them frantically. Bob was standing next to her and Henry. Maggie and Rita walked back to the fence.

"Drops of blood," Shola said, her face shining with excitement. "Not visible with the naked eye, but the magnifier picked it up." She showed Rita the screen. Small circles, and oval shaped dark marks appeared against a similarly dark background – the wood of the fence.

"Are you sure that's blood? I know blood turns black, but that could be anything." Rita sounded sceptical.

"Aha," Shola looked at her triumphantly. "Ye of little faith." From the pocket of her sterile suit, she pulled out a thin, small object that looked like a cigarette lighter. "This canister sprays a chemical reagent that turns green when it falls on blood. That's because it reacts with the haemoglobin molecule, the pigment that gives blood its red colour." Shola's eyebrows danced, and so did her dreadlock ponytail. "Did you know that?"

"Yes, Miss Smarty Pants, I did know that. And haemoglobin carries the oxygen, as well as iron. Does this reagent react with the oxygen, or the iron?"

"Ooh, we are clever today, aren't we?" Shola grinned. "Sadly, the oxygen disappears on the exposure, and the iron oxidizes, giving blood its dark colour when left out. The colour of rust, in other words. And that oxidised iron is what this reagent discovers."

"Not just any flecks of rust?" Rita frowned.

"No, because oxidized iron is different from rust. This is definitely blood. And most importantly, we can get DNA from it."

Rita looked at Shola, her eyes brimming with excitement. DNA would be valuable, assuming this blood was from the abductor. And assuming the blood was from a human being, and not an animal.

Shola pointed to the fence where she had found the blood drops. Henry was circling the spots with a white marker pen. They were close to the top, near the tree branches, and there was a smear of them halfway down the fence. Without the technical instruments, Rita knew she would never have seen these.

She went close to the fence and observed closely. The marks were higher than what an animal would be able to make, if they were grazing past the fence. Rita felt the old drumbeat of the chase in her blood stream. This was an important finding. Now all she needed was a DNA match with one of the suspects.

“Well done,” she told Shola.

CHAPTER 10

Shadows were lengthening across the field by the time the uniforms had finished searching the field. Inspector Bennett walked up to Rita, who was speaking to Janet, the neighbour who worked in Jack's office as a receptionist.

"Nowt out there, guv," Bennett said, taking off his cap and wiping the perspiration from his forehead. He took a swig from a bottle of water. It had been a hot day and Rita was grateful for the work they had done. Maggie and Rizwan were still out there, helping the uniforms.

"Nothing at all?" Rita was disappointed.

"Not a thread. No clothes, no drops of blood that are obvious, nothing really. We're into the woods now, and getting close to the A road after that. So far, nothing again. I heard you think there might've been a car parked behind the house? Maggie told us."

"Yes, and if the car belonged to the abductor then maybe they escaped via the road. So looking down where you are might not be worth it, but you never know." Rita smiled at him. Bennett looked tired, they all did. It had been a long day. "But that's for sticking up with it."

"No worries. It's just taking up a lot of manpower, that's all. But we're almost done."

Bennett left, and Rita turned back to Janet. "Sorry for the interruption. So, you saw this man who came to the Crosby home, right? What did he look like again?"

"Slim, dark jacket, less than six feet not very tall, basically. I told Jack all of this."

"Yes, thanks but I wanted to hear it from you. Tell me what you saw, please."

Janet leaned against the doorframe. She was in her sixties, Rita thought, with straight hair up to her shoulders that showed no signs of thinning. She had a house gown on, and she wore glasses, with slippers on her feet.

"It was about two weeks ago. I was putting out the bins, and heard raised voices. A man was shouting at Stuart, who was also having a go at him. The man kept saying it's my son, and I'll do what I want. I couldn't really hear what Stuart was saying, but something along the lines of he doesn't want you, and so on. Then Nelly came out, and tried to drag Stuart back in. He was having none of it."

"The other man – you've never seen him before?"

Janet shook her head. "No. But from what I heard he seemed like the boy's father."

"What sort of a car did he drive?"

Janet thought for a while. The sun was sinking rapidly, but it was still warm. Despite the warmth, Janet still had a cardigan around her gown, and she wrapped it around herself.

"It was dark blue. That's all I remember."

"Was it a big car, like a Range Rover, or maybe a van?"

"No, it wasn't a van, that's for sure. Neither was it one of those big four wheelers everyone drives these days. It was like a normal four-seater."

"Old or new?"

Again, Janet paused for thought. "You know, it was actually an old banger. A bit like me," She laughed, and Rita smiled.

"The car had seen better days, that's for sure. I wish I could remember the make for you. Or the registration number. Mr Banford already asked me about those." Janet shifted on her feet and Rita thought she was getting tired.

"Would you like to sit down?"

"Yes, if you don't mind. My knees aren't what they used to be." Janet smiled apologetically, then turned and walked inside the house. Rita entered a narrow corridor, and shut the door behind her.

It was a bungalow, and the paisley carpet was old, but otherwise the house was well maintained. Photos of grandchildren hung on the walls, and the white wallpaper wasn't old. Rita walked past a living room, a bedroom, and into the lounge with patio doors leading out to the garden. Sofas and armchairs faced a TV that was switched on to the news. Janet picked up the remote and turned the TV off.

Rita sat on the sofa, and faced Janet on the armchair. "Can I get you a glass of water?" Rita asked. Janet waved a hand, refusing.

"How long have the Crosby's lived here for?"

"About one year. I see Nelly taking the boy to school in the mornings. Sometimes, I see Stuart come back from work. He drives this black car. It's new, and I think it's an Audi."

Rita nodded. She had seen a two-year-old black Audi A3 in the Crosby's drive. The car looked relatively new. She hoped Bob had taken the tyre prints to compare with the car at the rear. Stuart's car wasn't old, but they needed to check the treads urgently.

"Do you ever speak to them?"

"Not really. They're busy with their lives, you know. And I work three days a week still. Keeps me busy. My John died two years ago, and all I have now is my cat Tabby and myself." Janet smiled, but Rita could see the sadness in her eyes.

"Sorry about your loss. Do you have family around? I saw photos of the grandchildren. They're sweet."

"My son lives in Nottingham," Janet said brightly. "And yes, I see his two girls in the holidays. Three times a year, really. But it's not that frequent."

"You must have friends here, on the street.

"Oh yes, we have a neighbour's group. We stay in touch on social media. It's so much easier these days."

Rita thought for a second. "Do the other neighbours say anything about the Crosby's? Has anyone met them before?"

Janet thought for a while, then shook her head. "No, can't say they have. The Crosby's are new here, you see. They kept themselves to themselves."

Rita had her notebook open, and she tapped it on the open page. "Can you remember anyone visiting their home recently? Or seeing anyone outside their house?"

Janet was thoughtful. "Apart from the postman..." Then her eyebrows crinkled, and her face lowered. "Hang on. I saw Nelly leave the house one day, in a car. A man was driving it. I can't remember the car, before you ask me. The man was young. It wasn't Stuart, and it wasn't the bloke Stuart had a fight with outside their house."

"Can you describe this man?"

"I'm sorry, love. My eyes aren't what they used to be. He was young, with short, dark hair. A white man. The car was nice, it looked sleek and I think it was black.

There was no one else in the car. That's all I remember."

Rita's mind was churning. Could it be Nelly's brother? Or someone else?

"When did you see this car pick up Nelly?"

"About mid-day, a couple of weeks ago. I don't remember Nelly coming back with him., though. Pretty sure that day she came back with the boy. She took the bus to school and back, as Stuart took the car, I think."

Rita smiled at Janet. "You've been very helpful. Thank you."

CHAPTER 11

Darkness had fallen, but the office was busy. Rita was staring at the screen on her laptop. Shola had sent in her report already, which was great news. The door opened, and Richard walked in with three pizza take away boxes.

"Fantastic," Rizwan said, and Maggie joined him in taking the boxes from Richard. Richard walked to Rita's desk and put some change on her desk.

"Change from a twenty for three large pizzas?" Rita raised her eyebrows.

Richard grinned. "That's why it's cheaper to live up North, guv. And I got an offer as I ordered three. Got the chicken Caesar salad for you."

He put the box and cutlery on her desk. Rita's tummy was rumbling. The others had already opened the boxes and were munching on their slices. Rita had opted for the healthier option. She eyed the pizza enviously, but was glad she was having the salad.

While she ate, she checked the report from Shola. She glanced at her team. “Have we got DNA samples from everyone? Including at the school?”

Richard spoke between mouthfuls. “Yes. I’ve sent them all to the lab as urgent samples. We should get reports by day after tomorrow. Shola should have the matches the following morning.”

Still three long days, Rita thought. If they hadn’t found Matt by then…she didn’t want to think about that now. Her tired mind was starting to get overworked.

Richard said, “Bob confirmed that the tyre prints are from Stuart’s car, and the prints from the back were not the same. A different car tyre left those marks.”

“That makes sense,” Rita said, sipping her water. “Even if Stuart did abduct the child, he would be bloody stupid to use his own car.”

“No witnesses have come forward about the car,” Richard continued. “I spoke to Steve Bennett, and Dave Adams, the two uniformed Inspectors in charge. Many residents were out at work, and those who were at home were in the back gardens and so on. And there’s no CCTV on the road.”

“Still, someone must’ve seen something. We have to keep looking for witnesses.” Rita shook her head. “What about CCTV on the main road?”

Richard, who had stayed at the nick to coordinate with Traffic and other forces, spoke again.

"We don't have the description of a car, which makes it difficult. We have seen Stuart's car however, first when he leaves for work the morning of Matt's abduction, and then later, at 12.30, when he returns. His black car turns off the main road, and into Osgood Lane, then disappears as it's a CCTV black spot. But we know that he appeared at home shortly thereafter."

Rita opened her up her notebook and thumbed to the right page. "Janet, the neighbour I spoke to, said the man arguing with Stuart that day drove an old, blue saloon. He took Matt in his car, so the man must be Mark Alridge, the biological father. Have we got hold of him yet?"

"Nope," Richard sighed. "He lives in York, so uniforms there have been to his house. He lives in a two-bedroom flat, a converted Victorian house." Richard lapsed into silence, and Rita read the look on his face.

"Mark's not there? And they can't find him?"

"Correct. I've sent you his photos, and other details."

Rita clicked on her keyboard, munching her food. As the pangs of hunger had cleared, her mind was functioning better.

She checked Mark's details. He was a good-looking man, with large, brown eyes that stared directly at her from the screen. His slender nose tapered into full lips, and his shaven cheeks were bordered by a strong jaw.

Under his police record, she found something interesting. “He’s been cautioned twice for violent behaviour in a pub, and he served a sentence for GBH.” Grievous Bodily Harm.

Rita looked up from the laptop. “Why was this not reported before?”

Richard said, “He used a different name in the PCNs. That’s why they didn’t show up. He didn’t have a custodial sentence for the GBH. He served out a community order, cleaning parks and sewers, and then he was released. Must’ve had a good lawyer.”

“Yes.” Rita checked the records. Mark had put his name down in the police files as Arnold Walsham. He had got into fights outside a pub, and then punched someone in the street, again outside a pub. The third offence had led to the charge of GBH.

“Have you checked the CSODS with the new name?” Rita asked.

Rizwan answered. “Nowt there, guv. He’s not a kiddy fiddler, whatever else he might be. I wonder why he used a different name for the cops though. What did he have to hide? If he didn’t have a police record, why bother with a false identity?”

“So the police wouldn’t harass him in the future. So he didn’t get into trouble at work.” Maggie said. She grimaced at Rizwan. “What sort of a detective are you?”

"The kind that looks behind the obvious, unlike you," Rizwan shot back.

"Ooh," Maggie made an O with her lips, then held her hands up like claws. "Somone woke up on the wrong side of the bed today. Getting grumpy are we?"

Rizwan looked at her with heavy lidded eyes, shaking his head as Maggie smiled at him sweetly.

"I mean," Rizwan said a little sheepishly, "Only seasoned criminals give a false name to the cops, don't they?"

"Not always," Maggie said, looking smug. Rizwan narrowed his eyes at her.

Richard said, "I know what Rizwan means though. If he's not been in trouble before, why act like he has?"

"Any houses or rental agreements under Arnold Walsham's name? What about cars, and the DVLA?" Rita asked. She was scrolling on the internet as she did so, typing Arnold Walsham's name. Her hands stilled as she got a hit. A wood artist called Arnold Walsham had a website with photos of his wooden sculptures. They were birds, horses, and other animals, all intricately carved. She saw Mark's face staring out from the About section on the page.

"Bloody hell. He's an artist as well." Rita murmured. "Come and have a look at this."

The team gathered around her desk and they checked the screen as Rita went through the pages.

"That's definitely him," Richard said softly. "But why on earth does he use this name? Kind of weird."

"A bit like an author using a pen name," Maggie said. "Although I have to say, this is a little odd."

Rita scrolled to the bottom of the screen. There was a number to call, and it was a York dial code. She pulled out her phone and called the number.

It went to answerphone, and a woman's voice said, "Thank you for calling AW Designs. Please leave your name and number and we will get back to you. While you're waiting, why don't you visit our warehouse? Discover Arnold Walsham's art, and see for yourself what the hype is about."

An address followed. Rita typed the post code on the map, and then zoomed in with the satellite vision function of the map. In an industrial estate, she found a warehouse with a triangular steel roof, and it looked deserted.

"If he's not at home," She whispered, "What're the chances he's there?"

CHAPTER 12

The man who abducted Matt wanted to call himself the Keeper. He was on his laptop, chatting with another man who had also abducted, and then killed two boys in Nevada, USA. They had been chatting for a while. This man, called Tyke, had been a member of the Gathering – the group that Joshua Dixon, the original Keeper, had formed. The man wanted a name for himself. He asked Tyke what it should be.

"Robert McFarlane called himself the Guardian. Then Dixon was the Keeper. You could be the Protector?"

"Nah," the man tapped on his keyboard. "I want to pay my homage. My name should be one of theirs." His fingers hovered over the keyboard. He was careful in his communications. He kept his real name hidden. He was talking to Tyke on the dark web now, but he was always cautious.

"The Keeper," he whispered to himself. That he was, definitely. He would keep Matt for as long as he could. His inspiration had come from the sick and depraved souls who preyed upon the vulnerable teenagers in the Gathering. The web group set up by Dixon. He had killed a teenager already, and it had increased his appetite. Blood begets blood, he thought to himself.

He typed rapidly. "I'll be the Keeper again. Maybe the Keeper II. That sounds good. Right?"

"Hell yeah," Tyke wrote. "You got to live up to that name. You've only killed one so far. Long way to go, buddy."

Wind whistled in through the cracks of the old window. The timber frame was rotting in the derelict house. The half broken wooden shutter slammed against the window sill. The man cursed, and rose. He saw a light in the distance and his eyes narrowed. It was a car's headlights. It moved far away, on the main road that was distant from the farm house. He relaxed as the car kept moving, and didn't get closer.

He signed off from the chatroom on the dark web, promising Tyke to be in touch with him soon. He checked the news, and went to the North Yorkshire Police website. As expected, he saw the posters of Matt's face plastered all over the website, with appeals for information. Crimestoppers had the same posters, and so did the local newspapers.

He couldn't hide the glow he felt inside. He was getting to be in the limelight. The teenager he murdered was a heroin addict and prostitute. She was a good taster, but she was also a nobody. She wasn't even reported as missing. No one cared. Maybe he should've left the body in a public place, instead of digging her a shallow grave in the woods. But a public place would have cameras, and he couldn't risk getting discovered. Not yet, anyway. He smiled as he thought of his plan. All in good time.

He went downstairs, and into the courtyard. The barn door was closed, and he had to put his weight behind it to open it. He liked his farmhouse. Yes it needed attention, but it was a good little hideaway. His father had left him a couple of these. He had brought the girl back here. When the urge to kill overtook him, he couldn't resist himself. He remembered her eyes widening with shock as his hands tightened around her throat. She fought back, but he was stronger. Then that final gasp, the soft exhale with which her chest stopped moving, and her arms became flaccid.

When the adrenaline subsided, he was filled with remorse. He cried for a while, then dried his tears. He picked up the body, and put her on his shoulder. She was a thin, waif like person. He took her to the woods, and laid her out while he dug the grave.

As he stepped inside the dark barn, he thought of her now. Her deathly white face, staring dark eyes, mouth filing with dirt as he shovelled it over her body.

He switched on the torch light in his hand, and went to the rear of the barn. Two large cages rested here. Inside one of them, the little boy lay, curled up with his knees tucked under his chin. The man kept the light off Matt's face. He was still fast asleep.

Good, the man thought to himself. The boy needed his rest. Matt would make him headlines. The Keeper would become a household name. He turned the light off, and stood there in the darkness, listening to the night sounds.

It was time to get in touch with the Keeper, Joshua Dixon. It was time to put his plan into action.

CHAPTER 13

The warehouse was in Burniston, a small village north of Scarborough. Richard rang the uniforms team, alerting them to check the warehouse. He got a call back soon, and from the look on his face, Rita could see it wasn't good news.

"All Units are busy," Richard said, with a resigned expression. He stifled a yawn.

"Go home, all of you," Rita said. The time on her wristwatch said half past seven. "Be back here bright and early tomorrow."

They protested, but Rita was firm. "It's been a long day. Go home now."

She waited for them to file out, then she called Jack. He answered on the first ring.

"I was wondering how you were. Long day?"

"You could say that. Listen, I was wondering if I could ask a favour. Are you busy this evening?"

"No, as it happens." He paused, and a note of caution entered his voice. "What's going on?"

Rita bit her bottom lip. Jack was a criminal lawyer, and he had helped Rita in several cases. She didn't want to involve him, but…in fact, all she needed was a lift. She didn't have to tell him what this was about.

"I can take a taxi to this place, it's near Whitby. Sorry, don't mind me. I shouldn't be calling you. Alright, good evening."

"Whoa, whoa, hold on. What's going on?"

"Nothing. I just have to see someone. It's a work-related matter. I shouldn't have asked you, sorry." Rita closed her eyes. She really should've just made her own way there.

Think next time, Rita, she told herself in silence. Don't let your subconscious ring Jack just because you want to speak to him.

"This is all very cryptic, Inspector Gupta," Jack said, a note of laughter in his voice. "A work related matter? Are you doing something you're not supposed to?"

"What? No. Look, just forget it."

"Did your D Sup not give you clearance, so you don't want to involve the uniforms? Or your team. Eh?"

"Shut up," Rita sighed. She knew Jack was messing, and she didn't have time for it. She would go to the warehouse, have a quick nosey around, and if she was in luck, might find something interesting. If she did, she would call for back up. That's it. She was tired, and not thinking straight. She shouldn't have called Jack.

"Look, I've got to go. Chat tomorrow, okay?" Before Jack could protest any further, she put the phone down. She took her extendable baton, the radio, her keys, and made for the door. She opened it and stood there, gaping.

Jack was standing there, a wide grin on his handsome face. "I happened to be around, so thought I'd drop by." His eyebrows wiggled, and his nice lips moved as he smiled. Rita tried not to respond. She locked the office and walked past him. Jack fell into stride with her.

"So, DI Gupta, where are we going?"

"I can go by myself."

"Of course you can. But that doesn't answer my question."

They walked through the front reception, and Rita waved at the duty sergeant, who waved back. They went down the steps to the car park. Jack pulled on her elbow, and she stopped.

"Right," he said. The street lights were on, and she could see his face. A tightness had appeared around his jaws, and his eyes glinted.

"Wherever you're going, we can go together, okay?"

Rita sighed. She didn't want to make a scene. "I don't want to get you involved."

"It's too late for that now." He raised a hand before she could speak. "I was going to knock on the office door anyway. Now you can tell me what's going on."

Rita shook her head. The tiredness was seeping into her bones, and her head felt weary. "It's the boy's father, Mark Alridge. He's given us the slip, I think. He's got another name, and PCNs under that name." She told Jack the story, and his eyes widened.

Then he pressed his lips together. "Strange behaviour that, for an artist. I mean, getting arrested and charged for GBH. He does wooden carvings, for crying out loud."

"Yes, it is weird. But you never know. He won't be the first artist who's messed up in the head."

They started to walk, and Rita knew Jack was going towards his car. He said, "So you want to check out his warehouse, see if he's hiding out there?"

"Yes."

"But surely, he will expect that. And if he is there, you should go with back up."

"I've asked already. There's no uniform unit around that's free." She saw the look on Jack's face, and grimaced.

"Don't do that. I need to go and have a look. Like I said, I'll see you tomorrow morning."

Jack's eyes dimmed, and so did his voice. "You remind me of the way you were years ago. You haven't changed."

"What's that supposed to mean?"

His words were gentle, like a caress to her skin, and they made her shiver. "You were always headstrong. Like when you looked for your mother. I think even the cops were scared of you. And you were just a teenager then."

He reached out to touch her shoulder. She didn't move. His warm hand rested on her shoulder.

"Look, all I'm saying is that don't rush into it. Why don't we ask once again if a uniformed unit is available now? They might be."

"Okay," she sighed. In her heart of hearts, she knew he was right. In truth, her heart was breaking when she thought of Nelly. No parent should have to put up with this. It was the reverse of what she had been through – the disappearance of her mother. She knew what it was like to feel the loss of a loved one.

She also knew there was no time to lose. She called on the radio, and the duty sergeant told her they were attending an armed robbery, and one unit should be free in half an hour.

"Meet us on site." She gave them the address. She looked at Jack. "Happy now? Will you give me a lift, or shall I take a cab."

"Good work," he said. "Come one, let's go."

They walked to Jack's nice BMW, and he wasted no time in getting it on the road. There was some traffic in the town centre, but when they hit the A171 road upto Whitby, Jack opened up the throttle. The four litre, sixteen valve engine growled as it leapt on the asphalt.

It took them twenty minutes to get to Burniston. It was a sleepy, quiet village, one that Rita had never visited. Hills bordered them on both sides of the road. As the car slowed, Rita wound the window down. The air was fresh, coming off the sea and the craggy cliffs. The houses looked well maintained. Like so many of the coastal, small hamlets up North, Rita imagined Burniston would be picturesque and pretty in the daytime.

Jack had slowed the car down as they trundled through the almost deserted high street. A corner shop was open, as was a pub. Two pubs in fact, almost opposite each other on street corners.

"Cut the headlights," Rita whispered.

Jack looked at her. "Is that necessary?"

"Just do it, and go into this side street. Quickly."

Jack pulled into the narrow alley between a row of shops. He cut the lights and engine. It was dark outside now, and they were at the end of a short, blind alley, with blue doors that were good entry for the shops on either side.

"If Mark has friends in town, then they might be in the pub. They'll know we're outsiders when they see us in the car, or when we walk into the pub."

Jack nodded. He was used to the ways of the smaller towns and villages. Everyone knew each other here.

He said, "So, either we stay out of the pubs, or only I go in. No offence, but you're still dressed like a cop. And Mark's friends might well know that a female detective is in charge of finding his son." Jack's eyes narrowed. "What are you suspecting here? That Mark abducted his son?"

Rita took a deep breath. "Well, it's an option we need to consider. He fought with Stuart at their door, while his son was in the car. That shows he's got a short temper. He's been convicted for GBH. And then he used his other name in the police records. He might have more to hide than we think."

Jack nodded in silence, still thinking. They got out of the car, and Jack decided to leave it there, as there were no parking restrictions, and it was walking distance to the industrial park.

They walked rapidly, and the wind had picked up, streaming up from the cliffs, buffeting against the sides of the buildings. Although only the streetlights were on, Rita could see the closed shutters of the small boutique stores and cafes.

It was a far cry from the gritty streets of Scarborough. Burniston would be nice in the summer, in daytime.

Now however, the wind was making her feel cold. As often happened in the coastal North East, sudden clouds had gathered from the sea, and the breeze was now freezing. Without realising, she had inched closer to Jack for warmth. She felt him stiffen, then relax. She glanced up at him, his face was rigid, facing ahead. His arm began to lift, then fell back to his side. Was he going to put his arm around her? Would she mind if he did?

A small voice inside told her she wanted him to. But a louder voice said this was neither the time or the place. She didn't know when the right occasion would be. Like so much of her life, perhaps she was overthinking this.

She grabbed his right elbow, entwining her arm with his. He relaxed then, and she felt warmer.

"Not far now," Rita whispered. She had looked at the map on her phone while Jack drove. They turned a corner, and went down a hill. The landscape changed, with open fields appearing on both sides. At the bottom of the hill, the warehouses appeared, separated from the street by a high fence.

"How're we supposed to get in?" Jack whispered. "I'm hoping there's going to be a gap in the fence somewhere."

"Yes, let's look."

Rita had a torchlight, but she didn't want to use it. There were no streetlights here, and the meagre starlight was now obscured by clouds. Her eyes were used to the dark, and with Jack, she walked swiftly, both of them checking the iron railings that made the fence. At the sides, the fencing disappeared into the woods behind. Rita stopped when Jack called her name.

"Look," he whispered, pointing to one of the dark squat buildings inside the compound.

They stood like silent, menacing ghosts, as if watching them intrude on their land. At first Rita didn't get what Jack was pointing at. Then she saw it. A glow of light from the ground floor of the warehouse just beyond a row of stacked pallets. The light seeped in from the bottom of the gates, and it moved. Someone was moving around. Then abruptly, the light went off. Rita listened intently. Apart from the night sounds, and the wind, she heard nothing.

Jack gripped the railings and tried to shake them. "What're you doing?"

In response, he put one foot on the lower rung of a horizontal rail, which crossed the vertical rails at roughly one foot intervals. Jack started to climb. He went up a few steps, almost to the top, then climbed down. Rita saw sweat glistening on his forehead.

"See that garbage dumpster?" Jack pointed at the square black object on the other side of the fence, that came up above his waist height.

“If I can get over the top, then I can drop down onto that. I could climb down to the other side as well. But if I wheel it to the fence, I can maybe give you a hand.”

Rita looked around her. Jack was right. They could waste valuable time searching for a gap in the fence, or tackle it now. She nodded, and he took off his jacket, and wrapped it around his waist. Then he started to climb.

CHAPTER 14

Jack heaved himself over the top, and then started to scale down the other side. He did it with an alacrity that didn't surprise Rita. Jack was lean and muscular, and had clearly looked after himself.

Once Jack was on the ground, he bent low at the waist, and ran to the dumpster. Pushing it to the fence however was a difficult task. He strained at it, but the object wouldn't budge.

Rita started to climb. It wasn't easy, and the railings were cold and hard to grasp. She had to make sure her rubber-soled feet maintained their grip. The iron was slippery. She got to the top, and not thinking about the undignified manner in which she had to get her leg over, she did it quickly. Her right hand twisted as she did so, and she almost cried out in agony. She stood there for a while, both feet on the railing, holding on for dear life, cursing herself.

"Are you okay?" Jack whispered from below. Without replying, she started to climb down. She had read somewhere that the downward journey was always harder on the body, and it was right. She couldn't see where she was going, and had to feel with her feet. She flinched when she felt Jack's hands on her waist, but then relaxed as he guided her down the final rungs.

"Bloody hell," she wiped sweat from her brow. "Remind me to do this in the daytime."

They kept low, and ran to the edge of the warehouse. Jack flatted himself on the floor in front of the roll up gates, and tried to see underneath. A short distance away, Rita did the same, as the gates were wide. She couldn't see the light anymore, but her ears picked up a sound. She pressed her ears to the ground, and the sound became clearer. Shuffling, like someone was walking around, inside. Would an animal make that sound? Not a fox, it had to be a large animal. Rita knew of the large cats rumoured to be around the North Yorkshire Moors. She got rid of that idea swiftly. The big cats wouldn't be out here, so close to human habitation.

Which meant someone was in there still, moving around. Jack got up, and signalled with his hand that he was going to the right. Rita nodded, and went down the left side. The warehouse walls loomed long and foreboding to her right.

Across the path, there was another warehouse, sunk in darkness like the other. She moved quickly, and came across a steel door. Gingerly, she tried the handle, but it was locked and bolted. She kept going, till she was near the end. The compound ended here, and there was a similar fence at the back, and woodlands behind it.

As she turned right, the smell of rotting undergrowth assaulted her nostrils. As she walked down, moving the leaves that fell over her face, she also detected the stench of animal waste. Her feet squelched in the wet path. Then she found the ladder going up to the walkway. She sent a text to Jack, who replied in a few seconds.

Rita put her hand on the cold iron and started to climb. She was almost halfway up when she heard a sound behind her. It was Jack, and he came up quickly to join her. Together, they climbed the narrow staircase to the metal doorway at the top. Rita felt the breeze tugging at her hair, cold on her cheeks. She put her hand on the cold metallic handle. This time, the handle turned. She bit her bottom lip, waiting for the creak as the door opened.

There was a creak, but it wasn't loud. The door was oiled, and had been in use recently, she thought. She pushed it further. An impenetrable darkness lay behind it. Jack reached out and pushed the door again. Rita went first this time, feeling with her feet. Her eyes got used to the new darkness, and she could make out a steel walkway, the kind that wrapped around the upper floor of a warehouse.

"Don't use your torch," Jack whispered. Rita didn't reply. She felt Jack's hand on her back as she stepped inside. Gingerly, she made her way to the right. As she stepped slowly, she could see the floorspace down below. Shapes covered the floor, squat, rectangular and square masses. She couldn't make out what they were, but they seemed to be covered up.

Rita got to the steps that went down. It was a single flight, and she stopped often, hearing only Jack's steps behind her. The dark shapes now loomed bigger. They seemed to be covered in tarpaulin, lashed down with rope. She wondered what they could be.

When she got to the bottom, she crouched against the wall. Jack joined her. Rita could smell engine oil, and old chopped grass and vegetation. She wondered if the shapes were farming machines, now wrapped up for transport elsewhere.

Her ears strained for sound, but she heard nothing. Yet, she knew there was someone here. Or had been here, just before they entered. She motioned with her hand, to show she was going right. The implication was for Jack to go the other way, but this time he shook his head. He grabbed her shoulder and leaned close to whisper.

"We stick together. The person could still be inside."

After a moment's hesitation, Rita nodded. She took out her extendable baton, and flicked it to the full size. Then she rose and moved slowly, her senses on fire. They stopped at the corners of the shapes, which now smelt strongly of oil or gas. They came across a clearing, and she saw wooden benches and worktops.

Now she could smell sawdust, and feel the dust beneath her feet. She inched closer to the worktops. Is this where Mark worked on his wood carvings?

At the rear, she could see shelves, and they had small objects on them which were only vague, black shapes.

Rita stepped out of the shadows and started towards the worktops, when a shape darted out from the right. It was upon her before she could react. She spun around, but she wasn't fast enough. Jack had sensed it, and pulled her back.

The figure brushed past her, and would've slammed into her if Jack hadn't dragged her out of his way. She collided against Jack, he lost his footing, and both of them crashed to the floor.

CHAPTER 15

Jack and Rita scrambled to their feet. Rita ran after the figure, shouting at it to stop. The figure knew its way around. Rita collided against a bench, and pain shot up her left ankle and knee. She almost fell, holding on to the bench for support. Jack ran past her, and she followed, half limping, half running.

Up ahead, she heard the sound of a door opening, and she felt the breeze blow inside. Jack was way in front of her now, and she saw him go through the gate, chasing after the figure. She heard shouts, and the sound of scuffling.

Then she was at the door herself, which led to the rear. Jack was picking himself up from the floor. She heard the railings shake, and looked up just in time to see the figure perched on the top, then jump over. She heard him fall on the other side with a grunt, and then some curses. Then she heard him run away. She pulled out her radio, calling for support. It was a pain that the uniform squad hadn't arrived as yet.

"Charlie Sierra Tango to Zero One," the radio squawked. "ETA is seven minutes."

Rita gave them the location quickly. "Go around the back please. He's running into the woods. I don't know where it ends, but see if you can cut him off."

"Roger that, guv."

Jack was up now, brushing wet leaves off his back. He now smelt rotten as well, like the old vegetation.

"You stink," Rita said, stepping closer to him. "Are you okay?" Unconsciously, she touched his head, then slower still, his face. Jack breathed heavily, but didn't move. Her hands rested on his face for a second or two, his skin warm under her touch. She felt sweat trickling down the side of his jaws. His hand reached up and held hers, then lowered it slowly.

"I'm fine," he said in a low voice. He still held her hand. Rita was sharply aware of the heat of their bodies, and the unsaid feelings that lay between them, pulsating like the warm night air.

Slowly, she moved her hand from his, and he didn't resist. The touch lingered in Rita's hand, and she made a fist, as if she wanted to savour it. Not now, a voice whispered inside her.

"He's gone," Jack said. He tore his eyes from her, and looked at the top of the fence. "I could've gone after him."

"No, you did the right thing."

"Actually, he kicked me, then I slipped and fell. Not quite the hero you had in mind, eh?" Jack grinned, and she couldn't help reciprocate. It's what she loved about him, his lack of ego. But she didn't want to see him hurt, especially on account of her.

"Where did he hit you?"

"He just kicked out from above when I started to climb and grab his legs. I lost my footing and fell."

"Sure you're alright?" She moved closer, touching his shoulder.

"Totally."

They heard the sound of a siren, getting louder. Then flashlights broke through the darkness above their heads. Running footsteps sounded in the space between the warehouse. Rita and Jack walked out from behind the warehouse, and into the space. Two uniformed officers approached them. Rita showed them her warrant card, but the officer waved it away.

"Sergeant Nizar reporting, guv," the tall man said. "He managed to give us the slip. We diverted another unit to the rear, but the woodlands are big, and it's going to take us ages to search in the dark, even with more units."

"And he might well be further away soon," Rita said. "Unless he tries to hide. We keep looking on the road that exits from the woods."

"It's the A171. He could flag down a truck for a hitchhike. The woods stretch down to the road in a broad arc," Sergeant Nizar explained. "I've asked for extra units, but they're all busy."

Rita thought for two seconds. They didn't have time to wait. She felt in her bones Mark had been hiding in the warehouse. He would know the woods well, and chances were he was already on his way to the main road. What if he had a car parked somewhere? She had the description of his car from the neighbour, Janet, but not the registration number. If she had the number, she could've asked Traffic to use ANPR.

"How many cars do we have here?" She asked, her breathing still short and fast.

"Only one here and another patrolling the A171."

Rita glanced at Jack. "Then we will join you. I'll radio for more units to be release from York, but by the time they get here it might be late. Join the other unit now, Sergent, and we'll meet you there."

Sergeant Nizar turned to leave but Jack called out after him. "Our car's a dark blue BMW M4, just so you know."

Nizar waved and Rita shook her head. "Show off," she said. She mimicked his voice, making a face. "I've got a BMW M4."

Jack spread his hands. "What? I don't want to get chased by the cops." He shook his head. "Unbelievable."

Rita put her torch on, and went back inside the warehouse. She heard the squad car screeching off, sirens on. She wished they would turn the sirens off. That was giving Mark notice they were nearby.

Inside, Rita flashed the beam around. Jack groped along the walls, looking for a light switch. He didn't find any. Rita got closer to the wood worktops, against which she'd almost fallen. Her light illuminated the shapes on the shelves beyond. They were wood carvings, some elaborate, like floral designs, and others bigger, like wooden statues of birds and squirrels.

"Why would a man who makes these want to abduct his son?" Jack murmured the question that was bubbling to the surface in her own mind.

Rita didn't like the answers that came to her. But there would be time to deal with them later. First, they needed to find Mark, and hopefully, he had Matt with him.

With Jack, she ran around the warehouse, in the frail hope that Matt was here. Jack managed to find the light switches near the front gates of the warehouse. The powerful overhead lights came now with a clapping sound. Rita blinked under the sudden glare. Another sound came from the front, loud and grating. Jack came back, looking sheepish.

"Sorry I pressed the gate button by mistake."

A quick search revealed only more packed machines, and pallets stacked on the side. No sign of Matt, or any of his clothes. But Rita did find a sleeping bag. With gloved fingers, she looked inside it. It felt warm. A man's boxer shorts were inside. Next to it, in a plastic bag there was a toothbrush, shaving kit, and toiletries. Rita put them in evidence bags, and stuffed the bags in her coat pocket.

"Let's join the search," she said to Jack. He nodded, and they ran to his car.

CHAPTER 16

The shrill alarm got Rita up at six am. She had slept soundly, for once. She slapped a hand over the offending device, and it shut up. She lay in bed for a few seconds, eyes blinking open. It was just starting to get light outside. The June sun was finding gaps in the curtains, but the light was still shy, as if mustering up courage to brighten up her room. Rita thought over the events of last night as she swung her legs out of the bed, and stood up, stretching.

They didn't find Mark. She had no doubt it was him in the warehouse. But she was sure he didn't have Matt with him. After the three cars – Jack's, and the two squad cars, searched the entire area the best they could, reinforcements arrived from York.

They shut down one lane of the A171 and renewed their search with spotlights and a canine unit. The dog found Mark's scent from the clothes in the warehouse, and also in the woods. But the trail petered off on the road. By that time, it was close to midnight, and Rita was exhausted. Jack dropped her off, and she apologised for taking up his time, which he brushed off with a wave.

"Never a dull moment now you're here," he said, with a wink. After he left, Rita just had enough strength to get changed, then she collapsed on the bed.

As she showered and got ready, the now familiar anxiety needled at her. Matt was still missing. So was Mark, but what good was chasing him if he couldn't lead them to Matt? And maybe Mark was hiding Matt somewhere else. Ergo, it made sense to chase Mark.

As Rita dried her wet hair, she wondered again why Mark was on the run. And why he had used a false name with the police. She could think of one person who might know. Nelly Crosby.

Rita left her flat and walked to the bus stop. She still didn't have a car, and she needed to get one. Scarborough wasn't big, but the countryside around it was, and the views were spectacular. She missed driving around, especially with the lack of traffic here. As she waited for the bus, she called Nelly once, despite the early hour. In her experience, the parents of missing children didn't sleep well. She wasn't surprised when Nelly picked the phone up.

"Hello? Who's this?"

"DI Gupta of North Yorkshire Police. I saw you yesterday at your house."

"Have you found Matt?" The edge in her voice was unmistakable. "Where is he?"

"I'm sorry, we haven't found him. But we are looking as hard as we can. We did find his father, Mark. Well, sort of. We found that he had a police record. He was arrested once, for GBH, or beating someone up. Did you know about that?"

There was silence for a few seconds. "No, I didn't. When did this happen?"

"About five years ago."

"We weren't together anymore. I don't know what he's done after we broke up."

"Yes, but did you see any threatening or violent behaviour when you were together?"

Nelly sighed. "To be honest, yes I did. That was the reason why I left him. I couldn't cope with his mood swings."

Rita paced the pavement, walking away from the bus stop. It was a half hour walk to the station, but she decided to do it. She could talk to Nelly on the way.

"Did he ever hit you?"

Nelly was quiet, and Rita heard her breathing, and the sound of deep, buried fear.

"It's okay," Rita said. "What you tell me will never be made public. Don't worry."

Nelly's voice had a wobble in it. "He did, once. It was a mistake, he said, and he was sorry. He never did after that. But it got me scared, whenever he lost his temper. He could lose it quickly, and go from being nice to a monster in seconds." Nelly gasped, then stopped. Rita thought she pressed her hand over the phone receiver to stop Rita from listening. Then she came back on.

"Why didn't you tell us this yesterday?"

"There was no time. And it's not relevant, is it? I broke up with him, and it's past history."

"It is relevant because he might be after Matt now. We didn't see Matt last night, but we found Mark in the warehouse. He manged to give us the slip." Rita explained what happened. She was going up a hill now, and the south side harbour came into view. She slowed her pace, saving her breath.

Nelly gasped. "Oh my god. He's got Matt, hasn't he? He's hiding him somewhere."

"We can't jump to conclusions," Rita said. "There might be another reason why Mark ran. But yes, it is one of the possibilities. It's upmost in my mind, I can assure you. We need to find Mark, but our priority remains to find Matt."

Even as Rita spoke, she knew the seconds and minutes were ticking down. With each passing hour, the chances of finding Matt were getting slimmer. Somehow, she had to reverse the tide.

"But where could he be?" Nelly wailed.

"Can you think of a place that Matt used to visit? Somewhere he liked to take Matt, for example?"

Nelly was silent for a while. "Nowhere specific, to be honest. We used to take little Matty to the beach, and on walks up to the castle. The usual things. I can't really pin point a place."

"Have a think, please. Let us know if you remember anything, it might help."

"Of course."

Rita transferred the phone from one hand to the other. Her palm was getting sweaty. The sun was also warmer now, rising over the sea. The view ahead was beautiful, the sea framed by the dark cliffs surrounding it in a pincer grasp. But she had no time for scenery.

"You never reported your trouble with Mark, did you?"

"No." Nelly was quiet. "Part of me now thinks I was wrong not to do it. I could've alerted the police about it." She sniffed, then sobbed, her voice breaking. "Oh god. Do you think this could all be my fault?"

"No," Rita said firmly. "You didn't do anything wrong. In fact, you did the right thing by leaving him." Most victims of domestic abuse, she knew, didn't leave their abusive partners. That was the real tragedy.

"Did Mark get into any trouble while he was with you? Did the police ever come to the house?"

"No. I would've known as I was always in when Matt was little. Mark was alright after Matt was born. But slowly, he reverted to his old ways. He could be mean when he was drunk. He never hit me again, but he did throw a vase in my direction after an argument one night. He was drinking too much, and coming home late from the pub. That's when I knew I had enough."

Nelly lapsed into silence again, and Rita gave her some time, knowing this was hard for her.

"Go on," she encouraged, eventually.

"I was afraid he wouldn't leave. So I took Matt and went to stay with my parents for a while. I had to threaten him with a restriction order."

"Did you get lawyers involved?"

"I didn't have to. When I mentioned the order and legal stuff, he backed down. He agreed to leave the house, as long as he could see Matt. I didn't move back in until he had cleared out."

"Where were you living at the time?"

"In Barrowcliff. We were renting. I took over the rent, and moved in after Mark had gone. Matt went to school there. It was a good community. Then I met Stuart, and moved to where we are now."

"Thanks. I wish you had told me all this when we met, but I realised the situation wasn't quite right. Does Stuart know about all of this?"

"Oh yes. He doesn't like Mark. In fact, he had an argument with Mark one day when he came to pick up Matt. Mark was late, and Matt was waiting for too long. Mark didn't like it as usual. I was afraid that day that he might kick off again. He hasn't changed."

"Yes, I heard about that." Questions were circling in Rita's mind. Matt still liked spending time with his father. He went with Mark willingly. Whatever Mark's faults were, he loved his son, Rita thought. She had to keep the balance right here. Mark's problems might be with women, not with his child.

"Did you know that Mark did wood engravings and statues?"

"Yes. He had a workshop as well, in Burniston I think."

"That's right. That's where we found him. He uses his false name as the wood engraver now – Arnold Walsham. That's also the name he gave to the police after he was arrested.

"I've never heard of that name," Nelly said. "It makes me think I barely knew him."

"It might've been a name he adopted after he left you. Don't worry. We will continue our efforts to find him. And hopefully, he leads us to Matt."

"Yes," Nelly whispered. "Please find my son."

CHAPTER 17

Matt wasn't drowsy anymore. He was in a strange place, and every time he moved, he hit something. He tried to get up, and his back struck something hard. He lay back down again. The smell was strange, unlike anything he had smelled before. It was also a little dusty, and he sneezed once.

He moved his hands and feet. He could stretch his legs out, but they soon hit something solid. He tried to raise his head, and he could, but if he lifted it too quickly, it hit the same solid object above. However, if he manoeuvred himself slowly, he could sit up. He did so. His hands moved around. It was dark, and he realised he was in some sort of cage. He could sit with his back almost straight, but he couldn't stand.

Where was he? And why was he here?

He had called for his mother several times, but got no response.

It was dark, and he knew it was night. His eyes had adjusted to the dark. He couldn't see much, but he knew there was a roof over his head; it felt like he was in some large room.

The first pangs of hunger had arrived, and he wished he could eat something. His throat was parched and dry.

"Mummy?" he called out. His voice was almost a croak. Matt drew his knees towards him, holding them tight, and placed his chin on them. It wasn't cold, but he shivered once. Was this some sort of game? It must be. Mummy and Stuart were playing with him.

"I want to get out of here!" he shouted. Again, nothing responded but a faint echo. Then he heard a sound. It sounded like a dog scratching on the ground. A heavy door was being pushed open slowly. Then lights came on overhead.

The sudden brightness blinded Matt. He screwed his eyes shut. When he opened them, he saw the bars of the cage for the first time. He also saw a man's legs, and he was wearing dark blue jeans. Matt looked up to see the man's face, but he moved quickly. Matt couldn't see his face or recognise any features.

The man had a key, which he used to unlock the cage. A bar slid open, and the man put his hand inside, touching Matt's shoulder. Matt looked up at him and realised he knew who it was. He stared back at the man in blank confusion, unable to speak.

“Come on, get up,” the man said in a quiet voice. Matt couldn’t move. The man grabbed his elbow and pulled him up, roughly. Then he picked Matt up and put him on the floor. Matt looked around him. Spades, hoes, and rakes were arranged on either side, along with small wooden enclosures that were meant to keep animals. He had seen pictures of these. Was he on a farm? That strange smell—was it from animals?

The man grabbed his hand and pulled him along. Matt didn’t question him. He was glad to be out of the cage. The barn was long. They went through a small passage and came out into the front section. He could smell hay now, and grass. There was an upstairs, with a ladder leading up to it.

“Sit down,” the man said, pointing to a table with two chairs. Matt did so, and the man gave him a glass of water. There was a microwave, and the man had some food inside it. He took it out—it was baked beans and sausage. Matt didn’t really like it; he preferred pasta. But from the man’s expression, he knew there was no point in arguing.

The man put the plate of food and water in front of Matt. “Eat that now,” he said, turning his back to him.

“Where’s my mummy?” Matt asked. The man kept his back to him and didn’t answer. Matt looked at the plate and heard his tummy rumble. Slowly, he began to eat.

CHAPTER 18

HMP Wakefield is a Category A prison. Some of Britain's most evil minds are incarcerated within its high walls. None of them will ever set foot outside the prison for the rest of their lives. Most of these highly dangerous men, and they are mostly men, live in separate quarters, where they are not allowed to mingle with other prisoners openly. The only prisoners they see are the ones in their own block. Each block has five prisoners, and each have their own personal guards.

Joshua Dixon stretched his arms to the ceiling in his room. He was doing Yoga, like he had been taught by the instructor at the prison gym. Joshua liked staying fit. He attended the gym daily, when he was allowed to. He liked staying fit, something he had learnt in the police force.

The knock on his door broke his concentration. He finished his asana, then got up. His room had a skylight recessed into the side wall, higher than any man could reach. Apart from that, the room had no windows. He had a bed and table, chair, whose legs were screwed to the ground.

The viewing box in his metal door slid open. The cold eyes of the guard appeared on the other side.

"Your visitor has arrived. Are you ready?"

Joshua smiled to himself. He was looking forward to this. His visitors were carefully selected – only close family were allowed. His sister visited him every month, and lately that had increased to twice a week. Joshua pretended to be sad if he didn't see his sister. He had learnt it was easy to fool the prison psychiatrist, who was responsible for his overall health. Joshua was on antipsychotic and antidepressant medications. He had to take them daily, even if he didn't want to.

"Give me ten minutes," he said. "I need to have a shower. She's early." He looked at the watch recessed into the wall. It was ten to two pm.

Joshua had a quick shower and got ready. He knocked on the door, and the viewing box slid open.

"Show me your hands," the guard said. Dixon did so. He moved back as the guards entered slowly. The first one grabbed his hands and put handcuffs on them. The other patted him down, then searched his room. He knelt on the floor and looked under the bed, lifted the mattress, slid his hand under the pillow cover. Dixon had some books on the shelf. He was reading about different religions, and he was enjoying it. He had come to the conclusion that all religions had the same spiritual conclusion – a spiritual unity of human beings with eternity.

He watched as the guard went through his books, and then his notepad, where he wrote letters to his family. Dixon knew every letter was read by someone before they were posted.

The guard who put his handcuffs on put a neck immobiliser on Dixon's shoulder, and the other one helped to fasten it at the back. They made sure Dixon could breathe, and wasn't uncomfortable.

Dixon had headbutted another prisoner in the canteen, hence the precaution. He felt trussed like a chicken going in the oven. Still, it meant he could see his sister.

"No funny business," the guard called Pete said. "You know what happens."

Dixon did. After the headbutting, he had lost canteen privileges. He could only eat inside his cell. That wasn't nice. He stepped forward calmly when Pete pushed him. The other guard, called Dan, fell in line behind Dixon.

They went to the end of the corridor, and through the metal double doors, which swished open when Pete held his ID card to the reader. They went two floors down to the ground floor. After another set of double doors, they entered a wide corridor. At the end, there was another checkpoint, with a glass observation desk in front. Security guards milled inside, some of them looked up as they came closer.

Dixon's handcuffs were made of plastic. He had to walk through a metal detector, raising his cuffed hands above his head. Then he walked out and was frisked once again. Finally, he was shown into the small chamber where he had to wait with a guard. The red dot above the door turned green, and the guard opened it, and pushed Dixon through it. He was now in the visitor's room. He was allowed barrier free visitor privileges. His eyes lit up when he saw his sister.

Janice half stood as he approached her. They weren't allowed to touch each other. But Dixon could receive gifts. Each visitor had to go through the same airport style security. Every gift was checked carefully by the security staff. In reality, nothing but food products passed through.

Janice leaned close to Dixon, putting her elbows on the desk. Her fleshy jowls hung down, and her big, red lips split into a smile.

"He's done it," Janice whispered, her face inches from Dixon's. "He's got the boy."

"Good," Dixon whispered back. "How is he getting in touch with you?"

"He comes to see me at night. Nice looking bloke, actually." Janice's large cheeks moved as she smiled. Her long, hooked nose had grown bigger with alcohol abuse. She had been in rehab several times, and relapsed often.

"He's also got in touch with Robert McFarlane," Janice whispered. "I don't know how. He wouldn't tell me."

"Clever man," Dixon smiled. He was glad the Brotherhood was now looked after. Robert was a father figure to him. It was Robert and the others who started the evil, abusive ring called the Brotherhood.

"He sends you this," Janice said. From her handbag, she took out a small, square block of homemade lemon drizzle cake. The guard looked interested, but then glanced away. That cake had been examined carefully, and scanned under x-ray.

"Good," Dixon smiled. "You did well. Did he give you the money?"

"Yes. Four hundred quid. He'll send it every month, he says."

"Excellent. Are the police treating him as a suspect?"

"They've been around. No, he's not under suspicion. He said he knows what to do."

"Great."

They talked for a while longer, then it was time for Janice to leave. She had to pick up one of her children from school. Janice had five children, but four of them were in care homes. Janice had custody of one child.

Dixon was handcuffed again, and led back to his cell. He put his ear to the door, listening to the steps fade. Then he put the cake on the table. He sat down, and carefully removed the wrapper. The cake was moist, and he dug his finger inside easily. There was a tablet inside, the size of a large pill. He took the pill out, and cracked it with his teeth. Inside, there was a tiny, rolled up scroll. Dixon flattened it on his table top. He had to smile when he read it. He was inspiring the next generation, even though he was locked away for life.

I will ask for ransom. If not, I will say the boy will die. I will call myself the Keeper. Is that okay?

CHAPTER 19

The Major Incident Room at Scarborough's Police Station was full to the gills. It was the second day in a row that the MIR was this full, and Richard had told Rita he couldn't remember the last time that happened.

Behind Rita, on the projector screen, Mark's passport photo was displayed. Rita had already told everyone about last night's escapade.

"He can't be far. There's not that many roads around Burniston. His car's an old banger, according to Janet, the secretary. We found the car on DVLA," Rita nodded at Maggie, Rizwan and Richard, sat on the front row. Maggie had given her Mark's car's details as soon as she walked into the office.

"It's a dark blue Honda, 2008 reg. Traffic haven't seen it on the A roads as yet. Namely the A165 and A171." Rita pressed on the remote, and pulled up a map of the region.

"There are smaller country roads as you can see, and they don't have cameras. But he can't get far on them, unless he's hiding in a farm. That could well be the case, there are plenty of derelict barns and farmhouses dotted along the coast. We have teams from Leed, York and Whitby joining us, and the Coastguards."

A hand went up, and it was Inspector Bennett. "He could have escaped into North Riding Park. The terrain is mountainous, and there's plenty of rivers. Hiding there would be easier for him, and harder for us to find."

"We need to get eyes up there," Rita pointed to the sky. "Are the drones operational?"

Richard answered. "Yes. They are moving in the air around Burniston now, and there's two of them. We can get two more, if necessary."

"Let's do that, ASAP. Any updates from the Coastguard?"

Rizwan answered. "Nowt as yet. Their helicopters have been up since first light, and done the whole coastline. They have two boats, and they've checked with the harbourmaster at Scarborough and Whitby. Mark Aldridge didn't own a boat, anyway."

"But he could steal one. He's a local lad, he'll know about boats, and where he can find a cave to hide in. Relay that to the Coastguards, please."

"Aye, guv," Rizwan said. "There's no caves around the beaches on Burniston, as far as I know."

"But there are cliffs, and that area is part of the North York Moors. We need to look at the wild beaches. I think the helicopters and drones will be very useful for us." Rita paused.

"But more important than Mark is finding Matt. Anything from our extended door to door, yesterday?"

From the shaking heads, Rita knew the answer. Her heart sank, but she battled against it.

"We need to keep going. Someone must've seen something, somewhere."

Bennett raised his hand, and voice, again. "There's a path around the coast called Cleveland Way. It's a rambler's path. It goes past Burniston, and all the way up to Whitby, I think. Only ramblers though. If he's only walking, he could be on that path."

"Right. We keep looking. I want reports every hour. All Points Bulletin are out. If Mark tries to get on a train, plane or take the ferry to Europe, we're going to know. Let's find him ASAP."

The D Sup, Nicole, hadn't arrived, Rita noted with relief. The meeting broke up, and they went to the office. Maggie and Riz went to the canteen to pick up coffees. When they were all back, Rita went to the white board.

"Mark hid from us, and then ran away for a reason. He had guessed, I think, that we knew his previous history. Wouldn't take long to find out, obviously, and he was right. He thinks he might get arrested, given his violent behaviour."

"And what if he did?" Rizwan said. "That doesn't make him a child abductor?"

"Exactly," Rita pointed the marker pen at him. "And remember what Matt scribbled on the wall by his desk. *I miss Daddy*. Matt liked being with Mark. It's possible that Mark wasn't getting enough custody and he had planned to abduct his son all along. He knew that Matt would come with him willingly."

Maggie shook her head. "And leave his mother? A little boy wouldn't just do that guv."

"Unless he was told they were going on a holiday and would be back soon. Matt doesn't know. Besides, he might well have been asleep when he was abducted."

Richard said, "But where is Mark hiding Matt? If he's got him, that is. Wouldn't he have been with Matt, instead of sleeping in the warehouse?"

"Maybe he came to collect his things," Rita said. "And we surprised him. His toiletries were there, with his sleeping bag." Rita frowned as she thought. The bag looked slept in. Was Matt living there with Mark? Maybe Mark moved him, then came to get the sleeping bag.

"Let's go back to the day before," she said, rolling the sheets back up, to get to the timeline of Matt's disappearance. She tapped the pen on the sheet of paper where times were written in red.

"Nelly goes to her neighbour's house for half an hour. Between half ten and eleven. That was all the time Mark had to climb over the fence and take Matt away. And yet, Traffic haven't found his car."

"They might," Richard said. "They should be done soon. There was a car there, behind the fence, correct?" All heads nodded. "And the tyre prints are not that old. So there was a car there the day before. It would be there for a reason, as it's not the normal place to park a car."

"And the only reason I can think of," Richard continued, "Is that Matt's abductor was either snooping, or he actually got Matt and disappeared."

Rizwan was looking at his laptop. "Hang about. I just heard back from Mark's employer at York University, where he used to be a security guard. He didn't actually work for the University, he worked for a firm that handles the contract. Anyway, he's not been to work for the last three days. And he drove to work. The car's reg number matches what we found on the DVLA."

"An old car, like the one waiting behind the fence," Rita said. "Has Bob got back about the tyre prints?"

"Yes hold on," Maggie said, scrolling through her screen. "Nope, there's no match."

Maggie's face turned pale, and she blinked a couple of times. She got up from her chair rapidly. "Excuse me," she said, and literally ran out of the room. The two men looked at Rita and shrugged. After a while, Rita went out of the office. She walked down the corridor till she came to the bathrooms, and saw Maggie coming out. The constable looked flushed, and she tucked a few strands of hair behind her ears. She was surprised to see Rita.

"You alright?" Maggie asked Rita.

"Yes, I'm ok." Maggie grimaced and put a hand over her belly, smoothing down her blouse. "Something I ate last night, that's all."

Rita nodded. "OK. See you back in the office."

CHAPTER 20

Mark Aldridge gripped the steering wheel of his blue Honda car, and stared out over the green foliage that covered the windscreen. He had hidden the car in the undergrowth, in the slope of the woods that went down to the cliff over the bay. He had done a good job, and the police cars, or the helicopters overhead, still hadn't found him. But he had to be careful. The police had infra-red heat maps, and he could still show up on their cameras.

He couldn't be out here for long. He should be in a public place, while the idiot police looked for him out here in the open. A high street, or market, would be his best chance to hide, but he needed to get there first.

He could drive out of here, down the dirt track, and then into the farm road that led to the A171. Or maybe the Coastal Road, which was smaller, and with less traffic. Both roads went to Scarborough. He had to get to a bigger town, somehow. Out here, between the coastguard and the cops, he would be caught like an insect in a spider's web.

He thought of last night, and shivers ran down his spine. He should never have gone back to the warehouse. The cops had arrived there, and they had been clever, not to turn up with sirens blazing and lights flashing. It was a couple, and he thought he had seen the woman somewhere before.

Mark closed his eyes, breathing fast. He had been lucky to escape. Melting away into the night was easy, he knew the woodcutter's path through the woods. He would've started driving last night, but the bloody cops had shut down the main road.

He needed to get down to Osgodby, to put in motion the last phase of his plan. He had a strategy, and it was starting to pay off. Nelly and Stuart were running scared. The two bastards, who thought they could keep his son away from him. When he thought of Matt, his heart twisted in sorrow. The old wound opened up inside him, and he bit his lower lip as his head dropped.

He could make this right. He would come through, and be a good father to Matt, no matter what nightmare they were living through now. It was a storm, and it would pass. He knew that. He had to believe in it. Tears blurred his vision, and he gripped the steering wheel tightly.

He would show that Stuart what he was made of. Trying to keep Matt from him? Well, Mark would have the last laugh.

Every sinew in his body was itching to drive the car out, and start down the road to Osgodby. But he would get caught, in this car. He wondered if he should steal a car, and while that was an option, it might get him into more trouble. Residential streets and car parks had cameras, and he would be caught in them. No, there had to be another way.

He would have to hitchhike. The solution was brilliant, and simple. He thought about what to do with the car. It was his escape, and also for Matt, but it was now a liability. The cops were looking for it, and the cameras would pick it up easily. No, he was better off leaving the car here.

Mark got out of the car, and took his backpack. Then he set off for the main road, at a brisk jog. He walked along the A road, cars zipping past him. When he saw the lorries coming, he stopped and raised his hand. One truck pulled over to the hard shoulder eventually.

The truck driver yelled over the sound of his engine. "I'm going down to Hull."

"Great," Mark hauled himself inside the cabin. "Drop me off near Osgodby, please."

CHAPTER 21

"What?" Rita's hand rested on her waist, and she frowned as she listened on the phone. "When did this happen?"

Lucy, the FLO who had just turned up at the Crosby house, was on the line. "Nelly found it this morning, guv. It was in the letter box. It was after she spoke to you. She showed it to me."

"Does the letter have a return address or stamp on it?"

"There's no return address. It's only signed as the…"

"The what?" Rita asked impatiently.

"The Keeper II. Strange name that, guv."

Rita felt she'd been hit by a sledgehammer. Her eyes closed and she leaned against the table. Her head was spinning, and she sat down quickly, then opened her eyes.

"Guv, are you there?"

"Yes." Rita cleared her throat and composed herself. "Tell me again what the letter says."

"I want a hundred thousand pounds, or Matt will die slowly. I want the money tomorrow, at the North Cliff Park at 4PM. Leave the money under the park bench next to the bandstand.

Once I get the money, I will tell you where Matt is, and you can pick him up. He will be safe, I promise – but only if you get me the money.

If you tell the police, or if I get caught, my associates will start torturing Matt. In two days' time, you will receive his severed little finger. Every day you delay, you will get a new finger, till he has none left.

The Keeper II."

The last two words hit Rita like a sledgehammer. Blindly, she groped for the chair behind her. She didn't care that the others in the office were looking at her strangely. She sat down heavily and cradled her head in her hands.

"You're sure the letter is signed as the Keeper II?"

"Yes, guv."

Rita screwed her eyes shut. It felt like a screaming bullet had smashed against her skull, the noise drowning out all other thought in her head. She rubbed her forehead.

"Okay, I'm on my way. See you there."

“Oh, and guv? There’s also a photo, a print out of a digital photo I think, like it was taken from a camera. It shows Matt. It’s a close up of his face.”

“I see,” Rita sighed. “So this isn’t a hoax then, I guess.” They had started getting hoax calls already, on the national lines.

She hung up, and put the phone carefully on the desk. Maggie, Richard and Rizwan were staring at her. She told them about the ransom letter.

“It’s signed as the Keeper II. I don’t think that’s a coincidence.”

“You mean, the guy we caught the last time? The freak PC, Joshua Dixon?” Maggie was aghast. “But he’s dead. How does someone know about him?”

Rita’s mind was twisted like loops of spaghetti. “He was a part of that group called The Brotherhood. Remember them? A bunch of sickos who preyed on vulnerable teenagers, abused them, killing them to offer them the final freedom.”

They were quiet for a while. Everyone remembered that case well, particularly as the cost had been a personal one to Rita. She and her father, Jay, almost died in the process.

“Interpol and the National Crime Agency managed to take down most of that network,” Richard said.

“Well not all of it, clearly,” Rita snapped. “Otherwise, this gutter snipe wouldn’t be calling himself Keeper II, would he?" She glared at him, then snapped her eyes shut. "I'm sorry," She shook her head. "I didn't mean to shout. I'm just a bit..." Rita was lost for words as her hands cradled her forehead.

"This is a whole new angle. I can't believe…" her words were lost as she thought of the implications.

Who had known about the Keeper? The police, obviously. Who else? The psychopaths inside The Brotherhood. The Keeper was now in prison, and his prolonged absence would have made his followers suspicious. The fact that many of the followers were arrested later on, and their network largely dismantled, only meant some of them had found other ways of staying active.

These evil people still lurked in the shadows…and had one of them kidnapped Matt?

It had to be. Otherwise, they wouldn't know about the original Keeper. Joshua Dixon. An unassuming young man, who had masqueraded as uniformed police constable. She knew where he was – in the ultra-secure HMP Wakefield, one of UK's eight Category A prisons.

Who was now pretending to be him? Maybe the answer lay in Dixon's convoluted, despicable mind.

Rita got to her feet. The others were watching her closely, aware of how personal this was to her all of a sudden. The air in the office seemed dense, heavy.

"Maggie, come with me. You two please stay here and coordinate with Traffic. Let's find Mark Aldridge asap."

"Is Mark the Keeper? I mean, the one who signed the letter?" Rizwan echoed the thoughts in all of their minds.

"Maybe. He's become desperate now that he's being hunted. But it doesn't make sense that he would hurt his own son. Someone else is involved here, I think."

Richard said, "Mark could just be lying about the torture. He's doing it to get money out of Nelly and Stuart. If he scares Nelly, then she might do something desperate. Does she have that sort of money though? Doesn't seem like it."

"That's a good point," Rita said. "Nelly might have money we know nothing about – like an inheritance. Mark knows about it, and hence is trying to scare her into coughing up."

"He's taking a risk though. A big one," Rizwan said. "He could easily get caught. That tells me either he knows the plan will work, or he's so desperate he doesn't care."

Rita raised a hand. "In the end, our key job is to find Matt, safe and sound. I don't care about Mark or even the Keeper. Come on, let's go."

"No word from Traffic as yet about the car behind the Crosby's house," Rizwan called out as Maggie and

Rita walked out of the office. "Or of Mark's blue Honda."

"Good," Rita said, turning. "Tell them to keep looking."

Two squad cars had blocked off Seaview Avenue, on either end. Uniforms stood guard by the blue and white crime scene tape. The reason was obvious, and Rita's heart sank when she saw it – reporters. They had descended in their droves, brandishing microphones, cameras, boom sound sticks, the whole lot. Outside white vans, female reporters were checking their make-up, and some were doing rehearsals with their camera men. They turned like a pack of wolves as Rita and Maggie drove up. Instinctively, the media vultures seemed to know that Rita was a police detective.

Two uniformed sergeants had to hold the baying mob back, as they all rushed towards Rita. Questions were hurled at her as she ducked under the police tape.

"Where is Matt Crosby?"

"Is Matt dead?"

"Do you suspect the parents?"

"When are you going to hold a police conference?"

Rita ignored them. The reporters jostled for space, and the uniforms struggled to contain them. Another three uniformed constables joined their colleagues, to hold back the reporters.

Inspector Bennett appeared, looking stressed. “They started arriving about an hour ago. It was a couple at first, then there was a wave of them.”

“They report on social media as soon as they’re on site and that alerts the others,” Rita said grimly. “I’m surprised it took them that long. Keep them away from the house. I feel sorry for the parents. They can’t even go outside now.”

They walked to the house, Rita aware of the neighbours standing outside and talking. They stopped as Rita and Maggie walked past. At the Crosby’s house, Lucy opened the door before they could knock.

They went into the kitchen and living area at the back. Stuart was pacing the room, his colourless face pinched and nervous. Nelly was sat on the couch, legs folded underneath her, staring at the floor. Stuart stopped and glared at them when they walked in.

“He wants money,” Stuart blurted. “A bloody ransom. I mean, how can you not know who it is? He’s sending mail here for crying out loud.”

“Sending post doesn’t mean we can locate him,” Rita said calmly. “We will find him, don’t worry.”

“Don’t worry?” Stuart’s chest heaved, and it seemed like he was having a panic attack. “This arsehole’s saying he’s going to chop Matt’s fingers off. How can we not worry?”

Rita glanced at Nelly, who was sitting there wide eyed, observing them. Rita suppressed the urge to slap Stuart, to get him to calm down.

“I can understand your concerns,” Rita said. “But panicking now isn’t going to help. If you stay calm you can also support your wife.” Rita flicked her eyes at Nelly, who didn’t seem interested anymore.

She was staring out the window, ignoring them. Rita thought of their conversation this morning. Nelly had a bad relationship with Mark. What was it like with Stuart? There didn’t seem to be much in the way of love between the couple – or was she being too judgemental? It was in the way they sat far apart from each other, avoided meaningful looks or glances – in fact, any eye contact at all, and that bothered Rita. She made up her mind to speak to Nelly in private.

“Right,” she asked Lucy. “Where’s the letter?”

CHAPTER 22

The words were written in block capitals, using a normal ball point pen. Wearing gloves, Rita held the paper up to the sunlight. No watermarks, and no smudges to take fingerprints from. But she would give it to Shola anyway, to see if she could do anything with the paper.

Rita picked the photo up carefully. It was bigger than a passport size photo. It showed Matt's scared face, and Rita's heart twisted in sorrow. The poor, frightened boy. He had dark shadows under his eyes, and stains on his cheeks from where he had been crying. It made Rita want to give him a hug. Her eyes closed. She could only imagine what Nelly and Stuart were going through.

The photo's background was blurred, and dark. It had been taken with a flash, as Matt's face was brightly lit, but nothing else was visible. Apart from his face and neck, Rita could only see the top of his T shirt. Matt didn't have any other marks on his face. His hairline and scalp looked untouched. She put the photo in an evidence bag. She knew Shola would magnify every inch of that photo, and run it under an electron microscope to see if she got anything from the background.

Rita read the letter again, a shiver running down her spine. She gave the letter to Maggie, who inspected it. Rita walked over to Nelly. Stuart was still fidgeting and Rita ignored him.

“When did you see the letter?” She asked.

Nelly turned her head to Rita. “I came down to make tea, then Lucy arrived. I opened the door for her, then decided to check the letter box. It’s on the side wall, just outside the front door. That’s when I saw it.”

“What was written on the envelope?” Rita realised she had not seen the envelope as yet.

“It said – To Matt’s Parents. That’s all. No return address, nothing.”

“What did you do with it?”

“I showed it to Lucy, and we opened it together.”

“I didn’t touch it,” Lucy said. Rita nodded at her. One less fingerprint set to exclude. She walked over to the kitchen counter and checked the envelope. It was a simple, cheap, white A4 envelope. There was a second-class postage stamp. On the front it was addressed to Matt’s parents, with nothing written on the other side. Rita looked inside the empty envelope. No smudges of ink. Shola would probably find no fingerprints, because the sender would surely have worn gloves.

"You must know where that envelope came from," Stuart said, coming closer. "You lot can track these things, right?"

His eyes were red rimmed from lack of sleep. His jaws were working, his thin cheeks caved in, making his eyes look bigger. He was on the edge. Rita felt a little strange, observing him. Nelly and him had been together for two years, so he only had that time to know Matt. Clearly, he saw Matt as his son.

"Unless we know which specific post office it came from, we can't do much," Rita said quietly. She glanced at Nelly, who was listening to them. "But we can go through all the post offices in town, and around Scarborough. They will have cameras. That will take some time, but we might get some leads. We have to be patient."

"Patient?" Stuart's Adam's apple bobbed up and down. "We only have till tomorrow 4pm. What are you going to do?"

"We do not negotiate with kidnapper's," Rita said. "I know this is incredibly stressful for you, but you need to keep your wits about."

"That's easy for you to say," Stuart said, running a hand through his hair. But he stepped back, and slumped on the chair.

Rita looked at Nelly, who was looking defeated as well, staring at the floor.

"You don't know who this person is," Rita said. "I can tell you that the webpage we set up, and on the telephone line, we are starting to get hoax calls." The couple looked up at her.

"That's one of the problems with a national alert," Rita said. "We have to weed out the hoax calls from the genuine ones."

Nelly spoke. "Could this be a hoax letter? I mean, I can't see how, unless he's forged Matt's photo, somehow."

"No," Rita said. She didn't want to tell them about the Keeper. Not right now, anyway. "The photo looks genuine. He has been quite specific about the location to drop off the money. He probably thinks you'll give in to his demand. I would suggest you don't."

Stuart frowned, his jaws working again. "Eh? What do we do about Matt, then?"

"What if you give him the money but don't get Matt back?" Rita raised an eyebrow. "He's only said he will tell you after he gets the money where Matt is. That sounds dodgy to me."

"So, you think he's lying?"

"I think it's worth baiting him. Leave a bag at the location. See if he turns up. If he does, we can grab him. Personally, I think he will have the location under surveillance, just like we will. If he's clever, he will spot us, and stay away. But he might not see us. He might make an error. Then we get him."

Stuart's feet tapped on the ground, and he stopped when Rita looked at him. He gulped. "I think we should pay him the money. What if we can get Matt back?" He looked at Nelly, and for the first time, Rita thought there was a silent exchange between husband and wife. But Nelly looked away, as if she wasn't interested in what he might have to say.

An uneasiness was starting to prickle at Rita's spine. She turned to Nelly. "What do you want to do?"

Nelly sighed. "I don't know. You're right – he could just take the money and run. Can we get in touch with him? This…Keeper, or whatever he calls himself."

"What for?"

"To ask him to send us proof where Matt is, like you said. Or that he has Matt, for definite."

Rita thought for a few seconds. "We could send out a message in our social media channels. See if he responds to that. The only problem is the media attention we have now." Rita pointed to the main door, and street behind. "Once we address the Keeper," Rita shuddered as she said the name, and hoped no one noticed it. "Then the media will also know. They will go into a frenzy, and we might get a lot more hoax calls then. I have to say, none of the hoax calls so far have been for a ransom."

"I suggest we do that, then," Nelly said.

The sound of voices came from outside. Lucy showed in an older man. His hair was white, and he was bulky in the shoulders. He wore a blue jacket and jeans. There was an authority in his appearance, he seemed a man used to telling people what to do. Nelly rose from her seat, and the man went up to her, without giving Stuart a second glance. Nelly embraced the man, whom Rita assumed was her father.

"Daddy," Nelly said softly. "Thanks for coming."

"I got your text an hour ago. I came as soon as I could."

"This is Inspector Gupta," Nelly introduced Rita. "This is my dad, Graham."

Graham shook hands with Rita. He had an iron grip, and his blue eyes flashed at her. The sharp cut of his clothes, and the well-trimmed beard, made Rita think this man was wealthy. He didn't waste time getting to the point.

"Do you think the ransom letter is genuine?"

"That's what we were discussing," Rita said. "There's no doubt this man has Matt. I don't think that photo is a fake. However, we have to be cautious. A photo can be manipulated. If someone had access to Matt's photos," she stopped to glance at Nelly and Stuart, "then they could photoshop them, alter them to look like the one sent with the letter."

A new-found respect gleamed in Graham's eyes. "What do you think the chances of that are?"

"Well, its family members who have childrens photos," Rita said. "Has a photo album gone missing recently, or has anyone's phone been stolen?" Rita looked at the couple again, and both of them shook their heads. Neither looked happy at Rita's suggestion, and Stuart spoke up.

"Are you now saying the kidnapper – this Keeper, as he calls himself, doesn't have Matt, and he's posting a fake photo?"

"I'm saying we need to consider that as a possibility. That's why we have to be cautious in our dealing with him. We can bait him, but that doesn't necessarily mean he has Matt."

Nelly got up and stood beside her dad. Rita noticed how father and daughter completely ignored Stuart. Something was very off with the family dynamics here.

Nelly said, "Hang on. How could the kidnapper have Matt's photo if he doesn't have him?"

"He got Matt's photo from somewhere," Rita shrugged. "We have posted his photo online, on Crimestoppers's, the police website, you name it." She raised a hand as Nelly went to speak. "Yes, I know that he looks sad in this photo, but you would be surprised at how well photos can be manipulated these days."

"Have you sent Matt's photo to any of your friends recently?"

Nelly shrugged. The dark shadows under her eyes were more pronounced today, as was the tired droop in her eyes. Yet, her breathing was fast and shallow. Like Stuart, she was also on the edge. The difference was she was trying her best not to show it. Brave woman, Rita thought to herself.

"Only to my parents. The usual kids' photos. To a couple of my friends as well, but they don't live in Scarborough."

"Can you please check with your friends to ensure their phones have not been stolen, or been hacked?" Rita frowned. "Actually, can I please have a look at your phones?"

Nelly, Stuart, and finally Graham as well handed their phone to Maggie, who stepped forward to collect them.

She opened the phones one by one, with their passwords. Maggie helped Rita as they went to settings, and then checked the software embedded in the phone. Both of them knew the tell-tale signs of phone getting hacked – the battery became hot, and the phone started to slow down, or develop glitches when showing photos, checking emails, and so on.

"Nowt here, guv," Maggie whispered, handing Nelly and Stuart's phone back to Rita. "I can't see any malware or spyware. I don't think they've been hacked."

Rita was finishing up with Graham's phone, and then nodded. Maggie handed the phones back to them.

"So what do we do now?" Stuart asked, his voice high pitched. Graham gave him a disdainful look, the kind of expression a parent reserves for a spoilt child. Stuart noticed it, and he seemed to cower under Graham's vengeful stare. Nelly stood silent, expressionless.

Rita said, "Tomorrow we take a bag to North Cliff Park. An empty bag is fine. One of you has to take it. Do as the Keeper instructed. Put the bag under the seat, and then walk away. Let's see if he turns up."

CHAPTER 23

Mark Aldridge stayed in the layby overnight, where the truck dropped him off. He curled up in his bog coat, and covered himself with leaves and bushes. It was a warm night and he managed to get some sleep. He woke up with the first light. The trucks were already rumbling past, and the A road was busy. There was a mobile burger joint, and he bought himself a hot dog for breakfast.

As he ate, Mark considered his options carefully. He needed to see Nelly again. He had to keep control of himself and not scare her. Remorse filled his heart when he thought about how he had treated her. If only he could go back in time... But that luxury didn't exist for anyone. He couldn't change anything, and the path he had chosen for himself had only one resolution.

He had to see things through to the end. He didn't know the final destination yet, but all he wanted was for Matt to be happy. And he knew Matt wasn't happy in that house.

He had to make amends with Nelly, and the brief flicker of hope flamed to life in his heart, giving him some warmth. If—and it was a big if—he could speak to Nelly and make her understand, make her see his point of view. Perhaps she might take him back. He would go back on the antidepressants, see a psychiatrist, do whatever she wanted him to do. If necessary, he would even check into a hospital, if that's what she wanted.

The problem lay in contacting her. The police would be monitoring his phone, and hers as well. As for that Stuart, Mark didn't trust him at all. There was something in his eyes when he looked at Matt that gave Mark a sick feeling in the pit of his stomach.

He tried to act too friendly, patting Matt, and the boy pulled away. He did it in a subtle way, but Mark could see. He knew Nelly was also aware, and she must not like it either—not that she had ever confided in Mark. And why would she? Grief and rage tormented his soul. Nelly was the key to this—and he had let her down. If only he could speak to her—just once.

He got up and walked the last few miles to Nelly's house. Correction: Stuart's house—or at least that's what he liked to say.

Mark remained convinced Nelly had made a mistake. Stuart wasn't a safe character, and he doubted Stuart treated Matt very well.

Life depended on the choices we made, Mark thought as he trudged up the slope of the hill, the sea on his left, houses on the right. No one could know what consequences a choice would have, and we all had to do what we thought was best. But sometimes, the choices we made took us down the wrong path. And our personalities were the key determinants of the choices we made—our reactions, our hopes, and our fears.

Maybe if we could change ourselves, then it would be easier to live with the consequences of our choices.

Yes, Mark knew he had to change himself.

His impulsive, often dangerous behaviour had to change. He was only at peace when he was in his workshop, engrossed in his woodcarvings—the way the chisel slid over the wood, the shapes that emerged from under his hand, how the hard material seemed soft as putty, growing with every breath of life he infused into the grains of wood. Art was his salvation, but his personality was his downfall.

How could he subtract himself from his own life? He had to change, and he could be better in his dealings with people. With Nelly, first and foremost. Matt was his flesh and bone, but he had also shouted at Matt on occasion. He had apologized and showered him with gifts later on. He would never hit Matt; he knew that. He would rather chop his own hands off. Tears blurred his eyes as he thought about his son. How he loved that angelic face, that sweet smile. He needed to see Matt, without delay.

He stopped under a tree, pulled out his phone, and checked himself in the selfie view. God, he looked awful. He brushed down his hair the best he could. From his water bottle, he splashed some water on his face, smoothing down his wild locks. He took off the jacket, wrapped it inside his backpack, rolled up his sleeves, and flattened his shirt collar.

As he got closer to Seaview Avenue, he noticed the number of cars on the road. He had expected a police presence outside the house, but this was different. He stopped, fear suddenly spiking in his veins. White vans with satellite dishes on top were parked on the sides of the road. The police had blocked off the entire street, and uniformed officers stood guard outside. Reporters with cameras and microphones were harassing the police, but they kept ignoring the journalists.

Mark stepped into the alley between two houses and bent down, pretending to tie his shoelaces. Cars honked to disperse the crowd. He recognized some of the neighbours, but luckily they weren't looking in his direction. His heart sank as he realized there was no way he could get to Nelly's house. He shouldn't be here long. However, his only hope was to go around the back—the place where he had stopped with his car to look inside the house.

He put his baseball cap on, kept his head down, and walked slowly so as not to attract too much attention. He walked past the houses and came upon the dirt track that led to the rear of Nelly's house. Here too, a police car was parked, and more reporters were milling around, stopping pedestrians to ask questions. There was no use, Mark realized. His heart felt like it was weighed down with stones. There was no way for him to get in touch with Nelly. But he did have her number on his burner phone. He didn't want to use it, because he knew the police might be able to use the signal from her phone to triangulate his location. But what other choice did he have?

A woman walking her dog passed him and gave him a strange look. Mark lowered his face again and walked away faster this time. He couldn't stay here any longer. He had to get away. He got back on the main street without any further incident and walked back to the dual carriageway. He was able to flag down another truck, which took him back to Scarborough.

He got dropped off in the outskirts and walked until he was close to the high street. He knew there would be CCTV in town, so he stopped by a small café and went into the bathroom to get changed. He had a spare set of clothes. He was beginning to smell—he needed to have a shower soon. He went back outside and sat down with a cup of coffee. From his corner seat at the end, he could see the TV above the counter. A mindless game show was on the screen, but it was interrupted by the news. He almost dropped the coffee when he saw his own face on the screen. It was his passport photo, taken a few years back, but there was no doubt it was him. He was clean-shaven then, whereas he now had a five-day stubble. The news anchor was saying something that he couldn't hear, but he could read the caption that ran beneath his photo:

Mark Aldridge—suspected kidnapper of Matt Aldridge, his son. Please notify the police at 999 immediately if you see this man.

Mark felt his fingers turn to ice. The cup shook uncontrollably in his hand as he put it down with a clatter. He noticed some of the other patrons were looking up at the TV, and one of them pointed at it, making his companion look too.

Fear consumed Mark, and he lowered his head, shielding his face with his hands. He stood up abruptly and walked out of the café, avoiding everyone's eyes. He came out into the street and bumped into a man walking from the opposite direction.

"Hey, watch yourself!" the man called out angrily. Mark mumbled an apology, kept his head down low, and pulled his hat over his face. He walked away as fast as he could, then broke into a run after he crossed the street.

CHAPTER 24

Stuart Crosby watched as his arrogant and detestable father-in-law chatted with the police officers. Graham barely looked at him. Who did he think he was? Bloody old fart. Stuart watched the female Inspector, Rita Gupta, speaking to Graham. She was persistent, he had to give her that. He knew that she suspected both him and Nelly of doing something. But she could suspect all she liked – she had no proof.

He sidled closer to Nelly, as she was standing next to her dad. He eyed his wife, hoping she would respond. She did, and his heart lifted, but only for a few seconds. Then she looked away again, quickly. Stuart had enough of this. He pulled at her elbow gently.

"Can I have a word please?" Nelly clenched her jaws. She didn't answer, but Stuart knew she didn't want to make a scene. She walked out the patio doors with him, into the garden. Graham watched as they left. The two detectives were now talking to each other.

“Are you okay?” Stuart asked as soon as they were outside. The sunlight fell on his face and it was nice to be outside.

“Yes, fine,” Nelly replied tonelessly, staring into the distance. “Why wouldn’t it be? I mean, it’s only my son that’s missing and now there’s a ransom note.”

Stuart sighed and rubbed his forehead. “Don’t be like that,” he hated the whine in his voice, and corrected himself. “I know what you’re going through. I don’t know why you’re shutting me out.”

“I’m not.” She folded her arms across her chest. “It’s just too much to deal with right now. What do you want me to say?”

“I loved Matt like a son. You know that.”

Nelly frowned and turned her head to stare at him. “Did you, Stu? Did you really? You had a funny way of showing it then, didn’t you? How much time did you really spend with him? Matt wanted a father figure. All you did was work all day and then spend time with your mates in the weekend.”

Stuart huffed. “That’s not true, and you know it. I tried. If he didn’t want to spend time with me, what could I do?”

They were starting to have a full-blown argument now. He glanced uneasily behind him. The detectives were still speaking to each other, and luckily, Graham was deep in conversation with the FLO, Lucy.

“You could’ve tried harder,” Nelly said. Spots of crimson were now appearing on her cheeks, and her chest heaved with emotion. “You could’ve taken him to football practice after school, by leaving early from work. Many dads do that. In the weekends you could’ve taken him to the cinema.” Nelly waved her hands in the air. “I don’t know. Do things that normal dads did.”

“I tried!” Stuart didn’t mean to raise his voice, but it happened. He was glad he’d shut the patio door behind him. “But he wouldn’t listen, would he? He just wanted to see Mark, not that he turned up that often anyway.”

“Your fighting with Mark didn’t help your relationship with Matt, and you know it,” Nelly’s voice was scathing and her eyes poured vitriol on him. “All you needed was patience, and spend time with Matt. But you did neither. You thought moving in with us would just magically make you his father figure.”

She stopped then, and their eyes locked. She had been the one to ask him to move in. She had wanted to move into a new house. Now she knew she was talking bollocks, Stuart thought. He wanted to argue with her, but what was the bloody point?

“I wanted, and still want to be his father figure. You know that. Okay, I admit I need to spend more time with him. But it’s been hard at work, right?”

Nelly shook her head, then her eyes closed as misery suddenly crumpled her face like a piece of paper twisted in a fist. She held her head, and a sob broke out from her throat.

“Hey,” Stuart put his arms around her. She was stiff at first, but then yielded to him. He pulled her closer, feeling the warmth in her body for the first time in three days.

“I’m sorry, okay? Let’s get through this together. I’ll do more with Matt, and whatever he wants, I promise. But let’s not fight. There’s enough trouble to deal with right now.”

Nelly nodded, and sniffed as she wiped her face. Her head rested on his chest, and he held her tight. Then they disengaged, and walked back inside the kitchen. Graham was looking at them suspiciously. Bloody idiot, Stuart thought to himself. Wish you weren’t here.

The detectives were leaving. He realised that Inspector Gupta had been watching them through the patio door.

“We’re going now, to check all the evidence at the station. I will be in touch shortly. North Cliff Park is already under surveillance. But don’t tell a soul about this letter, no one outside these far walls. Got that?”

“So, er, we’re not going to negotiate with the kidnapper?” Stuart asked.

“No. I’ve thought about it, and it’s only going to make matters worse.” Inspector Gupta’s dark eyes bore into him, like she could see the back of his skull. It made him nervous, and he tried his best not to show it.

“We have new leads that we are following up as we speak. Please give me a couple of hours, and I will be in touch again. Don’t leave the house, please.” She looked at Nelly to make sure she was listening. She nodded, and then left the with the other detective.

When they had gone, Stuart left Graham and Nelly to their own devices. He went outside, and fished out his packet of cigarettes. He avoided the police standing outside the house, and waved at a couple of the neighbours. Then he walked down a side alley, and looked back to make sure he was alone. He leaned against the wall, and pulled out the burner phone. With trembling fingers, he rang the number.

“I told you not to call,” the male voice said.

“The cops are not going to negotiate,” Stuart said, his words short like his breathing. His heart was hammering like a piston. “They want to lay a trap for the kidnapper. I told you this was a bad idea.”

The man was silent for a few seconds. “Yes, it was bad, because it was your idea. There was no need for it.”

“Look,” Stuart swallowed the leaden weight at the back of his throat. “I don’t think this is going to work out. “You need to release Matt. The Daily Tribune has offered a reward for anyone who can help. We can collect that money.”

“There will be a lot more than that. Wait till the national charities get involved. We’re talking tens of thousands.”

“But that might not happen. And what if the police find out? I have a horrible feeling that DI Gupta suspects me.”

“Why?” The voice was sharper. “You didn’t do anything stupid, did you?”

“No, of course not.” Stuart couldn’t stop the shaking in his voice. “But we need to watch her.”

“I told you – stay away from her. Speak as little as you can.” The man was silent for a few seconds. “I think we need to meet up. Tonight at 9PM. At the usual place.”

“But-

“Don’t question me,” the voice was harsh. “Just be there. Things are getting difficult now. We need a new plan of action. Make sure you’re there.”

The threat in his last words were unmistakable. “Ok,” Stuart said, letting out a ragged breath. “I’ll be there.”

CHAPTER 25

Matt felt cold in the room. He heard the wind whistle in through the cracks. It was early morning, and the sun was just coming up. He could see the sun rays through the curtain blinds. The single bed had a thin mattress, and his duvet was threadbare. Matt pulled up the cover over his chin. He listened closely, but he couldn't hear the man. Matt tried to speak to him, but he didn't answer. Matt knew his parents were looking for him. He desperately wished he could see his mum and dad again.

It was good seeing Stuart. That made him hopeful. But when he called to Stuart he ignored Matt. Stuart acted strangely. He stared at Matt like he was seeing a ghost, then the man grabbed Stuart's arm, and spoke to him. After that, Matt didn't see Stuart.

And he didn't want to see Stuart again. Matt was so drowsy when he was taken from home, he didn't know what was happening. But when he opened his eyes, he knew Stuart was carrying him downstairs. Stuart said they were going on an adventure. They went up on the apple tree in the garden, and then over the fence. Matt stayed on Stuart's back. The man helped Stuart to put Matt in the car. Then Matt fell asleep in the car again.

This wasn't an adventure anymore. Matt didn't like this place. He didn't know what was happening. He felt Stuart and the man were strange, and bad. But Matt knew the man. He was nice before. Why was he acting so weird now?

Matt was glad of one thing – he wasn't in the cage anymore. The man had put him in this room upstairs in the farmhouse. The building was in a terrible state. The wooden floor had holes, and cobwebs hung everywhere. The floor felt cold under his bare feet last night. He didn't sleep well, but it was still better than the cage.

Matt listened for a while. The sunlight was now obscured by clouds, and the wind still remained. Matt could hear water dripping somewhere. But he couldn't hear any footsteps. He remembered the TV show where the boy and girl escaped from the castle. They did it while the monster was sleeping. Could he do the same?

Matt took the covers off and got up. The floor creaked as he stepped on it. There was a chair and desk in front of the window. Matt lifted the blind and peered out. There was a courtyard below, and the barn opposite the farmhouse. The barn doors were shut. Matt craned his neck and saw a car, but it was hidden behind what looked like a shed. He could see it from up here, but anyone coming up to the farmhouse would miss it.

He put on his clothes. Then he opened the door a crack. He could see another two rooms, and both doors were shut. The bathroom door was open, and Matt went in there to wee. He didn't flush the toilet. He came out again, and stopped to listen. Was the man still here? Maybe he was asleep.

Matt walked slowly across the landing, trying to make as little sound as possible. It wasn't easy, the wooden floorboards were old. But Matt had the benefit of his small size. He crept to the stairs, and then made his way down.

He was scared by the long cobwebs that hung from the corners, and he froze when he saw a big spider. Matt didn't like spiders. On the downstairs landing, there was a big hole where the floor had caved in. Matt walked around it. The kitchen lay to his left. He peeked inside, it was empty. He had dinner here last night. A bowl of soup and bread. It wasn't nice, but as the man said, there was nothing else.

To his right, lay the passage that led to the front door. Matt walked past the living room, his heart thrashing wildly against his ribs. Could he really get out of here? And what happened after that? How could he get back to his mummy? He had to walk till he saw another car, and ask for a lift.

Matt's breath came in gasps as he got to the front door. He pressed the handle, and it turned. The door was open. He couldn't believe it. It was a heavy door, and he had to pull it hard, twice, before it opened.

He stared outside. The sun hid behind clouds, and the day was gloomy suddenly. There was a wooden porch, and after it, two steps that went to the cobbled stones of the courtyard. After the courtyard, he saw a road. It was a narrow, single lane. Matt thought his heart would pop out of his mouth. He shut the door behind him, and stepped on the porch. He went down to the steps, and then he was on the courtyard.

He walked faster now, taking care he didn't slip on the cobble stones. Then he was on the road, and his heart leapt in joy. Now, he could make a run for it.

He didn't hear the steps behind him. A hand grabbed his jacket and yanked him backwards. Matt cried out as he fell on his bum, and it hurt. He looked up fearfully as the man's face appeared over him. His cheeks were red, and he was breathing faster. He pulled Matt to his feet.

Matt cowered, afraid the man would hit him. But the man simply stared at him. He was breathless, but Matt didn't see anger in his eyes. Without a word, the man pulled Matt inside. He struggled, but the man dragged him forcefully. Once inside, the man locked and bolted the front door.

He turned to Matt, who shrank against the wall. The smell of dust and old wood was heavy in the air. The man crouched in front of Matt. He was calm, as if nothing had happened.

"Don't try that again. I will lock you in your room if you do. Understood?"

In silence, Matt nodded. The man stared at Matt, and he lowered his face. The man got to his feet, and pushed Matt gently, nudging him towards the stairs.

"Get ready, we are moving out of here."

Matt stopped and turned. "Where are we going?" He asked eagerly. Maybe this ordeal was finally over.

But the man didn't say anything. He shoved Matt a little harder, pushing him towards the stairs.

CHAPTER 26

Rita was walking through the car park, heading back to the office, when her phone rang. It was her dad, Jay.

"You go inside," she told Maggie. "Update the others. I'll see you in a second."

Maggie nodded and carried on.

Rita walked to the rear of the car park and leaned against a lamppost.

"Hi, Dad," she said. She was glad he'd called. He had tried twice before, but she'd been too busy to answer. She felt a familiar warmth as she heard his voice. After being estranged from him for decades, it was nice being in touch with him again.

"I saw the news," Jay said. "About that missing boy. You must be in the thick of it, correct?"

"I am, unfortunately," Rita sighed. "How did you hear of it?"

"On social media first," Jay said. "And now it's on the news as well. So this man abducted his own son, is that right?"

"We can't jump to conclusions. What we do know is that he is on the run and refusing to speak to us. The boy's still missing. The media have turned up, and you know what that means."

Jay made a sympathetic sound in his throat. "Don't let the stress get to you. You can only do the best you can. I've not seen your name in the papers yet. Will you be doing a press conference soon?"

"Yes, later this afternoon. That will be broadcast on the news as well."

"I'm going to see you on TV?" Jay couldn't hide the pride in his voice. It made Rita smile.

"It's hardly prime-time TV, and I'm not doing anything glamorous. Don't go around telling everyone to switch their TVs on."

"Oh, you're going to have a global audience when I tell my relatives in USA and India," Jay chuckled.

"Don't, Dad," Rita admonished.

"I'm only joking. I won't tell a soul. I don't want the general public to know, but I guess after the conference your name will be common knowledge, correct?"

"And the Detective Superintendent's, who will be doing the conference with me."

Rita stopped and looked at her watch. It was ten to midday. She had to get a move on.

"Are you okay? How are Anna and Aaron?"

Anna was Dad's second wife, and they had a boy called Aaron, who was a second-year university student.

"They're all fine, thanks for asking. It was actually Anna who saw the news first and let me know. She's a little worried about you as well."

"I'm fine, so don't worry. Dad, I've got to go. Talk soon, okay?"

"Take care, darling. Call me if you need anything."

Rita hung up and walked back inside, hands thrust in her pockets, head bent as her mind returned to the strange dynamics of the Crosby family.

There was no doubt that Graham and Stuart did not get along. To say that Graham despised Stuart might not be an overstatement, but Rita didn’t want to rush to judgment. It was a difficult time for the family, and she knew from past experience that people could act strangely in such circumstances. She had called Rizwan and told him to dig into Stuart's and Graham's backgrounds.

She stopped at the drinks machine, as her throat was parched. Her pager buzzed, and she gave a silent groan when she saw who it was.

"Come upstairs immediately," the D Sup Nicola Perkins had written.

Rita grabbed a bottle of water, took a swig, and then dashed up three flights of stairs. It made her thighs burn, but she was glad for the exercise. She wasn't getting any time to go to the gym these days. She knocked on Nicola's door, catching her breath before going inside when she heard Nicola's voice. She shut the door softly behind her.

To her surprise, there was a man inside, wearing a sharp black police uniform with a medley of badges on the left chest. She didn't need to be told who he was. Alistair Grant, the Chief Constable of North Yorks Police, rose and came forward. He was tall and slim, with closely cut brown hair. Rita suspected he was in his late 50s, but he had kept himself fit. His clean-shaven cheeks gave way to a strong jaw, and his light grey, inquisitive eyes scanned her face. He was a good-looking man, but she knew he didn't tolerate fools.

"Nicola has just given me a summary of the case," he said. He shook hands with Rita, then indicated the chair. She sat down next to the Chief Constable, aware that there was no higher authority in the North Yorkshire Police force. The fact that Grant was here meant the top brass were getting hot under the collar. Pressure from politicians tended to do that. Rita didn't know the full story, and she didn't need to. From her time in London, she had an inkling of how the corridors of power operated. If there was a problem, they wanted the news channels to stop chattering about it—without delay.

Grant kept his focus on Rita. "I understand the boy's father, Mark Aldridge, is the main suspect now. Are we any closer to catching him?"

"I believe it's a matter of time, sir," Rita said. "His car has not been seen on ANPR, but we have an all-points bulletin out for his passport, driving licence, and all the credit cards he owns. True, he could be using cash, but sooner or later we will catch him."

"And do you think he's got the boy?"

Rita considered her answer. She had to be honest with Grant. "If you want my personal opinion, I don't think so."

Grant frowned, and the corners of his lips tightened. Clearly, he didn't like the answer. Across the table, Rita sensed Nicola stiffen as well. The petite Detective Superintendent clasped her hands on the desk.

"Yesterday, you told me it was more than likely Mark had abducted his son," Nicola said.

"I said it was a possibility, that's all," Rita replied, turning to look at her. "Other evidence has come to light. We need to look at the parents again. The stepfather, Stuart, is acting nervous, while the mother seems ice-cold. Something is not right with them. We're digging into their backgrounds, as well as the father-in-law's."

Nicola interjected, "But Mark's car was identified as the vehicle behind the fence, is that correct?"

"Yes. But that doesn't mean he abducted Matt in that car." Rita raised a hand as Nicola went to ask another question. A wave of crimson mottled Nicola's face, and Rita knew she wasn't happy about being interrupted. Rita couldn't care less. This wasn't the time to score brownie points by asserting authority.

"If Mark had his son, he wouldn't have come down to the warehouse. He would be far away by now, maybe taking the ferry to France or Ireland. Besides, he doted on his son. Despite his faults and past violent behaviour, I don't think he would hurt his son. Matt liked being with his father."

Rita turned to lock eyes with Grant.

"The father-in-law, Graham, also had access to the house and contact with Matt. We need to regard him as a suspect as well."

Grant seemed to be weighing up her words as he stared back at her. Then he changed the subject.

“What about the ransom letter?”

“We’re checking the CCTV on all post offices as we speak. The handwriting experts are looking at the letters, but they are in block letters, so typography won’t show much. The paper and envelope are very standard. As for the photo,” Rita stopped to gather her thoughts. “It’s recent, but it might’ve been edited to make Matt look distressed. But I don’t think so. It looks genuine.”

“Which means you consider the sender of that photo to be the abductor. Correct?”

“Yes, sir.” Rita knew where this was heading and she decided to pre-empt it. “We have North Cliff Park under surveillance. In particular, the area around the bandstand and the bench next to it. We will lay the trap, and hopefully he falls into it.”

Grant kept his eyes on Rita. “And the abductor signed his name as the Keeper. We know who that was. Only an insider would have that sort of knowledge.” Grant paused.

“After PC Dixon, or the Keeper, we must remain vigilant. Anyone in the Force that either of you suspect?”

“No sir,” Rita said. “PC Dixon was an aberration. Since his case, every recruit, new and old, has been scanned for fake names, ID's, you name it. Extreme vetting, so to speak. Nothing dodgy has shown up as yet." She coughed into her fist, once. "This person, the so called New Keeper, was probably a part of their online group – the Gathering.

Grant nodded, but he seemed far from appeased. The tight line in his lips remained, and he turned to Nicola again. Rita was getting a sense of foreboding now.

Nicola cleared her throat. "The Keeper, PC Dixon, were close to McFarlane, your mother's killer. Hence, you have a personal connection to this case."

The words dropped like bombs from the sky, whistling into Rita's fevered mind. She almost flinched, and steeled herself, absorbing their impact. She could feel Grant's eyes on her. She struggled to remain impassive. Her lips parted as she exhaled her warm breath, heart cannon balling against her ribs.

Nicola continued. "Are you sure your personal connection is not affecting your judgement?"

"No ma'am. I'm fine. We need to find Matt without delay, and that's my priority."

Nicola's hostile eyes bore into hers. "Earlier, you said if we find Mark, we find the boy. Your opinion has changed very quickly, despite the fact there's no sign of Mark."

The bitch was criticising her in front of the big boss, when she should be supporting her. Bilious anger rose in Rita's throat, and she silenced the response, then the snarl, that came to her lips.

"It's a fast-moving investigation, Ma'am," Rita bit her words out, staring Nicola down. "Opinions can change depending on evidence, and my feel for the suspects, given my twenty- four years of experience."

Nicolas' jaws hardened and her eyes flashed a warning. The air was dense with the tension of a conflict and Grant seemed to sense it.

"DI Gupta." His voice was calm, dragging Rita back to his attention. "You understand that we are reliant on you, as the SIO, to make the correct decisions. Nicola merely wants to be sure you're doing that. She has your best interests in mind." He angled his eyes to Nicola, who pressed her lips together, and nodded once.

My best interests? Well, she's got a funny way of showing it.

Grant said, "Why do you think the abductor is calling himself the Keeper?"

"I think he looks on Dixon as his hero, just like Dixon looked up to Robert McFarlane. In fact, Dixon's incarcerated in HMP Wakefield. I would like to go and see him." Rita glanced at Nicola as well, who was listening intently.

Rita continued. "I think the ransom letter is just a play to ruffle feathers – ours and the family's. He's stretching himself thin. We can get him. Let me speak to Joshua Dixon, just to see his response and if he knows anything."

"Why would he tell you anything?" Nicola demanded.

"He's a narcissist. Loves himself. If I can chip away at his sense of pride, he might get upset and make a mistake. It's worth a try."

Grant nodded. "Very well. But time is running out, DI Gupta. We need to find Matt without delay."

"I know, sir."

"I want some answers by tomorrow," Grant said. He reached for his hat, and put it on his head, adjusting the peak. He did look rather dashing in his smart uniform, Rita had to admit. Grant nodded at Nicola, who inclined her head, stiffly. Grant was a tall man, and when he stood, he seemed to fill up the room. He said goodbye to them, and left, shutting the door behind him. Rita stood.

"Will that be all, Ma'am?" She hid the smugness in her tone. Grant had actually listened to her more than he did to Nicola, and Rita knew that would irritate her weirdly vengeful boss.

"Yes," Nicola snapped. "Get ready for the press conference."

CHAPTER 27

Rita's mind was meandering through dark areas as she slowly walked down the stairs. She had to go and see Joshua Dixon today. She had rung the prison governor at HMP Wakefield and got clearance to visit him.

Rita needed permission before she could visit the ultra-secure, Category A prison. But how much would Dixon, or "the Keeper," as he had called himself, know? Joshua didn't have any access to emails or the internet. Even the books he read were carefully vetted by psychiatrists before being passed to him.

He didn't have a phone, and the letters he sent out were scrutinized to ensure they only went to close family members or next of kin. Random people were not allowed to get in touch with him, and he could only communicate with select family members that the prison security staff had approved. In short, he had no contact with the outside world.

If Dixon didn't know, then who was the Keeper? Could it be Mark Aldridge? It was certainly possible. She knew very little about Mark, even though they had dug up his brushes with the law and his fake name. A search on HOLMES – the Home Office Large Major Enquiry System – didn't reveal anything.

And if it wasn't Mark, then who could it be?

One thing Rita knew for certain: the Keeper was someone who knew the family well.

He was playing his evil game from behind the shadows, probably getting a lot of pleasure from watching everyone squirm. People like him got a kick out of that feeling of control, of power. He was the puppeteer with the strings, and ordinary human beings were his puppets. Rita's teeth ground together as frustration mounted. There was something obvious she was missing here, a vague outline whose shape she could see, but the monster lurking inside was still evading her.

"I'll find you," she whispered to herself, her hands becoming fists. She breathed out, shaking her head. She increased her pace, taking two steps down the stairs.

In the ground floor corridor, she heard a male voice call her name. She turned to see Jack Banford hurrying up to her. He wore a charcoal grey suit that clung to his body like a second skin. How did he keep himself in such ridiculously good shape? Jack came up to her and flashed a warm smile that made the corners of his eyes crinkle.

"You okay?" he asked. She nodded, and they walked together in the direction of the canteen. They got a coffee and found a table in one corner. Rita glanced at her watch.

"I'm going to Wakefield. I need to pick an evil person's brain," she grimaced.

"Are you going to HMP Wakefield by any chance?" Jack didn't miss much; she had to give him that.

"Yes." She told Jack about her conversation with Alistair Grant and Nicola.

Jack whistled as his eyebrows rose. "The Chief Constable was here? That's a big deal."

"I know. The pressure is definitely on now. I've got half an hour to do the press conference, then I'm off to Wakefield."

"Any signs of Mark Aldridge?"

Rita shook her head. "No, but we will find him. His car's not been seen anywhere, and he's got no other means of transport. The cameras would have caught him at a train station or an airport. He can't be that far."

"Unless he's hiding in the moors somewhere, biding his time. But he'll run out of food and money. Unless, of course, he's got Matt. You're right, he has to make a break for it sooner or later."

"And that's when we'll catch him," Rita said, draining her coffee.

They stood and walked to Rita's office. Jack said, "Janet has asked a couple of friends on the street if they noticed anything unusual. One of them is a night owl. She was saying something about a man coming to the Crosby's house in the evening. Stuart wasn't there at the time, because his car was absent."

A distant concern prickled Rita's mind. "Yes, Janet did mention that. A man came to see Nelly, and she went off somewhere in his car. She doesn't remember her coming back, but she must have, as Matt would have been at home. It was in the evening. So, Janet's friend saw the same thing?"

"Yes, according to Janet. She tried to ring you but didn't get through, so she told me."

"Thanks. I'll ask the team to check with Janet's friend. Please send me the friend's details."

"She's Alison and lives three doors down. I will do." Jack started to move away, then said, "I'll be finishing with my client downstairs in about 45 minutes. Do you want me to give you a lift to the train station? I assume you're taking the train to Wakefield, right?"

"Yes." Rita hesitated because she didn't want to get used to Jack doing her favours. He read her mind and came closer.

"I don't mind, you know that." His eyes rested on her, frank and open. She didn’t see any demands there or expectations. She hoped it stayed like that, despite the attraction she felt for him.

"Yes, I'd like that," she found herself saying.

"Good, see you soon." He smiled and walked away, then turned. "And good luck with the press conference!"

Rita rolled her eyes, then waved back at him. Inside the office, there was a smell of coffee and doughnuts. Richard and Maggie were busy at work, staring at the screens and talking on the phone. Maggie put the phone down as Rita came in.

"We have an unconfirmed sighting of Mark Aldridge. A neighbour who was walking her dog near the crime scene thought she recognized a man who looked like Mark. He had a baseball cap and a big black jacket on, as if he was trying to disguise himself. He walked away quickly."

"He came near Seaview Avenue?" Rita put both hands on her waist. "Maybe he wanted to visit the Crosby home." Her eyebrows furrowed. "Why would he do that? Too much of a risk to take, surely."

"The neighbour's not sure if it was him. But he looked familiar, and she's seen Mark pick up Matt in the past."

Richard stood from his desk and stretched. "I just spoke to Inspector Bennett. Uniforms have spread out near Seaview Avenue, looking for Mark. If he's around or hiding somewhere, we'll know soon. They've also got their sniffer dogs in the fields behind the house."

"Good," Rita said. "I'm going into the press conference. Then I'm off to HMP Wakefield."

CHAPTER 28

Rita got off at Westgate Train Station and decided to walk. The day had become cloudy and overcast, with the wind disturbing the branches of the trees. She was glad she had her jacket on. The foreboding grey walls of HMP Wakefield loomed in the distance. She walked rapidly and arrived within about 15 minutes. The security guards checked her warrant card, and she was allowed in. She passed through airport-style security with a metal detector, surrendering her warrant card, purse, phone, and radio. She folded her jacket and placed it inside her tote handbag.

Two burly security guards then escorted her through an empty courtyard and into another building with a succession of gates. Finally, they took her into an elevator and up to the third floor, where she was searched again by a female security officer. A man then led her into a corridor that resembled a residential block, though the grey lino floors and whitewashed walls gave it a drab, institutional look. The man knocked on a door marked "Dr Vick Patel, Psychiatrist" and held it open for her to enter.

Dr Patel was slim and wore a dark suit. He was about Rita's height, 5'9", with grey hair receding at the temples and sharp, attentive eyes. He smiled perfunctorily and gestured for Rita to sit down.

"The governor, Mr. Meacham, said you'd be coming," Dr Patel said. "I understand you're interested in speaking to Joshua Dixon. This is about the missing boy in Scarborough? Matthew Crosby?"

"Yes, that's right," Rita replied. "Mr. Dixon had formed a secret society of violent people who engaged in abuse. He called himself 'The Keeper.' The abductor has sent the parents a ransom note signed as 'The Keeper' as well. I don't believe that's a coincidence."

Dr Patel steepled his hands, thinking. His voice was calm. “But how would a child abductor know about Dixon? His name was not revealed to the press, was it?”

“That’s the whole point,” Rita said. “You must know that Dixon was part of a gang of abusers called The Brotherhood. We dismantled their network, but some dangerous individuals still remain, and they might have regrouped.”

“And you have evidence of that fact?”

Rita spoke slowly, hiding her irritation. “Not as yet. But what do you think the chances are of this being a coincidence?”

“Do you have any contact with this person called the Keeper?”

“No. The ransom note was written in block capitals. But you must agree, there’s every chance the abductor knows Dixon, or at least was aware of his activities.”

"I can see why you think that. But how is Joshua going to help you find this person? He might not have any idea. The abductor might be a part of that group, but will Joshua really know who he is? And even in the off chance that he did, how will he know where that person is now?”

Rita couldn’t hide the rage that blossomed inside her. She clamped down on her teeth to say something she might regret. She knew Dr Patel was just doing his job. Dr Patel had to treat Dixon as a human being, not as the monster that he was. Rita didn’t understand that, and right now, she didn’t care.

"A little boy is missing," she ground her words out. "Please consider the trauma the parents and family are going through. Do you have children, Dr Patel?”

Dr Patel blinked, and she could tell her words had penetrated the psychiatrist’s calm façade. “Yes, I do. I’m not belittling what that family is going through, or the little boy’s predicament. I am merely trying to understand how interrogating Joshua is going to help.”

Dixon's first name sounded so innocent. Almost biblical. Revulsion crawled on Rita's skin as she thought of him. And anger blossomed again in her mind, at Dr Patel's continued attempt to protect his patient.

"If Matt was your son," Rita said, "Wouldn't you want the police to pursue every angle?"

From his silence, Rita had her answer. He exhaled once, and his expression softened. "I'm not deliberately trying to be difficult. I am also audited by the board of governors for every visiting right that is granted to Joshua. I hope you understand."

Rita knew that the forensic psychiatrist was high up in the management ladder of these prisons. He was being more than a little facetious, she thought. But she needed his cooperation.

"I do. But you must understand that a little boy's life is at stake. After 48 hours, the chances of finding him are very low. We don't have much time."

Dr Patel nodded, and then stood. "I think that's reasonable. Please, follow me."

They walked to the end of the corridor, where a security guard unlocked a gate leading to a small hallway with two rooms opposite each other. Dr Patel knocked on one, and the security guard opened the door.

It was a windowless room, dimly lit by slits near the ceiling. There was a bed on the floor, a metal desk bolted down, and a chair similarly fixed to the floor. There was an ensuite bathroom, and as Rita entered, she froze. Joshua Dixon stepped out from the bathroom and into the room. He observed Rita curiously, and then a smile—a twisted, evil smile—spread across his face, making her stomach churn with nausea. She fought the impulse to look away or punch him. She kept her face impassive and met his gaze.

He looked better than she remembered. His shoulders and arms were thicker, likely from regular exercise. So much for being on suicide watch, she thought. Prison food must be doing him some good.

Dr Patel spoke. "Joshua, this is Detective Inspector Rita Gupta. I think you know her. She has a few questions for you."

Joshua stared at Rita, his blonde hair gelled back, his blue eyes glinting. "No problem," he said softly.

Dr Patel glanced at Rita. "There will be a security guard outside, and the door will be ajar. Don't worry, they won't hear your conversation." He pulled Rita aside and stepped out of Dixon's view. The security guard handed Rita a portable alarm with a red button that fit in her palm. "Press this if you feel threatened at any point," Dr Patel said.

Rita nodded and returned to the room. She sat down while Joshua rested on the bed, his back against the wall, a smug expression on his face. He said nothing, just observed her. Rita kept her voice calm and dignified.

"Do you know anyone called 'The Keeper'?"

Dixon smiled—a horrible, greasy grin that revolted her. He knew the effect he was having on her, and his grin widened.

"I am The Keeper. You should know that by now."

"There’s another Keeper, I’m afraid." Rita spread her hands. "It seems like you’re not the only one. Not anymore."

The smile faltered on Dixon’s face, then recovered. "What do you mean?"

"Someone calling himself 'The Keeper' has abducted an eight-year-old boy. Do you know who it might be?"

As expected, Dixon seemed pleased. A new light appeared in his eyes. "How interesting," he whispered.

Rita said nothing. The seconds passed as they stared at each other. She could hear her own heartbeat and the ticking of a clock recessed into the wall.

"Who's taken the little boy, Joshua?" she asked.

"Wouldn't you like to know?" Dixon smiled.

"Someone is taking your place. Your position as 'The Keeper' is under threat. Your followers are laughing behind your back." Rita shrugged, acting as if it didn't matter to her. "They're posting online about their new leader, 'The New Keeper.' You're nobody anymore."

The smile faded from Dixon's lips. His jaw clenched, and Rita felt a surge of satisfaction.

"You're a sad man withering away in a prison cell," she added softly. "Your reputation is in tatters. Your followers think you're nothing now."

Dixon's face darkened. He stared at her without blinking. Then unexpectedly, he smiled again.

"Is that a fact? My followers don't like me anymore?"

Rita didn't like the smile that remained on Dixon's face. It was a knowing smile. She acted like it didn't bother her. She shrugged again.

"It's what they're saying. Your followers... or, I'm sorry, they're not your followers anymore, are they?"

"You don't know what you're talking about," Dixon said, relaxing back against the wall.

His eyes were open and alert, and they searched her face. But there was something casual, and carefree about his posture. It was almost as if he had known what she wanted to say. A deep paranoia was staring to fester in the back of Rita's mind. No, it couldn't be. This was a Category A prison. There was no way Dixon could know what was happening outside.

Or could he?

"Do you know who he is?" Rita leaned forward. "Do you want some young upstart to take your place? Destroy your reputation?"

Dixon's eyes widened, then narrowed. Something shifted in him, and Rita wondered if she had scored a point. He looked away, then back at her.

"That’s why you’re here. You want me to betray my followers."

Rita shook her head. "No. I don’t care about you, or your followers. I couldn’t care less about the new Keeper. I just want the boy back."

Dixon's knowing look returned, and Rita didn’t like it. She stared back at him. "You had followers who liked little boys. We know that. You must remember a name or two."

Dixon smiled again, that horrible grin. "Maybe I do, maybe I don’t. Either way, I don’t see why it matters."

"Give me the names."

"Now, now, Rita," Dixon said, using her first name. "That would be telling, wouldn’t it? I used to be a police officer. I never betray my sources. You taught me that, remember?"

Rita swallowed the wave of nausea rising inside her throat, maintaining her calm façade. "Tell me what you know."

"I wish I could help you. But I can't." Dixon waved his hand dismissively, as if it were unimportant. He was trying too hard to be nonchalant, Rita thought. The conviction was growing in her mind. Dixon had an idea who this person was.

She raised her eyebrows. "Do you really want him to take over? You worked hard for your position. And now he's just going to walk all over you." The last statement was a challenge. Rita leaned forward. "Tell me who he is, Joshua."

The hard look returned to Dixon's face, but then the smile crept back, making Rita want to slap him. "I'm getting tired now," he said. "I'm not well. I need my rest." He got up and knocked on the door, then went back to his bed.

The guard came in, and Dixon pointed at Rita. "She's harassing me. My head hurts. I want to sleep."

Rita glared at him but felt the guard's eyes on her. "I'm sorry, ma'am, you have to leave now."

Rita stood, disgust churning inside her like a whirlpool. Dixon lay down and pulled the blanket over himself, casting her one last smug look. The guard turned to leave, and Rita followed.

CHAPTER 29

Rita was back in Dr Patel's office. "He knows who the abductor is," Rita said. "He's not giving anything away, but I can tell from the way he's acting." She frowned. "And I think he was either expecting me to come here, or he's actually enjoying this."

Dr Patel marble smooth façade had a chink in it. His forehead contracted slightly, like the corner of his eyes.

"That's quite a statement. I know of course, that Joshua has a malignant narcissistic personality disorder. If he knew the abductor, he would be pleased that he was using his nickname. But the MO is very different. Joshua killed young women. This man has abducted a little boy."

"Yes, but they belong to the same club, so to speak. Please, Dr Patel, I need your help on this." Rita kept her voice firm. "I would like you to monitor all of Dixon's communications. You, personally, not the security staff. If you find anything suspicious, please let me know."

Dr Patel stared at Rita for a while, then seemed to acknowledge the uncompromising look on her face. He sighed. "Okay, I will. You must know that he is not allowed to send letters or emails to anyone, or even to call them."

"Yes. Who visits him?"

"His sister, Janice. She is carefully checked each time she attends. She brings him some books, which I have checked. They are on different religions. She also brings him cakes, and chocolates, sometimes a roast dinner. Nothing else is allowed. Not even her phone, when she visits him."

Rita thought about that. The nagging suspicion that Dixon knew about Matt wouldn't leave her. And if Janice was his only contact with the outside world, what if she was bringing him information from outside? Rita was well aware of the stringent security measures in the prison. And yet…what if there was a code between Janice and Joshua? Or they found another way to communicate – like hiding messages in photos?

"Please check everything that Janice brings to Joshua. Check his room, and I mean every corner." Rita allowed a note of pleading to enter her voice. "He knows, Vick."

Dr Patel shifted in his seat. A new light gleamed in his eyes when Rita mentioned his first name. "I'm telling you. He knows."

*****

It was getting dark by the time Rita returned to Scarborough. A drizzle had started, and she didn't have an umbrella. She took a cab from the station and hurried inside. Richard, Rizwan, and Maggie were working away at the office.

Rita had picked up a few packets of biscuits and snacks from the shops. She handed Rizwan some money to get coffee, and he left with Maggie.

Richard brought his laptop over to Rita's desk. He pulled up the CCTV camera footage and pressed play. It showed a blue, beaten-up old Honda driving down the A165. It took the turning for Osgodby Lane. The date was three days ago, at 11.30 AM, midday—the day of Matthew's disappearance.

"That's Mark Aldridge's car," Richard said. They watched as the car went down Osgodby Lane and then disappeared. Rita knew the smaller roads were in CCTV dark spots. An hour later, the car appeared again, leaving the neighbourhood and joining the dual carriageway.

Richard clicked on the keyboard and sped up the tape. The car exited the dual carriageway at the turning for Burniston. Again, several streets were in CCTV dark spots, and they saw the car one last time as it arrived at the warehouse that Rita and Jack had visited. Mark got out of the car and pulled out a backpack, then went inside the warehouse.

Richard sped the footage up again, and at 1:30, the car left the warehouse and vanished from view into the woods.

"Well, well," Rita said, leaning back in her chair. "The abduction happened between 10:30 and 11. That's what Nelly told us. So, Mark couldn't have done it, if his car was there at midday. But did Nelly get the times right?"

"I was thinking that. What if she got back later?"

"What was the time of her 999 call?"

Richard scrolled to the case report on his laptop. "11.10 am. So, Matt was gone by the time Mark arrived at the rear fence."

Rita pressed her lips together, eyebrows crinkled like her mind. "Unless...Mark got his son before. Someone else drove the car up to the fence. We always thought he had an accomplice, correct?"

"Yes. It looks like a man drove the car on CCTV – but there's no way of identifying Mark, even with close up and facial recognition. So, someone else might have been driving the car."

"Mark gets there early, waits for Nelly to leave. Then he joins his accomplice at the rear, and coaxes Matt outside. Drugs him, or simply takes him in the back seat, and they drive off."

Rita grimaced, and Richard nodded. "Yes, guv. Possible."

He said, "Matt could have been unconscious in the back seat. We can't tell from the CCTV. Or he might have been in the car boot."

"Yes," Rita said, stroking her lower lip with the tips of her fingers. "But if Matt went with his father willingly, then he wouldn't have had to sedate Matt, would he?"

"Maybe he felt it was the safest thing to do," Richard said. "He doesn't take Matt inside the warehouse, but then they drive off into the woods. There are two drones overhead in that area now, and three uniformed squads are searching the area again. We might have missed something the last time."

"Good," Rita said. She rose from her desk and opened the door to let Maggie and Rizwan in. They drank their coffee, and Rita nibbled on a biscuit. She was famished and needed some food.

"Is there any connection between Mark and Dixon? Or was Mark ever a member of the Brotherhood?"

"We looked already," Maggie said, and Rizwan nodded. "Nowt so far. We also checked under Mark's other name of Arnold Walsham."

"Okay. Let's get back to Stuart." Rita addressed Maggie, "Did you speak to Stuart's employer?"

"Yes," Maggie said. "He wasn't at work the day before yesterday. In other words, Stuart lied. When Matt was abducted, Stuart wasn't at work. No one seems to know exactly where he was."

Rizwan dunked his biscuit in his coffee cup, then swallowed it whole. He let out a sigh of satisfaction and glanced at his laptop screen.

"The house the Crosbys live in was bought by Nellie's dad, Graham. It's not Stuart's house. I've got the sales details here. The property is in the name of Nellie and Graham."

"How interesting," Rita said. Both Nellie and Stuart had led her to believe the property belonged to Stuart. The awkward body language between the couple now started to make more sense.

"In fact," Rizwan continued, "Stuart doesn't have a job, and he's up to his eyeballs in debt. I'm not sure how he's making ends meet. Our search on his credit files shows he's got four loans, of £20K each. He spends £1,200 per month on his debt repayments, and his employer confirmed that Stuart lost his job two weeks ago."

Rita's mind buzzed, and a red light began to glow. "So, his total debt is £80,000? And how much was the ransom note for?"

"£100,000. That would clear Stuart's debt and leave him with some spare."

"What's he spent his money on?"

Rizwan tapped on his keyboard and looked at the screen again. "Forensic accounting has traced his card to an online gambling website. That's where he lost a lot of money. He couldn't pay his credit card bills, so he had to take the loans. It seems Stuart's struggling."

Rita recalled the nervous, jumpy manner in which Stuart had behaved the last time she saw him.

Why did he lie about his alibi? What was he trying to hide?

The red alarm in her mind was now flashing urgently. Mentally, she kicked herself for not checking into Stuart sooner.

"Have you tried to get in touch with him?" she asked the team. Maggie and Rizwan nodded.

"He's not answering his phone," Maggie said. "Nellie doesn't know where he is, and neither does his ex-employer. We checked the pubs in Osgodby. He's not there."

Richard said, "And before you ask, I can't see a connection between Stuart and Joshua Dixon. Stuart was never a part of the Brotherhood."

Rita pressed her lips together. "Did Stuart have another name? I know he doesn't have a criminal record."

"Nope, no other name. And like you said, no PCNs."

There was a knock on the door, and Shola came in. The expectant look in her face, and the gleam in her eyes, made Rita sit up.

CHAPTER 30

Shola shut the door and leaned against it. "I thought you would like to know. We got a DNA match with the blood samples on the back fence. The result might surprise you."

Shola paused, and Rita could tell she was bothered by her discovery. "It belongs to Stuart Crosby, the stepfather." She looked around the room. "We checked it twice and tried to match it with everyone else in the family, including the biological father, Mark Aldridge. Stuart's was the only DNA sample that matched."

A collective, soft gasp went around the room. Shola looked at all of them, and her attention rested on Rita, finally.

“What?”

“We’ve just uncovered that Stuart is unemployed, has no money, and mired in debt. He also lied about being at work the morning Matt was abducted.”

Shola frowned. “So, you think…” her words trailed off.

"Yes. He could've driven back, picked up Matt, and just driven off. Maybe he waited till he saw Nelly leave the house, then seized his moment." Rita looked at the constables. "Can one of you please check with Traffic, and get CCTV of Stuart's car the day Matt disappeared?"

Maggie gave her a thumbs up and picked up the phone. She spoke to them briefly, then got up. "The duty team are looking into it now. I'll go and see them."

"Tell them to search for his car over the last week. If he went to someone's house, or met anyone, I want to know. Thank you."

Rita crossed her arms across her chest as Maggie walked out. Shola sat down on a chair. Rita stared at the floor, at the patterns on the lino. She had focused on Mark for too long. Stuart was on her radar, and she should've been more alert to his weird, nervous behaviour.

She had assumed he was disturbed by Matt's disappearance. She didn't like the fact that Stuart wasn't answering his phone. She needed to find him, urgently.

Shola's voice dragged her back to the present. "What about the mother? If Stuart is lying, then what about Nelly? After all, she could've set the whole thing up."

"What's her motive?" Rita thought out loud. "It can't be money, she co-owned the house with her father.

Nelly doesn't have multiple children with different men. She's not from a troubled family."

Shola said, "What if she wanted to get away from Stuart?"

"It's an extreme move to abduct your child just to break up with your partner." Rita frowned, and her head moved sideways. "No, but I take your point. We need to question Nelly again. She was seen getting into a car with another man two nights before Matt was abducted."

Rizwan spoke up. "Ah, yes about that. I spoke to her. It was her father. They went to the supermarket to buy food. We have CCTV of the car, and them, in the supermarket car park."

Rita sighed. "I guess that puts it to rest."

Richard looked at Rita and asked in quiet voice, "Guv, what did you think of Dixon? Do you think he knows this person called the Keeper?"

Rita was silent for a while. Everyone in the room, including Shola, knew about her history with Dixon. He was the protégé of McFarlane, the man who killed her mother. Both McFarlane and Dixon belonged to that sick, depraved society called the Brotherhood.

"He's hiding something, that's for sure," Rita said. "The problem is that he's now protected by the prison system. He's playing them skilfully, pretending to be mentally unwell."

“He is sick in the head,” Rizwan said drily.

Rita nodded. “Aye, that he is.” Her accent slipped into her old North Yorkshire slant these days pretty easily. Without knowing, she had seeped back into her Yorkshire roots. The accent curled around her tongue unconsciously. “Flippin ‘eck. He’s on suicide watch, would you believe it?”

Richard and Rizwan looked at each other and grinned. Richard said, “He’s a crafty bugger, you have to give him that.”

Rizwan sighed. “But these lunatics do kill themselves in prison as well though don’t they? Harold Shipman did that. Hung himself with a towel in his room. Good riddance, if you ask me. We keep this lot alive at the taxpayer’s expense, for what?”

“Now, now,” Rita cautioned. “Capital punishment killed a lot pf people when trials went wrong. But I get your point. It’s almost as if we should have another system for serial killers. It’s not like their crimes, or proving their guilt, are anything contentious. But anyway,” Rita sighed, looking at the ceiling. Her eyes hurt, and there was a headache spreading across her forehead. There was no divine inspiration in the whitewashed walls.

“If Dixon knows something, which I suspect he does, we cannot force it out of him. That’s the bottom line. Besides, we need to find where Matt is, and who the hell abducted him.”

Rizwan looked at his phone. "No call back from Stuart as yet. Traffic is looking at CCTV in town to see if they can get a visual match with his description."

Rita was deeply troubled by Stuart's sudden disappearance. "We keep looking, all night if necessary." She looked at the two men, who nodded vigorously.

Shola said, "So it's definitely Stuart then, right? It's his blood on the rear fence. And he lied about his alibi."

"We still have to keep an open mind," Rita cautioned. "Yes, Stuart is dodgy, there's no doubt. But there's a number of reasons why his blood could be on the fence. He could've cut himself while he was painting the fence, for example. Or fixing a loose post. We don't have any idea of how old the blood is, do we?"

"No," Shola said.

"But Stuart is guilty of something," Rita said. "If not the actual abduction, then summat else. He wouldn't lie about his alibi otherwise."

Shola cleared her throat. "I need to tell you about the rest of my findings. Matt's toothbrush and clothes verify his DNA, obviously. No drops of fluid in his room – like blood or other body fluids. But we did find hair samples from his pillow."

The door opened and Maggie came back in. She smiled at Shola, and spoke to Rita. "I've done it, guv. Traffic is poring over CCTV footage of Stuart's car as we speak."

"Good, thanks." Rita glanced back at Shola. "You were saying?"

"Matt's hair follicles, from his bed. As you know, hair has a blood supply, and it stores a lot of chemicals. I sent his hair for toxicology. It came back showing a high concentration of temazepam."

There was silence in the room for a while. Rita's guts twisted like they were in an iron grip, and she forgot to breathe. An emptiness spread across her chest.

"Temazepam?" She whispered. "Are you sure?"

Shola also looked like she had been punched in the guts, and was having trouble standing upright.

"Yes, I'm sure."

CHAPTER 31

Nelly Crosby sat ramrod straight, every line and groove of her face rigid with tension. Maggie spoke into the recorder, announcing the presence of herself, Rita, and Nelly. The time was 7:15 in the evening.

"Thank you for coming to see us," Rita said.

Nelly inclined her head forward a fraction. She was dressed in a blue summer jacket and a dark brown vest. She wore a long skirt that came down to her ankles. Rita couldn't see her feet, but she could tell they were moving, like the hands on her lap.

"When did you last see Stuart Crosby, your husband?" Rita spoke slowly, for the benefit of the recorder.

A graph of concern waved across Nelly's forehead. "This afternoon. He said he had a work meeting, and he left. He was going to be back this evening, but he's not turned up as yet. He might be in the pub with his work colleagues. Why are you asking?"

"I will explain soon. How much contact did Stuart have with Matt?"

Nelly's lips parted, as if she was going to speak. Then she pressed her lips together. She seemed to be weighing up her answer, trying to second guess what was on Rita's mind.

"We've been through this already, haven't we? Stuart was busy with work, as he was the main breadwinner in the family." Nelly's voice faltered at the end, as if her words were dropping into a void of her own making. She blinked and lost eye contact with Rita, who was gazing at her intently.

"So, he didn't have that much time with Matt?"

Nelly shrugged. "But he took him to football practice, and other places."

"Other places?" Rita echoed. "Can you be more specific?"

Again, Rita thought Nelly was trying desperately to see where this was going. Rita was happy to play along, just to gauge Nelly's reaction. In her mind, Nelly wasn't above suspicion. Rita didn't think she'd abducted her own son, but stranger things had happened.

"To his music lessons, and sometimes to swimming lessons. Both on the weekends." Nelly waved a hand in the air, trying to be casual, but she couldn't dispel the tension on her face.

"Was Stuart ever alone at home with Matt?"

Her eyes narrowed. "Why are you asking that?"

"Can you please answer the question?"

Nelly breathed heavily, her eyes flashing. "Sometimes, yes. When I went to see my parents or my girlfriends for a night out."

"What about during the day? Did Stuart ever feed Matt? Or give him breakfast?"

"Yes, sometimes. When we were together in the kitchen."

"Did Stuart ever take food or drinks up to Matt's bedroom?"

Nelly looked as if her chest would explode, and she panted. A wave of scarlet crept up her neck into her cheeks.

"What the hell is this? Has Stuart done something? Have you found Matt?" She gripped the corners of the table and tried to stand. Then she changed her mind and sat down heavily. Her knuckles remained on the table, blanched white as she gripped them together.

"What's going on? Tell me, please." Her last words rose up in a plea.

Rita felt sorry for her, but she also observed her reaction carefully. She didn't think Nelly was acting. The emotion was too genuine and spontaneous. She took a deep breath and released it.

"Do you know what temazepam is?"

Nelly looked surprised. The corners of her eyes widened as the tension left her face. Then it returned with a vengeance, and she frowned heavily. "Temazepam? Isn't that the drug that puts people to sleep?"

"Yes. It can make them drowsy as well. Doctors prescribe it to those who suffer from anxiety, mainly. It can also be given to insomniacs, but it can be addictive, so its use is heavily regulated by doctors."

Nelly blinked rapidly, but understanding was dawning on her face. The fear had returned, and Rita knew she had started to think of the impossible.

Rita said, "Matt had been given temazepam to make him drowsy. It could have been in tablet or liquid form, we don't know. Did Matt swallow tablets?"

A sudden rictus of fear spasmed across Nelly's face, and her neck muscles contracted. Her face was white as a sheet. She shook her head in silence.

Rita asked, "Then it must have been in liquid form. It could have been mixed into his food or in a drink. Temazepam is available on the street, and they are known as green eggs because of the capsule colour, and shape. They contain a gelatinous substance inside. The capsule can be squeezed, and the jelly mixed into food or drink."

Nelly looked like she'd been slapped.

Rita continued, staring into the woman's stricken eyes. "The concentration of temazepam in Matthew's hair follicles is high. He was given a heavy dose quite recently, we think. The only people who could have given Matt food or drink would be you or Stuart, is that correct?"

Again, Nelly seemed deprived of speech. Her mouth opened, but there was no sound.

Maggie asked, "Did your parents come to visit Matt recently? For example, the night before his abduction, or that morning? Could they have given him any food?"

"No," Nelly managed to croak. "No close relatives have been to see Matt recently. My parents see him sometimes, but they've not fed him."

"Then it has to be either you or Stuart that gave Matt the temazepam to eat," Rita said slowly. She kept her voice soft, her eyes holding Nelly prisoner. "Did you do that?"

Nelly tried to swallow, but she ended up choking. She leaned to one side, coughing and spluttering, retching on the floor. Rita got up quickly and held her shoulders, lifting her back into the chair. Maggie got a plastic cup of water from the drinks machine and put it on the table. Nelly shook off Rita's hands angrily.

"How dare you say that?" she croaked, tears glistening in her eyes. Pain contorted her expression. "Why would I do that to my own son?" She gripped her forehead, and her head lowered. She wept softly.

Rita gave her some time. Maggie took out a couple of tissues from her pocket and slid them across the table. Nelly didn't look up.

Rita was encouraged by the fact that Nelly hadn't asked for a lawyer yet. That wasn't necessarily a sign of guilt, but it did mean the person was being careful, and Rita wouldn't get anything more out of them. So far, Nelly seemed to have a clear conscience.

Nelly dabbed at her face and composed herself. She took a sip of water. "Is this really true? You found temazepam in Matt's blood?"

"We don't have a blood sample, but the hair follicles show high concentrations of a short-acting benzodiazepine. It's temazepam. Someone gave it to Matt to sedate him, probably so that they could abduct him easily."

Nelly stared at Rita, her bone-white features a mask of incomprehension. Then she whispered, "Stu? Stu did this?"

"Unless you can think of someone else who's been to the house recently. And even then, they must have fed it to Matt the morning of the abduction. Temazepam is short-acting, and it works quickly."

Nelly's eyes flickered down to her hands, and her head moved sideways, as if she were trying to shake the shock away from her brain. It didn't work, clearly. She gripped her forehead, and her head descended to the table.

Maggie asked, "Can you think of where Stuart might be? You said the pub. Did you have one in mind?"

Nelly straightened. "No," she whispered. "So that's why you rang me this afternoon, asking for Stuart. And there I was, thinking you wanted to speak to me because you'd found Matt."

Rita said, "I'm sorry. But I have a feeling if we can find Stuart, then we'll find Matt as well."

Nelly stared back at Rita.

"Does Stuart have any close friends? Someone whose house he goes to every now and then, stays in touch with?"

"Yes, he's got a mate called Dan. They used to work together, but they don't anymore. He lives in Scawby. I'm not sure exactly where. His last name's Patmore."

Maggie got up and left to make the call about the new contact. Rita folded her hands across the table and sighed. "Did you know that Stuart doesn't have a job? And about his debts?"

The shock remained on Nelly's face. "No," she croaked eventually.

When Rita told her, Nelly's eyes shut softly, and she muttered under her breath. Rita gave her some time.

Nelly took another sip of water. Her hands shook, and she spilled some on her clothes. She didn't seem to care.

"My dad told me to stay away from him. He didn't like Stuart. Thought he was a charmer and not straight. I should have listened to him." She paused and sighed.

"But I was lonely. Raising a child on your own isn't easy. I had no time for a social life. I wanted to be with a man again. Looking back, I now realize Stuart smooth-talked his way into moving into my house. Dad offered to pay for it, and Stuart said once his business was up and running, he would buy out my dad's share. He had this glossy website for a horseracing company. He said it might make millions one day."

Nelly smiled ruefully, then her lips curled up in disgust. "I can't believe I let him do that to me. First Mark, now Stuart. I don't have any luck with men, do I?"

CHAPTER 32

Maggie and Rita trudged their tired way back to the office after Nelly left. Rita stopped on the corridor and called Lucy, the FLO. She wanted Lucy to be at Maggie's house at the crack of dawn tomorrow. Lucy agreed. Rita also called the duty Uniforms team and gave an order for a squad car to be parked outside the house from now until Stuart returned.

"Poor woman," Maggie said. "She's not going to have an easy night."

"Yes. I hope she has someone to be with her. We didn't ask her that, did we?"

"I did, when I escorted her back up to reception. She was going to call a friend."

"Good."

They went up to the office, and found Rizwan still there. "The skip had to leave," Rizwan said. "His daughter's got a cold and he has to take her into hospital. He said to call him if anything happened." Rizwan stifled a yawn. "How did it go with Nelly Crosby?"

"I don't think she did it," Rita said. "Yes, she was in the best position to abduct him, and then cook up this story. But I don't buy it."

"Must be Stuart then, eh? What a scallywag," Rizwan frowned. "Which reminds me." His face became animated as he picked up his laptop and came over to Rita's desk. Maggie joined them.

"Been busy have you?" She elbowed Rizwan as he walked past her. "Not wasting time like usual then."

"Shut it." Rizwan showed the screen to Maggie and Rita. A CCTV image was visible, showing the screen split up into 4 boxes. They showed a busy dual carriageway. The time stamp was from two days ago, at ten past ten in the morning. Rizwan pointed to a black Audi.

"That's Stuart's car." He played the film, and they watched the car come off the A165 and make its way into Osgodby, and then on Osgodby Lane. The car disappeared from view soon, as the Crosby home was in a CCTV blackspot. The car appeared on Osgodby Lane again, at twenty past eleven. Rita leaned in to get a closer look.

Rizwan stopped the film and zoomed into the car. The driver wore a black hoody, pulled over his head. Rizwan zoomed in till the face became pixellated.

"Caucasian, and not wearing glasses," Maggie said. "But we can't even be sure if he has glasses or not. His head's lowered, like he wants to hide."

Rizwan zoomed in on another image. This time, the man had his face raised, and despite the dark glasses and hoody, his features were familiar.

“Stuart,” Rita whispered.

Rizwan played the film again. They watched as the car joined the A165, but this time going in the opposite direction, heading south. Riz speeded up the tape, and they saw the car take an exit for Bempton Cliffs. Shortly after that, it pulled into a narrow exit that wasn’t marked.

“No sign of the car after that. Traffic don’t know where that exit leads to. Tomorrow first light they will be in that area, scouring the place.”

“Excellent work,” Rita said. “At least we now know Stuart was in the area when Matt disappeared. But we still don’t have concrete proof that he took Matt. He could’ve had the boy in the boot so no one could see him.”

Rita steepled fingers across her face, and leaned back on her chair. “So, Stuart must’ve given Matt the Temazepam in the morning, during breakfast. That’s why Matt was sleepy that day. He came back, kept watch till Nelly popped out to the neighbour’s house. Then he went in, grabbed Matt, and escaped.”

“The Temazepam made the whole thing possible,” Rizwan said. “Matt was sedated. He didn’t offer any resistance.”

"Correct. The neighbours probably didn't see much as they were at work. Stuart was only coming back to his own house."

Rizwan frowned. "Yes, but how did he take Matt out the front door? Maybe he wrapped him in a rug or carpet. Then he put that in the car boot."

"He must've driven around the back, so no one saw him." Rita thought of Stuart's anxious, worried face in the morning. Was he capable of carrying out such an act? It would explain his behaviour. He needed a place to hide the boy. Somewhere safe, and somewhere that he could visit easily.

"What about Stuart's parents? Do we know where they live?"

"Stuart's from Newcastle," Rizwan answered. "And his parents are both dead. His friend Dan Patmore is at home. I spoke to him tonight. He's got no idea where Stuart is, but uniforms have been to Dan's house, and searched it. They just got back. They found nowt."

Maggie got up quickly, hand over her mouth. She almost ran out of the room.

"What's wrong with her?"

"She did that this morning as well. Something she ate last night, she said." Rita stared at the laptop, her mind still buzzing, but a mist of tiredness was obscuring her thoughts.

Where could Stuart be? She turned to Rizwan. “Any sign of Mark Alridge?”

“After the neighbour’s unconfirmed sighting, nothing else. Uniformed squads will patrol Scarborough town centre, and around Osgodby, all night. His car’s not been seen on the roads. He’s got to be around somewhere.”

Maggie came back into the office. Her cheeks were flushed, but she looked tired and bothered.

“Still feeling unwell?” Rita asked.

“Aye,” Maggie sighed, picking up her stuff from the desk. She put them in her handbag which was slung on the side of her chair. “Serves me right for eating a dodgy takeaway.” She kept her eyes averted from Rita and Rizwan.

“Are you getting diarrhoea or vomiting?” Rita asked.

Maggie had a wan, exhausted look. Rita thought she’d just washed her face, and some of her make-up had come off.

Her eyes had shadows under them, and she looked like she hadn’t slept for a couple of days. Rita could see she was unwell.

“If you’re not well then stay at home tomorrow. That’s an order.”

“I’m fine, guv,” Maggie said. “Just a little tummy upset, that’s all.”

“Tomorrow morning, if you’re not well, just rest,” Rita said. “You won’t be much good if you’re running to the loo every hour.” She raised her eyebrows. Maggie clutched the strap of her handbag, and nodded, then lowered her face. Her usual bright smile was missing, as if a veil had passed over her. Rita imagined it was tiredness, and the bug she had.

“Right. Home, all of you. See you bright and early tomorrow,” Rita pointed a finger a Maggie. “But only if you’re feeling alright.”

“I’ll be fine, guv,” Maggie repeated, and made for the door.

CHAPTER 33

Detective Constable Maggie Long got into her car and sat there for a while. The night was warm, and she could feel a bead of sweat trickle down the back of her neck. She could still feel the nausea in the pits of her stomach. She felt bloated and hot. She put the window down, and started driving.

Maggie lived with her parents in a village called East Ayton. It was down the A170, the dual carriageway that headed east from Scarborough, snaking through the edges of the huge North Riding Forest Park. As Maggie drove, the cool air calmed her heated brow. It was dark now, and she could see the yellow headlights of cars in the opposite lane, stretched out like beads in a garland.

Maggie knew she was in trouble. She was late on her periods. It had been five weeks, and counting. She had met a new man recently, and they had hit it off right from the start. He was a farmer who lived in a village not far from where she did. She had met him in one of the barn dance nights organised in the East Ayton church hall. Kyle was tall, dark haired and handsome.

He was older than her by ten years. He was a quiet man, and when she saw him, he was drinking in one corner by himself. She couldn't take her eyes off him.

That was five months ago, and the days had gone by swiftly. Maggie was hesitant to start a new relationship, especially as the last one had ended with her being ghosted. It turned out the bastard had a child with another woman, and lived with her too. She had no such problems with Kyle. He was divorced, no children, and lived with his elderly mother. She had stayed with him twice. It was nice on his farm. A farmer's life was hard, she knew that. Her grandpa had a farm in the Yorkshire Dales, which she visited a lot as a child. She could see herself living in a farm.

Not that she was thinking of marriage, or settling down. She was only twenty-six, and she still had a life ahead of her. She wanted to do well in her career. Her guvnor, Rita, was an inspiration. Maggie wanted to be like her one day.

She got home to the four-bedroom detached stone cottage she shared with her parents. She pulled into the drive, and turned the lights off. She got out of the car, and then on an impulse, went out of the drive, and crossed the lane that led into the woods. As she walked in the darkness, the sounds of the cars faded, and she was left alone with her thoughts.

She needed to do a pregnancy test immediately. She had picked up a testing kit on her way here. But she had a feeling what the result would show. For the last two weeks she had been feeling heavy and off. Her ankles got swollen, and she felt sick, often. Her breasts felt heavy, like they did before her periods. And none of this was going away.

Maggie leaned against a wooden gate that led to a farm. The open land stretched out in front of her, rising up to the hills beyond. The velvety blue sky was like a shroud over the hills fading into blue and black. She lifted her head to the pin prick of stars, and felt the first stab of tears.

She wasn't ready for this. This was an accident…it seemed harsh to call it that. She had been foolish, and not as careful as she normally was in these matters. Kyle had promised her he would be careful as well, but in the end, it was she who would bear the burden. Where did this leave her with Kyle? She adored him, of course. He was a lovely man. But did she love him? They were different in many ways. Maggie was an outgoing and sociable type. Kyle was more of an introvert, like many farmers were. His life was in the farm and with his animals. Is that the life she really wanted?

No. She wanted to get out of Scarborough one day and head for a bigger town like Leeds or Sheffield. That excited her, and it would also help her career. It was well known that detectives who worked in higher crime zone areas sharpened their skills quicker. How could she accommodate her career aspirations with having a baby?

She didn't know what she wanted. She was torn, and couldn't think anymore. She trudged back, listening to the crickets chirping loudly, and the night sounds of the forest slowly rising up. She got closer to the road, and climbed over the short wooden fence, then crossed it quickly.

Her mother was in the kitchen, but she didn't see her dad. He ran a pub near Peasholm Park in Scarborough, and was still at work. Maggie said hi to her mother, then went upstairs. In the toilet, she held her breath as she did the pregnancy test. When she saw the two bars in blue appear, there was no doubt anymore.

She flopped down on the floor, held her head and wept.

CHAPTER 34

Joshua Dixon was doing his push ups when there was a knock on the door. Dixon was sweaty, and gasping from the exertion. He got up as the viewing flap lifted, and one of the guards peered in. Dixon ignored him. He went into the bathroom and wiped his face and head with a towel. The flap was still lifted when he came out.

"We're coming in," the guard said. It was Pete, Dixon knew his voice.

"What for?" Dixon knew his rights. Although he was in a Category A prison, he still had plenty of rights and privileges. One of them was the right to privacy when he was in his room.

"We need to search the room."

Dixon didn't like that. While the guards could search his room at any time, and he knew they came in when he was with Dr Patel, or eating dinner, they didn't normally bother him when he was in the room.

"What for?" He repeated.

"No reason. We're coming in, stand aside."

Dixon knew he could argue, but a part of him was also intrigued what they wanted to look for. He suspected this had something to do with Inspector Rita Gupta's recent visit. He had left the lemon cake half consumed. As for the paper the message was written in, he had eaten it. The capsule the hidden note came in had been flushed down the toilet, wrapped up in tissue.

Dixon watched as Pete, and the other guard, Steve, opened the door. They came in, and he sat down on the chair whose legs were screwed into the floor. The guards searched the room methodically, starting with the books on the bookshelf. They peered behind the radiator. Looked under the bed. They removed the duvet and bedsheets, looked inside the pillowcases.

Steve pointed a chubby finger at the remains of the cake. "Are you going to eat that?"

Dixon shook his head. "You can finish it off, if you like."

Steve snorted. He produced a folded black bin liner from his pocket, opened it up and put the cake inside it.

Dixon pointed at the crumbs left on the desk. He hated seeing a mess. "You missed these."

Steve grimaced. He was a big guy, like Pete. Psychiatric nurses tended to be built like bears. Dixon had seen them subdue other prisoners. He was subject to the same treatment when he headbutted the prisoner in the canteen. But he wasn't scared. Steve glared at him, and he returned the stare.

"The cleaner's going to come later," Steve growled. "Stand up."

Dixon stood, and raised his hands in the air as Steve patted him down. From the corner of his eye, he watched Pete come out of the toilet area. The wash basin had a faucet recessed into the wall. There was a motion detector below it that turned on when Dixon waved his hand over it. The commode didn't have a lid, nothing that could be lifted or removed.

The flush button was also recessed in the wall, and motion controlled. Dixon wondered if any parts of the capsule had fallen out of the tissue. He was careful, and didn't think so. But his heart beat a little faster when he saw Pete standing by the toilet partition wall.

He heaved a sigh of relief when Pete went to the door, and Steve joined him. He could tell they didn't find anything.

"Happy now?" Dixon smiled. "Can I go to the canteen for dinner today?" He had lost his canteen privileges, which he missed. It was lonely as hell sitting in a solitary room, eating by himself.

"No," Pete said. They went out the door, then Pete turned. "Your visitor is due in one hour. We'll be back."

***

Janice had bought him a lasagne this time. It was inside a see-through Tupperware box. Janice slid the box across the table. She wore make up today. Black mascara, red blusher on her sagging cheeks, and bright red lipstick. She looked like a traffic light, Dixon thought, but kept his thoughts to himself.

"They looked inside that," Janice pointed at the box and shook her head in disgust. "The guard lifted it with a spoon to look under it. Can you believe it?" She eyed the guard standing at the end of the room. She grimaced, looking back to Dixon.

"I can. This is a Category A prison. There's a reason why no one breaks out from here."

"But he said you can do it. He's going to help you. Did the solicitor contact you? Mr Maynard, his name is."

The man who called himself the Keeper had put Janice and Dixon in touch with a crooked solicitor who had helped other criminals escape from jail.

"Yes, he did. He's good. But even he knows it's impossible to get out of here. He's looking at other options. How is our man?"

"He's getting bothered. His business partner is making life difficult for him." Janice explained the situation the man was facing with Stuart.

"That's not good," Dixon frowned. "Tell him he can't have any loose strings." He leaned forward and lowered his voice. “It’s now time for him to kill the boy as well. He needs to get out of here. The heat is rising. Tell him to learn from my mistake.”

CHAPTER 35

Rita was back home, lying on the sofa with a glass of wine. She smiled when she saw the text from her dad.

Saw you on TV today. You looked great!

She thanked him, and they chatted on text for a while. Rita had finished her microwave pasta dinner. She didn't have time to cook, and she was famished. Her eyes closed as she leaned back on the sofa. The wine was working its magic, but she still had the headache and felt exhausted from the day's events. Her eyes were closing of their own accord, she was struggling to stay awake. The TV was on, but the sound was on low.

Rita heard the sound of something falling. Her eyes popped open. She was in the kitchen and dining area, and the window was open here, but nothing had fallen from the table. The sound had come from living room area, across the hallway. As far as she knew, the windows there were closed. A gust of wind blew in from the kitchen window above the sink. Rita lived on the slope of a hill overlooking the south bay. It was a beautiful view, but the weather could change rapidly due to the proximity to the sea. She got up and shut the window.

She couldn't hear any more sounds. She went across the dark hallway, turning the lights on. The living room door was open. The lights were off, and she could see the faint glow of streetlights. The lights sloped down the hill, and the sea glittered in the distance. But Rita's eyes were on the flower vase that was on the carpet. Water had spilled out of it, and the flowers had fallen. She could feel the breeze inside the room, and without going into the room she could still see the open window.

She hadn't been in this room since she got back. She hadn't opened that window. A frisson of fear ignited in her spine. Hairs stood up in the back of her neck.

Someone was in the flat, and they had come in through that window.

She retreated, and went towards the main door. There, on the small table under the mirror, she had kept her handbag. Without taking her eye off the living room door, she rummaged around the handbag till she found her extendable baton. She took it out, and held the weapon in front of her, flicking it to the full length.

She checked the front door was shut. Then she went into her bedroom. The light was still on, and her bedroom was empty. She had a quick look, then checked the smaller guest bedroom. Here, the door was shut, and she opened it, then turned the light on, without going inside.

It was also empty, as far as she could see. The double wardrobe was closed, and she looked under the bed. She found nothing. She checked the bathroom quickly, all the while keeping an eye on the living room. Her senses were on fire, head swivelling around rapidly.

That left the living room. She tiptoed back to it. She listened hard. She heard a rustling sound inside. Her mouth ran dry as her heart thudded against her ribs.

"Who's there?" She called out. "Come out and show yourself."

The rustling sound stopped. "Come out, now!" Rita shouted. There was no sound all of a sudden. Rita's free hand groped on the wall inside, desperately trying to find the switch.

She found it finally, then flicked it. The harsh glow lit up the room. She blinked. She heard the rustling sound again. She braced herself, baring her teeth. Then she kicked the door with all her might, and burst into the room.

Her head jerked around, eyes scanning the room wildly. A breeze came in again through the open window, moving the curtains. Rita saw a dark shape outside, huddled near the base of the window. She had a ground floor flat, and the grass mound of the hill rose up towards the building. Rita rushed to the window;

baton raised. The shape detached itself from the window, jumping down to the grass verge underneath.

She saw a figure run away to the left, towards the front of the building, away from the streetlights at the back of the down sloping hill. Rita ran to her front door, yanked it open, and jumped outside. She saw a man running away. For a split second, she thought of giving chase.

But what if he had an accomplice? She had to lock her place up, and he would be long gone by then.

She watched in frustration as he sprinted to the end of the road. Her chest heaved with anger, and she clenched her teeth together. Adrenaline was coursing like lava in her veins. She would rip him apart if she got her hands on him. She ran back to the house. She turned all the lights on, and searched carefully again.

Apart from her, no other living being. She closed all the windows, and locked the front door. There was a back door as well, by the kitchen sink. It was locked as well. She took her torchlight, and went outside. There was a front garden area that extended to the sides. The building had four floors, with apartments on each. Hence the garden area was sizeable, meant for all the residents.

The sole building occupied a corner plot, and Rita went around it, flashing her torch around. She didn't go deep into the bushes where it was darker. She was angry, but she wasn't stupid. She flashed her light around the undergrowth carefully. A bush moved, and her heart stopped.

She jerked her light back to it, raising the baton in her right hand. Her heart was like a piston against her ribcage. Then she saw the fox, with its tail raised behind its back. Its eyes stared back at her, glinting, then it turned, and ran away.

That’s when she heard the footsteps behind her.

CHAPTER 36

Gasping, Rita swung around, the torchlight flashing in a wide arc. It caught a man who raised both hands over his face and cowered. Rita needed to identify him, and if necessary, strike the first blow. She advanced, baton raised like a sword.

"Who are you?" She shouted. Her mind was aflame with possibilities. Could this be Mark? Or perhaps Stuart? Or one of their accomplices?

"Stop, Rita. It's me!"

The familiar voice halted her. She lowered her torch beam, directing it to the man's torso. He raised himself up to his full height slowly. It was Jack. Rita panted, rage still bubbling away in her veins.

"Bloody heck. I thought you were going to Taser me." Jack stood there, watching her warily. He seemed to understand the situation. His head snapped to either side as he came forward.

"What's going on? Are you alright?"

"Someone tried to get in through the living room window." Rita breathed heavily; the baton still clutched tightly in her right fist. Sweat trickled down the sides of her face.

"What? Did they come in?"

"I think I scared him off. He tried to get in, but a flower vase fell off the table, and I got up to check."

Jack looked behind, at the light inside the flat. "Let's go inside."

They walked back, and Rita let them in with her keys. She got her radio from the kitchen counter and called Switchboard to let them know. The duty uniformed sergeant said he was on his way, but Rita declined.

"He won't come back, don't worry. Just arrange a patrol car to swing by. I'll file a PCN tomorrow.

"But guv, what if he does? It could be one of the suspects in the case."

"And if it was, how does he know where I live?" Rita asked. "That doesn't make sense. I think it was a burglar. Just a random event. I'm often home late, so he thought he'd chance it."

The sergeant sounded reluctant. "If you say so, guv."

"I'd rather you look out for him around the house. Please ask Traffic to check CCTV on my street as well. There're cameras here."

"Will do, guv. And sending a patrol car out."

“Was that wise?” Jack asked, leaning against the counter. The radio was on speaker mode, and he had heard the conversation.

“Yes,” Rita said firmly. “It’s true that Stuart knows my name and could’ve searched for me. My phone and address are off directory, like it is for all police staff. But these days its not difficult to find someone. But why would they come here, when they know I’m looking for them? Doesn’t make any sense.”

“You said the abductor had an accomplice. It could be him. Or her.”

“I doubt it.” Rita flopped down the sofa. “Why give themselves up?” She frowned. “Unless-

“Unless they wanted to harm you,” Jack said. “Rita, this is serious.” He sat down next to her on the sofa. “You need to consider that whoever tried to get in tonight is dangerous. He knew that you’re in the house. You had the lights on, right?”

She nodded. Jack said, “A burglar wouldn’t enter if someone was in the house. You know how they operate.”

Rita thought of the shape outside the window, as if it was caught between hiding and jumping over to come inside. She might have surprised him. He was expecting to come in without any trouble. But something about the man still bothered her. For some reason, he seemed familiar, when he was running away. She explained this to Jack.

"Did you see his face?"

Rita shook her head. "No. But something about him was familiar, that's all I can say. But I don't understand how anyone would know where I lived?" She glanced at Jack curiously. "How did you turn up here?"

"Not suspecting me, I hope," Jack grinned. "I was passing by on my way home from work, and you weren't answering. Hence, I decided to stop by. Hope you don't mind. You said you weren't busy this evening."

"Very rude of you to drop by unannounced. My downtime is my own, Mr Banford."

"We do things differently up North. Everyone's your mate here, didn't you know?"

"Like the man who just tried to get in?" Rita sighed, breaking the good humour. She felt dog tired all of a sudden. The adrenaline was fading, and the tips of her hands and feet felt cold. She closed her eyes, and leaned her head back against the sofa. She was glad Jack was here. She wouldn't tell him that, but she suspected he knew.

"I'm staying the night," Jack said. "I can sleep in the guest room. You have a bed there, right?"

Rita looked at him. She yawned, covering her mouth. "You don't have to do that."

"Yes, I absolutely do. And I will. You can try and kick me out, but I'll win because I'm bigger than you. You can't even call the cops because you are one."

"Now that's GBH."

"Debatable, if you instigate it. You're talking to a criminal lawyer, remember?"

"Aye, don't I just," She grimaced. "Bane of my life, you lot are."

Rita knew argument would drain her, and in any case, it would be futile. Jack was determined, she could tell from the hard set of his jaws. She rolled her eyes; secretly glad he was staying.

"Alright, if you insist. There's a microwave lasagne in the fridge if you want."

"Nothing but the best home cooked food Scarborough has to offer."

"There's also some wine," Rita indicated the table where a bottle of Claret was half finished. "See how I spoil you?"

There was a knock on the door. Rita went up to it, and Jack followed. It was the police, as Rita had expected. She could see the flashing blue lights before she opened the door. A bearded sergeant stood there, looking apologetic. His name badge said Betteridge.

"DI Gupta," Rita said. "Don't worry, it's all been sorted. Did you liaise with Traffic to get the CCTV footage?"

"Yes, and they're going through it right now. It'll be emailed to you as soon as they're done, which should be in an hour or so."

"I'll see it at work tomorrow then."

"We'll patrol around here tonight. We're the duty team and one of us will be in front of your house."

"No need for that, I've got company."

"Our guv ordered it," Betteridge said. "Inspector Bennett."

Rita smiled. "That's nice of him. Yes, I know Steve. I'll let him know. If you must, then do so. But I'd much rather you get the CCTV footage and chase the man who tried to break in."

"Roger that, guv."

CHAPTER 37

Stuart stopped running, and leaned against the alley wall, gasping. His shirt was soaked in sweat, and even the jacket was sticking to his back. He wiped sweat with his sleeve, and tried to think. He needed to get as far away from this place as possible, but he was exhausted. He should never have come here. But he was forced to. As he remembered the conversation with his friend, his skin crawled, and nausea pooled in his guts.

"You've messed this up, you know that?" The man had raged. They were in the lock down garage where he kept his stuff. This is where they met. It was a large garage, with enough space to park four cars.

"The cops suspect you now. That female detective, she's got a shark's nose for blood. She's going to come after you. Then we're done for."

Stuart had enough of this. The lying and cheating. He couldn't bear it. His voice had quivered.

"I think we should end this now. There's no point. I can't keep running around scared. Like you said, the cops are going to be on us sooner or later."

The man came closer. He was shorter than Stuart, but his eyes gleamed like a serpent's and he bared his fangs. Stuart gulped and stepped back.

"What're you talking about?" The man hissed.

"I mean, this. Taking Matt. It's got to end. Let's take whatever money there is and split it okay? You can have more than me. I-

The man's hand lashed out, gripping Stuart by the throat, and slamming him against the wall. His grip was like iron, and Stuart choked, then kicked out as the man's hand squeezed his neck powerfully. The man pressed his body against Stuart's, suffocating him, putting his face within inches of his.

"You think this is a game? We can just stop playing when we want?"

Stuart went to speak, but the man pushed his neck harder, and Stuart started to choke.

"Do you want to see the boy dead? Is that what you want?"

Miserably, Stuart shook his head. The man released his grip slightly to let Stuart breathe. "Good. The way I see it, we have one option. We run away with the boy."

The man stepped back, and Stuart took a gulp of air, and breathed again. He put his hands on his knees and bent forward, coughing and retching.

"I think that's a bad idea," Stuart said. "The cops will know. They've seen my car. They could-

"Shut up, you fool," the man thundered. "Go home now and keep your stupid mouth shut. You running away now only makes matters worse. I get away with the boy. You stay here, got that?"

"But what if the cops come after me? They might know that I came home that day."

"Let them. There're no cameras on your street, right? They're just going to make stuff up, put you under pressure. Just keep saying no, and get a lawyer. Keep saying you didn't do it. Got that?"

Now, as he panted, Stuart stared at the puddle in the alley and thought about it. After he left the garage, he made his mind up. He was going to go to the police and come clean. He made his way to Scarborough police station. But as he was coming out of the cab, he saw the female inspector. Rita Gupta. She was getting into a cab, alone. Stuart realised she must be going home.

"Follow that cab, now," he told the driver. The man did as told. Stuart got off a safe distance away from where Rita Gupta stopped. He walked by, and saw where she lived. He had tried to get in, and tell her everything. But when he saw her, he lost his nerve. She'd arrest him, wouldn't she? He would spend the next ten years behind bars. He could see it happening. He'd been a fool to come here.

He turned and ran away. Luckily Rita didn't come after him. Stuart straightened, and walked out of the alley, and crossed the road. He needed to go back home to Osgodby. He was near Peashome Park in Scarborough. He picked up his pace, pulling his hoody over his head.

He used the shortcuts, staying away from the cameras on the main road. But it was a long way back, and his legs were tired after the running. He had been optimistic when he thought he could do it by foot. He started to walk towards the main street, where he could find a bus station. He was walking through a long, narrow alley, and he quickened his pace. He had to get back home. He had turned his phone off, but now that it was on, he could see all the missed calls. The road after the mouth of the alley was visible, bright with streetlights.

Stuart stopped short suddenly. A figure had appeared ahead. A man stood there with his legs spread, silhouetted by the lights behind him. His long shadow fell over the alley. The man came forward slowly, like he was watching his prey. With a spasm of fear, Stuart realised who it was. He took a step back. The man advanced, with measured steps.

"Where did you go?"

Stuart swallowed, but his mouth was bone dry. His heart rate was going nuclear, thrashing in his chest like a fish caught in a net.

"I…I took a detour. Needed to clear my head."

"So you didn't got back home like I told you to."

The man was closer all of a sudden, and Stuart retreated further, then stopped. Why should he be so scared? He needed to stand his ground, damn it. He raised himself to his full height.

"You don't control me. I can do what I want. What the hell are you doing here?"

The man was now within a few feet of him. Stuart could see the sinister, evil grin on his face.

"I followed you. Just to see where you went."

The fear returned, crawling up Stuart's spine like a spider. "So, you're following me around now? A bit weird, don't you think?" He tried to keep his voice normal, and not shaky like he felt inside. His hands were fists inside his jacket pocket.

"You went to the police station, didn't you? Why?"

"None of your business."

"Then you followed a cab home. It was that female Inspector, Rita Gupta. You tried to get into her house."

"This is stupid. I've got to go." Stuart tried to brush past the man. He was ready for a confrontation. He would fight back this time, damn it. He pushed him, but the man was prepared. He deftly side stepped, and his arms were a blur of movement.

Stuart felt a blinding, tearing stab of pain slice across his lower belly. It came again, this time in his back, ripping into his side, as he cried out and stumbled forward. He fell to his knees. He raised a hand.

"Please, stop. Don't do-

A hand grabbed the back of his neck. The voice growled in his ears. "You're a traitor. You went to spill the beans, didn't you? Now the boy's going to die."

"What? No, wait. I didn't say a word."

Despite the pain convulsing his body, Stuart tried to turn around. Another blinding blow came swiftly, this time to the back of neck. A searing, rendering agony as the knife stabbed into his neck, driving his body down to the ground. Stuart's head hit the damp earth, and he didn't remember anything anymore.

CHAPTER 38

Clara was calling her name. “Rita, stop that.” Rita was an adult now, why did her mother have to speak to her like that? But she wasn’t angry. How could she be, when Clara was back, after all these years. Sitting at the dining table, like she’d never left.

“I’m only draining the pasta,” Rita said, looking behind. But her mother was now next to her, as if she had floated up there.

“This is how you drain it. Here, hold the strainer like that.”

Clara took the pan and strainer from Rita’s hands. Her hands briefly brushed Rita’s. It made Rita stare down at her hand. She hadn’t felt her mother’s touch for so long. She looked up, and Clara wasn’t there anymore. The pan and strainer had tilted to one side on the counter, pasta and fluids seeping down to the floor.

“Mum?” Rita called out. “Mum?”

Rita’s eyes flickered open, and she lay there for a while, looking at the ceiling. She could hear birdsong in the trees. The pale morning sun slanted in through a gap in the curtains. She was up before the six am alarm, and she couldn't go back to sleep.

She had the same dream so many times. Clara was back, and staying with her. The old emptiness returned, the cloak that lay heavy over her shoulders. With time, the cloak had worn thinner, and she had learnt to live with it. But last year, after she discovered her mother's remains, the chasm came back with a vengeance.

Discovering her mother's killer didn't fill up the chasm, it remained like a yawning gap. But at least she had closure. At least she had laid Clara to rest, and she could put flowers where she lay. She visited the cemetery every fortnight. Her father had come with her the last time he visited. That had been special. Rita counted her blessings that her dad was still alive, and she had made amends with him.

In life, one had to be grateful for what one had – not what one had lost.

She flung the covers off and got up. There was a lot to get on with today – finding Matt being the priority, but her mind returned to the man last night. The way he hesitated by the window. Like he couldn't make his mind up. If he wanted to hurt her, he would've come in. She had no doubt.

As she came out of the bathroom, she saw Jack's bedroom door ajar. She made sure her bathrobe was wrapped tight, and she peeked in through his door. He was sleeping with his back to her. The covers had slid down to his waist, revealing his broad back and shoulders. His skin was smooth, the contour of his muscles sleek. His chest rose and fell as he breathed gently.

Rita felt a loosening low in her belly, a slow release of desire. When was the last time she had been with a man? She turned away, and tiptoed back into her room. Now was not the time…well, she didn't know when the right time would occur. She sighed, and stepped into the shower.

She got ready, and went into the kitchen. The small red dot on her radio was flashing, and she turned the knob up to listen to the dispatches from last night. A couple of burglaries and a fight outside a pub were reported.

Rita made her coffee as she listened. The coffee mug stopped halfway to her lips as an urgent notice came through the speaker.

All units alert. IC1 male found deceased on Holbeck Hill, Scarborough. Knife wounds in abdomen and neck. Request assistance. Repeat – request assistance.

The following few messages were from various uniform units converging on the spot. Rita skipped a few and tried to hear if they had confirmed the victim's ID. None had so far. No wallet or phone was found on the victim.

It was seven now, and Rita had to leave for work. She called Maggie, but the constable didn't answer. Rita left a message on Richard and Rizwan's phone, informing them of the murder.

She heard sounds outside, and realised the shower was on. She made a quick breakfast of cereals and milk. Jack came into the kitchen, rubbing his hair with a towel.

"Thanks for leaving this in my room," Jack said, holding the towel up.

"You're welcome. Do you want coffee?"

Over a hot mug, she told him what happened last night. He frowned as he blew on the coffee, then sipped it.

"If it was the same guy who was here last night, that would be strange."

"Exactly what I was thinking."

They ate quickly, and Jack offered to drop her off at work. Rita agreed and they left as soon as they finished breakfast. She promised Jack she'd catch up with him after work that day.

The station was humming with activity. It was a Friday morning, and the sun was bright. Rita stopped by the main desk, and asked for the morning uniform team, who would've been handed over last night's cases. A uniformed sergeant called Tolson came up to her.

“We got some news, guv. The murdered man had a fake Rolex wristwatch, and a tattoo on his upper arm. It was a small dragon, red and blue coloured. Does that ring any bells?”

Rita thought for a while. “No. From what I gather – the man was dark haired, five feet eleven, and wore a black jacket and dark blue jeans with brown trainers. Is that correct?”

“Yes. We’re still searching for an ID. Fingerprints have shown nowt on IDENT-1. DNA swabs are awaiting a match on PCR. Should be available soon. Body’s at the morgue and the pathologist is aware.”

Rita thanked the man, and strode to her office. She called Nelly Crosby, who sounded sleepy.

“Hello? Who’s this?” Nelly mumbled. When she heard Rita’s voice, she was instantly alert.

“DI Gupta. What’s happened? Any news?”

Rita sighed. She wished that for once, she had some good news for Nelly. Sadly, that would still have to wait.

“I need to ask you something. Did Stuart come back home last night?”

“No, I don’t think so. Do you want me to check?”

Rita agreed, and Nelly came back online in a couple of minutes. “No, he’s not here. His beds not slept in. What’s going on?”

“Does Stuart have a dragon tattoo, coloured red and green, on his left forearm, under the elbow?”

There was silence for a while. “Yes.” Nelly said in a small voice.

“And does he wear a Rolex watch? A fake one, I should add.”

A gasp came from the other end. “What’s going on?” Nelly repeated. “What’s happened to him?”

Rita closed her eyes. “I’ll call you back when I have some more news.” She excused herself, not committing to Nelly’s questions, but promising to get back to her asap. The others hadn’t arrived as yet. Rita left a note for them, asking them to chase up CCTV near her house with Traffic, and she headed out to Scarborough General Hospital. She took a cab there, and went down to the morgue. Dr Das was surprised to see her. He was in his office, and he adjusted the glasses on his nose, looking up at her from his desk.

“You didn’t call?”

“I did try. You live in an underground cave which is not exactly mobile phone friendly.” Rita smiled, standing by the door. Dr Das rose, and they went outside. A line of gurneys rested in the large chamber, with stainless steel wash basins on the walls. Bright fluorescent lights gleamed overhead.

"I take it this is about the IC1 murder victim from last night."

Rita nodded, and they walked to one of the gurneys. Dr Das's helper, Stephen, waved at them from a desk. Rita waved back. The right side of the morgue was taken up with worktops containing microscopes, small weighing machines, desktops and printers. Framed photos of colourful flowers brought some life to the walls. Rita could never work here, but she knew the morgue was critical to her own work – a pathologist's eye uncovered clues that solved countless murders.

Dr Das put on his gloves and apron, then took the cover off a dead body. The skin was deathly white, and the clothes had been removed, and the man lay there, naked. Deep gashes had formed on the left side of his lower abdomen, and she could see the stab wounds on the back of his neck. She got closer, and the face became clearer. In death Stuart looked different, perfectly calm, resigned to his fate. But there was no doubt it was him.

"You know him?" Dr Das hooked an eyebrow upwards. Rita glanced at the slightly chubby cheeks of the veteran pathologist. Not much went past him.

"Yes. He was the main suspect in the abduction of the boy. Matthew Alridge. This man was his stepfather."

"Why was he the main suspect?"

Rita told him about the CCTV footage, and Stuart's lies. Dr Das's brown forehead creased. "So, you don't actually have an eyewitness, or any other proof that he took Matt?"

"No, but we do know where his car went after he left the crime scene. He took a turn for Bempton. We lost his car after that. I think Matt's somewhere there, where his car was that morning."

Dr Das's eyes flickered down to the body. "He was stabbed to death. He lost a lot of blood, and that was the cause of death. But the real question is – if he abducted Matt, and now he's dead – how will you find Matt?"

"Like I said, we're organising a search party in that dirt track near the Bempton exit off the A165."

"I know that road. Nice little area, leading to the Bempton Cliffs and the beaches. Not far from Bridlington."

"Yes."

"It's a long stretch of road. No CCTV there?"

"Unfortunately, not down the dirt track he took. Uniforms are heading out there as we speak."

Dr Das stared at Rita in silence for a while. The elderly pathologist had a keen mind, and had seen more than his fair share of murder victims. He pointed to the abdominal stab wounds.

"This was a vicious attack. The wounds are fresh. Death occurred around midnight. Someone wanted this man dead in a hurry. Your chief suspect. The one you think abducted the boy. Who would be desperate to kill him?"

Dr Das's question swirled in Rita's mind like milk stirred into coffee. The thought had crossed her mind, but now she had to face it. And slowly, like a mist lifting, the answer came to her.

"Someone who thought he knew too much. Like an accomplice. Or the real mastermind of the abduction."

Dr Das's dark eyes were sober, and he gazed at Rita.

"Exactly."

CHAPTER 39

Rizwan and Richard were at the office. Richard was on the phone, and Rizwan looked up from his laptop as Rita entered.

"The search parties are on the scene near Bempton exit off the A165. Although that exit goes to Bempton, the dirt track where the car was last seen is in a place called Reighton. There's a couple of beaches there. Nice place actually, Reighton is. Good holiday park there, on the beach. Big cliffs around the bay. I've been with the family a couple of times."

The name struck a distant bell in Rita's mind. "Never been there, but sounds familiar. Has the search party reported anything as yet?"

"Nowt. By the way, Maggie called in sick. She sounded groggy, if you ask me. Glad she's resting."

"Good, looked like she needed it."

Richard came off the phone. He looked anxious, his eyes hooded with concern. “That was Traffic, with the CCTV footage from last night. Apparently there was a break in at your house?”

“Not really. He didn’t come in.”

“Are you okay?” Richard asked.

“Yes, I’m fine, don’t worry.”

“Flippin’ ‘eck guv, kept that one quiet,” Rizwan said. “Did they get him?”

Richard answered. “No, but they have the CCTV of him here.” He clicked on his keyboard and got up the images. Rita and Rizwan stood on either side of his desk, leaning in to look. The black and white image showed a man from behind, running down the road. Rita recognised it as her street. The man looked familiar.

“Show him from the front if you can.”

Richard switched cameras, and now they could see the man frontally, his features darkened in the night, but the dark brown hoody, and black jeans were unmistakable. When Richard zoomed in to the face, even the blurred image was enough to identify the man.

“Stuart,” Rizwan whispered. “Bloody hell. He tried to get into your house last night, and now he’s dead?”

“Exactly.” Rita drummed her fingers on the table. She had expected this. A sixth sense had told her it might’ve been Stuart. What did he want?

Rita was now sure Stuart was killed because he came to her house to tell her something. His murderer assumed Stuart had spilled the beans. Just like Dr Das had suggested.

That also meant Matt was now in danger. His abductor would now try to move Matt. That was a problem, but it was also an opportunity. In his rush to move farther out, Rita hoped he would make a mistake.

“Go back to the CCTV of Stuart’s car after he left Osgodby the morning of Matt’s abduction.”

Rizwan pulled up a chair for Rita to sit down, and then stood behind Richard’s chair. Richard’s screen showed Stuart’s black Audi coming out of Osgodby Lane, and into the main roundabout that led to the A165.

“Ok now check the time stamp,” Rita said, pointing at the digital clock on the top right of the screen. It was twenty past eleven.

“Nelly came back home at 10.30, and looked around everywhere. She went to the path beyond the house. Safe to assume that would be around 10.45. If Stuart took Matt, he was gone by then, because Nelly didn’t see him, or his car. Question is, where was Stuart?

Because he doesn't turn up on the camera till 11.20, which is almost an hour later."

"Good point," Richard said, stroking his pot belly. "You'd think he'd want to get the hell out of there, as fast as he could, right?"

"I think he met up with the man who killed him. His accomplice, who helped him get Matt. That man took Matt away."

"So what are we looking for?" Rizwan asked. "Any car that left Osgodby Lane between half ten and twenty past eleven?"

Richard raised a quizzical eyebrow. "We've done that already, guv. That was the focus, in the last two days. Every car we've seen so far has been checked with the DVLA, and the owners."

"Well, we must've missed something. Go through them all again. And extend it to the whole day, because the abductor could well have left after dark, to disguise himself further."

Another thought had been circling in her head. She still didn't know where Mark Aldridge was. She asked Rizwan, and from the rueful look on his face, she knew the answer.

Richard said, "There's no sign of his car. He's hidden it, and it's definitely not been on the roads. ANPR would have identified it by now. And he's not turned up on the all-points bulletin either. So, he's not taken a plane or ferry anywhere, which means he's local, and he can't be that far."

Rita tapped her rubber-soled shoes on the ground and stared down at them. Potentially, Mark remained a suspect for Stuart's murder. "If he's local, he could have been in Scarborough and followed Stuart from my house. We need to find him without delay."

Rizwan nodded. "If he's capable of GBH, he might be capable of murder, especially if he hates Stuart and…" Rizwan frowned, as if a sudden thought had gripped him. "What if Mark was the accomplice?"

Rita folded her arms across her chest as the two men turned their heads in silent agreement towards her. Could it be possible?

Mark was not at home that morning. He had come down to speak to Nelly, he said, but he never got around to it. And since then, he had avoided Nelly and run away from the police. Then Rita shook her head.

“Mark didn’t like Stuart. They argued outside the family home, and even the neighbours noticed. I doubt they would work together. But regardless, we need to find Mark. I want to know why he’s on the run.”

"Have we put posters out for Mark in the town centre?"

"Not that I know of," Rizwan said. "Do you want me to organise it?"

"Not just that," Rita said. "I also want a door-to-door around the Crosby residence, and in Scarborough town. Mark wouldn't be sleeping rough in a residential area. There's plenty of room to rent in town, and he could be in one of those." She shook her head in frustration. She should have thought of this earlier.

Rizwan got to his feet. "I'll get a uniformed unit and go down to the town centre myself."

"Good," Rita said. “Richard, you’re coming with me to Reighton.”

*****

It didn't take them long to get there, given the absence of traffic on the A165. The sea appeared on the left, and Rita gazed at it from the passenger seat. The cliffs succumbed to the sea, and waves foamed against the rocks at the bottom. Her mind beat against closed doors of the case, desperate to break them open. She was missing something obvious.

Did Stuart take Matt? To do that, Stuart had drugged the boy in the morning, and then pretended to leave for work. That's why Nelly reported Matt was tired, and wanted to sleep. She went through the scenario for the hundredth time.

While Nelly was gone, Stuart gets back into the house, but he parks in the rear so his neighbours won't see. He goes over the fence, and scrapes himself in the process, hence the drops of blood that Shola found. He gets Matt, puts him on his back, and comes out of the rear the same way.

Was his accomplice already in the car? It was possible. He might've hidden in the backseat for the cameras. They got out, and then drove to where the accomplice's car was. That was clever, Rita thought. Because the accomplice's car was unmarked. Then Stuart drove off…but the accomplice wouldn't have dawdled for long, because he would've known the police would be searching soon.

As the exit for Bempton got closer, Rita had a sinking feeling. If Stuart's car didn't have Matt in it, this might be a waste of time. Richard pulled into the dirt track, which was now guarded by a squad car, with uniformed constables standing around, watching passing cars. Further down the road, Rita could see Bob Chandler's white van. Bob was kneeling on the side of the road, using his microscopic brush to sift through layers of dust. The uniformed sergeant in charge came up to her.

"Hello guv. This road goes straight down to a couple of abandoned farmhouses, then peters out into the woods. We've checked one of the farmhouses already. Nowt in there."

Rita looked down to her right, where the road curved around in a broad sweep and disappeared from view. Directly in front, she saw the sea, glittering in the sun.

"Is that the Reighton beach?" She asked.

The sergeant nodded. "Yes, that's the Reighton Sands Holiday Park."

Why would Stuart drive here? Rita wondered as she walked down the path. According to her scenario, the accomplice had Matt in the boot of his car, and he drove off with him. His car was unmarked, but Stuart's would under scrutiny.

Did Stuart drive here to act as a decoy? Or to meet up with the accomplice?

Rita said hello to Bob, who was engrossed with the task at hand. He looked up, squinting.

"Och, aye, if it ain't the queen of Crime herself," Bob grinned, and got stiffly to his feet, knee joint popping.

Rita rolled her eyes. Bob smelt of stale tobacco and sweat. "Flattery will get you everywhere, Mr Chandler. How's it looking?"

"Well, there's one car that's been down this road in the last few days. It's rained once so the prints aren't great. But beggars cannae be choosers, aye?"

"That's right. Apart from the tyre tracks, anything else?"

"No. But I'll keep my eyes peeled, like. You ne'er know what treasures the ground coughs up, aye?"

"If you say so."

Richard and Rita walked to the next squad car, which was parked on the side of the road. The uniform constable gave them a lift to the farmhouse. Uniforms were crawling around, but hadn't found anything. Rita spoke to them for a bit, then the constable drove them to the second farmhouse, which seemed in better condition. The roof hadn't caved in, for starters. It was also at the edge of the woods, where the road came to an end. A river ran through the woods, it's silver gleam winking in the sun. A canal had been dug, and it brought water into the farms.

Two uniformed constables were in the barn. Rita and Richard walked across the cobblestone front yard. The heavy oak door was open, and the barn had an upper floor, a wooden platform that was empty save the dust of decades. Along the right wall there was a bunch of rusty utensils – from pitch forks to spades. The two constables said hello to Rita.

"Nowt here but spiders and cobwebs, guv. We did scare a fox when we arrived."

Rita pointed to the upper floor. "Have a look in there as well. Anything at the back?"

"Nope. You can have a look if you want."

Rita did so. Her rubber soled shoes were slippery on the paving stones, and she had to be careful. The rear of the barn had derelict horse stables, and an animal pen, likely used for goats or sheep at night. There was a smell here, of old hay and mildew, but also something else. She sniffed more, and then suddenly she froze.

It was petrol. As if a car had been in here. The paving stones wouldn't have any car tracks, but that was possible. Rita went deeper into the barn. The horse stables were broken, the wood rotting. A couple of bicycles were stacked in one corner.

They were kiddies bikes, and Rita got closer to them. One of the bikes didn't have dust on them. It wasn't new, but neither was it old and rusty, like the other one. Rita put her gloves on. Her mind was ablaze now, her senses also on fire. She looked around carefully, then turned her attention to the bike. The red leather seat felt cold. She looked at the wheels, and then turned them. They were oiled, and this bike had been used recently.

Why would there be a kiddies bike in a derelict barn?

CHAPTER 40

"Guv, come and look at this," Richard called out.

Richard was on the floor, on one knee, staring at a row of cages that came up to waist height. The cages were stacked along the far wall, with two large grilled windows above them. The grills were covered with plastic sheets that had either borne the elements well, or they were new. A strange sensation was unfurling in Rita's chest. A dread, mixed with adrenaline.

She knelt on the floor in front of the cages. Rita assumed they were kept for small animals like sheep, or goats. They were large enough for a child to be kept in, Rita thought. A lump had formed in her throat, a black, solid weight that wouldn't budge.

The cages were empty, but the one Richard was pointing at had been cleaned, and the floor was lined with soft felt. This cage, and the two next to it, were larger than the others. They opened from the top, and the grill mesh had been replaced by iron bars.

They snapped gloves on, and Richard gingerly opened the top, which had a handle. The bars lifted. Rita's heart hammered as Richard reached inside, and pulled out a piece of paper. It was disguised in the white felt, and wasn't easy to see. Richard laid the paper out on the ground. It was small, about the size of a postcard. It was a child's drawing with crayons. It showed a boy with a man and woman on either side.

Rita felt the lump grow larger in her throat, and saline regret pool in her eyes. She stood up quickly, sniffing, and turning away. She wiped her eyes, exhaling. Her heart felt like it had been clawed to ribbons.

Had little Matt been kept here? It made sense now why Stuart would come here. Him and his accomplice had kept Matt here for a while, then moved him again.

Rita pulled out her phone, and called Shola. Richard was looking around in the other cages, and he was now joined by the uniformed constables.

"I think we know where Matt was kept for a while. We need you here to take swabs and do a sweep of the place."

Shola listened to Rita in silence. "Bloody 'eck," She sighed. "That poor child, eh? Alright, I'm on way. Send me the location please."

Rita hung up, then joined the others. There was a rear door in the barn, that led to the backyard. Wood logs were piled in one corner – but they were old and damp. There was a log fence that separated the backyard from the woods beyond, and the river running across it.

"One of you stay and have a look around," Rita said, addressing one of the constables. She strode out of the barn, and across the courtyard, into the main farmhouse. The door was shut, with a wooden beam across it. Richard and one of the uniforms lifted the beam, and they entered.

The landing floor creaked under their weight, and another smaller door led to a larger reception room. Old cupboards stood against the wall, glass windows smashed in, and lying on the floor. Cobwebs hung from the ceiling, thick in places, and hanging down to the cupboards.

The wooden floor had seen better days, with gaping holes in places. Windows on the opposite wall looked out into an overgrown garden. They walked through, and entered the kitchen. Wind whistled in through the cracks in the timber frame of the walls.

The large kitchen was unused, but Rita noted there was a fridge. It was plugged in. She opened it with a gloved hand, then covered her mouth and nose at the fetid smell that emerged like a cloud. Mouldy cheese and curdled milk lay inside. She shut the door, and looked around the kitchen. There was a dish in the sink, with cutlery. There was no dishwasher. Someone had been here recently, Rita could tell.

“Put a crime scene tape outside,” Rita instructed the uniforms. “No one come here now but scene of crime.”

She heard a creaking sound above her head. Richard was looking up already, and when their eyes met, she nodded. Richard crept forward, and they came to another landing, with stairs going up. The stairs had given way in places, holes emerging from the rot. The creaking came again, and Rita couldn’t tell if it was the wind, or someone was upstairs.

They came to the landing upstairs. Three closed doors faced them. They couldn’t hear the creaks anymore. Richard tackled the first door on his right, while Rita went to the one directly in front.

Slowly, she turned the handle. It wasn’t locked. Inside, she saw a single mattress on the floor, without a bed. The mattress was covered with a bedsheet, and a duvet lay on top. It looked slept in. There was also a desk with a missing leg, and it was half on the floor. There was a shelf above the desk, and it was empty. Rita tip toed inside the room, and looked out the window. This room faced the backyard, and she could see the barn from here. She whirled around when she heard a sound, and saw Richard standing at the doorway.

“You scared me,” Rita said, exhaling.

“Sorry, guv.” Richard’s eyes swept around the room. “There’s a bed in that room as well.”

Rita went out with him. The first room was larger, with a bigger bed. It was an old pine frame, double bed, with a bare mattress, and a duvet. This was also slept it. The rest of the room was empty.

Rita went inside, while Richard checked out the third room. Rita walked around, her shoes picking up dust, an old, musty smell in the place. She longed to open the window, but knew she would spoil valuable finger prints. The beds would be a rich source for DNA. She looked out the window, at the barn and the woodlands, then the sea – a sliver in the distance.

Matt had been kept here, she could feel it in her guts. And this bed had been used by the abductor – The Keeper – as he liked to call himself. Goosebumps spread across Rita's arms, and she shivered in revulsion. That's why he called himself the Keeper. He was keeping the boy as long as he could.

Richard came back from the other room. "Nowt there but old desk and cupboards and bric-a-brac. No one's been there for years, I think."

Rita's radio squawked, and it was insistent. She turned up the black knob to listen. Then her eyes widened. It was Rizwan's excited voice.

"We got Mark, guv. We saw him in town and followed him. You were right. He was staying in one of the flop houses in town, where you can get a room for cash. He's in custody now."

“Well done, Rizwan,” Rita smiled. “You get serious brownie points for this.”

“Doughnuts will do, guv.”

CHAPTER 41

Mark Aldridge fixed Rita with a hostile stare. He sat ramrod straight in the chair, hands folded on his lap. Next to him sat his lawyer, Mr. Steve Chisholm. Rita had seen Chisholm before, and Jack had warned her about him. Like most criminal lawyers, he loved poking holes in the prosecution's case.

Rizwan sat next to her. He spoke into the machine, introducing everyone and noting the date and time. Rita didn't blink as she stared back at Mark. Eventually, he looked away, a sneer on his face.

"Hello, Mark," Rita said. "My name is DI Gupta. We met briefly in the Burniston warehouse, but you were too busy running away. I'm glad we can meet at last."

Mark didn't care for Rita's ironic introduction.

"Why don't you just get on with it?" he growled. "The sooner we get this over with, the better for everyone." He gave Rizwan a dirty look. "Feeling clever, are yer? Instead of finding where my son is you go around chasing after me. Bloody stupid, if yer ask me."

Rizwan stiffened, but ignored him like Rita did.

Rita looked down at the report Rizwan had filed when they arrested Mark.

"You were seen coming out of a side street next to the bank in Scarborough town centre. You were followed to a bed-and-breakfast in town, where you paid with cash. According to your statement, that's where you slept the night before. Is that correct?"

Mark glared at her, then nodded. The snarl remained on his lips, as if every word Rita uttered grated on his nerves.

"What were you doing last night between the hours of 8 PM and midnight?"

Mark stared back at Rita. "I got a Chinese takeaway and ate that in my room. I went outside a couple of times to have a cigarette. But most of all," he leaned forward, the snarl appearing on his face again, "I wondered where my son was and why on earth you lot were doing nothing to find him." He shook his head in disgust.

"That's all you did last night?" Rita asked.

"I just told you, didn't I? I can't go out much because I know you lot are trying to find me. I'm keeping my head down, but I also need to see Nelly, to ask her and her stupid husband what happened."

Rita stared at him. “Where is Matt?”

Mark snapped his eyes shut, and his jaws hardened. “I don’t know. Don’t ask me that again.”

“Why have you been avoiding us?”

The snarl on Mark’s face deepened. “You know why.”

“Tell me again,” Rita said calmly.

Mark glanced at Mr Chisholm, who nodded briefly. A prepared answer, Rita thought.

Mark said, “When Nelly called me, I came over as soon as I could. I had an argument with Stuart. He blamed me for Matt’s disappearance. He thought I had taken Matt, and I knew where. I couldn’t believe it. He accused me and it made me angry. I lost my temper, and had a physical confrontation with him.”

Mark stopped and Rita looked at Mr Chisholm, who sat staring forward, ignoring everyone. He had chosen these words, Rita knew.

“You threw a punch at him, then tried to kick him,” Rita said. “It was witnessed by Nelly. You pushed Stuart against the wall, and had your hands around his neck. Nelly hit you with a broom, and that’s when you separated from Stuart. Then you ran out the door. Is that what happened?”

Again, Mark glanced at his lawyer, who inclined his head a fraction of an inch.

“Yes,” Mark said.

“Is that your explanation of why you were avoiding us? You only lost your temper, and had a fight with Stuart. Or is there another reason?”

Mark fixed Rita with an angry stare. “There’s no other reason. I knew you lot would add two and two and come up with five. You would assume I took my son.”

“And did you?”

Mark looked like his head was going to explode. A wave of scarlet was slowly rising from his neck, engulfing his space.

“I told you. No!”

Rita nodded calmly, as if Mark was speaking to her about the weather. She decided to change track.

"Where were you the day before?"

"In Burniston."

"And the day before that, 18th June, your car was seen going into Osgodby Lane, where Matt lived. Is that correct?"

A wary look came into Mark’s eyes. He glanced at Chisholm, who gave him a reassuring nod.

"No comment," Mark said. Rizwan opened the brown manila folder in front of him and shook out a collection of photos. They were from CCTV, showing Mark’s car going into Osgodby Lane on 18th June, at 9:30 AM.

"As you can see," Rita said, "We can prove that on the morning of Matt's abduction, you were in the neighbourhood. Osgodby Lane leads directly to Seaview Avenue, where Matt lived. Did you drive to the house?"

Mark didn't respond, the hostility remaining in his eyes. His jaws clenched. Rita could tell his hands had become fists on his lap. Mr. Chisholm leaned closer and whispered a few words in his client's ear. Mark blinked a few times.

"No, I didn't," he said.

"Are you sure about that?"

The snarl returned, Mark's lips curling upward as if there were an unpleasant smell in the room.

"I just said I didn't. Why the hell are you asking me again?"

"Its just a big coincidence that you were in the area the morning that Matt vanished."

Mark's shoulders dropped, and a look of resignation appeared on his face. "I wanted to see Nelly. Not necessarily Matt. I wanted to tell her that Matt didn't like Stuart, and she should get rid of him. But then I saw Stuart's car. I decided against it, and turned back."

Rizwan glanced at Rita. She asked, "You saw Stuart's car that morning? Where?"

“Driving out of Seaview Avenue. He was alone. I saw him, and drove right past the bend, and kept going. Decided against it.” He shook his head. “Little did I know that Nelly would call me later on.” He bared his lips. “And to think that guttersnipe accused me of taking Matt. What the hell was he doing?”

Mark narrowed his eyes all of a sudden. “Hold up. Have you checked on Stuart? He’s dodgy as hell. He could well have taken Matt.”

Rita said, “What did you do after you left Osgodby Lane?” She knew, of course. Mark had headed back to his warehouse in Burniston. He confirmed that, and she nodded. Mark was a troubled man, and prone to violence. But Rita didn’t think he was capable of cold-blooded murder. And if he had really abducted Matt, he wouldn’t leave his son alone and come to Scarborough.

She folded her hands on the table and looked at him directly.

"Why do you use the fake name Arnold Walsham?"

"It’s my nom de plume as an artist. For my wood engravings, I’m known as Arnold Walsham."

"And that’s the name you used when you were arrested for GBH. Is that correct?"

Mark didn’t answer, and Mr. Chisholm nudged him on the elbow.

"Yes," Mark said.

"Why did you use that name? It's illegal to give your nom de plume, or whatever you call it, to the police if you are arrested. Your legal name is the one on your passport."

Mark was getting angry again. "I can give whatever name I want. If you must know, I didn't want any trouble from the cops. That's the only reason."

"Have you been arrested before, under a different name?"

Mark frowned, then shook his head. "No, I haven't."

"Are you sure about that?"

Mark's lips opened, then curled upward in an expression of hatred. He was about to speak when Mr. Chisholm tapped him on the elbow. The lawyer smiled at Rita.

"DI Gupta, you're deliberately baiting my client after he's already responded to you. I must say, there's no need for that."

"It's perfectly reasonable to ensure nothing has slipped your client's mind," Rita said, tongue firmly in cheek. "Those who present false names upon arrest have a history of doing so in the past."

"Well, I bloody didn't," Mark bit out through clenched teeth.

Rizwan nudged Rita with his elbow. She let him ask the next question. He cleared his throat.

“So why did you come back to Osgodby?”

“I wanted to speak to Nelly. And also to Stuart, if he was around. I wasn’t scared anymore. I need to know where Matt is. But I couldn't even get close because you lot are all over the place." He raised a hand and jabbed a finger in Rita's direction. "I'm telling you, that Stuart is up to no good. I've seen the way he looks at my son and how he acts around him. It wouldn't surprise me in the least if he's taken Matt."

"Why do you think Stuart might have abducted Matt?"

"He's weird. He acts like he’s concerned about Matt, but he doesn't care. Matt tells me how he ignores him. I think his love for Nelly is also fake. She's made a mistake. She needs to kick him out, as soon as she can. He’s bad news."

Interesting, Rita thought. Mark wasn’t holding back. If he had murdered Stuart in cold blood, would he be so frank?

She knew there would be CCTV footage of Mark walking around the town centre. They knew his disguise now, and they could find him on the cameras, even if he was hiding his face.

Rizwan fixed Mark with a look. "Did you see Stuart last night?"

The corners of Mark's eyes narrowed, and Rita could see he was trying to guess where this was leading.

"No," he said. "I didn't see him last night, and I don't care if I never see him again. Why?" He glanced at his lawyer, who also seemed interested now. He looked at Rita, who ignored him.

Rizwan asked, "So last night, after you had your dinner and smoked your cigarettes, you went back into your room?"

"I walked around town for a bit, staying away from the busy areas." He shook his head. "Then I got tired and went back." He frowned again. "Why are you asking?"

Rizwan glanced at Rita. She inclined her head a fraction. Rizwan paused, making sure Mark had his full attention. "Stuart Crosby was found dead in the early hours of this morning. He had been stabbed to death in an alley near Holbeck Hill in Scarborough."

He paused to let the news sink in. Mark blinked several times, and blood drained from his face. His mouth opened, and he breathed heavily. He looked like he was going to vomit. Chisholm leaned into him and whispered a few urgent words. Mark closed his eyes and nodded. He was now regretting his previous judgment of Stuart, Rita thought.

Rizwan asked, "Were you in Holbeck Hill last night between 8 PM and midnight?"

"No," Mark gulped and said quickly. He raised his voice. "No, no. I bloody wasn’t. You can't pin this on me. I didn't like the guy, but I wouldn't murder him." His frantic eyes scanned from Rizwan to Rita.

"Can you please answer the question?" Rizwan repeated.

"No. Like I told you, I stayed in town and went to bed. I had nothing to do with this."

"Do you know who could have murdered Stuart?"

Mark squirmed in his seat like a worm at the end of a fishing hook. "I don't bloody know," he whispered, his face pale. "I don’t know where he was from or his background. He was dodgy, that much I knew."

"And how did you know that?"

"Just the way he looked, and things that Matt told me. He said that he lied to Nelly. He said he'd gone out when actually he had been in the house, on his laptop."

Rizwan glanced at Rita. This was important information. Rita took over. She asked, "Matt told you that?"

"Yes. I informed Nelly as well. She didn’t like it. She thought I was trying to stir up trouble in their relationship. Matt also said Stuart shouted at him a few times. But he never did it when Nelly was around. That’s what Matt told me."

Mark stopped, his lips moving without any sound. "But that doesn't mean I wanted him to be harmed. I had nothing to do with him getting stabbed. You know that, don't you?"

Rita and Rizwan said nothing. If they let Mark's discomfort grow, he would be more forthcoming, Rita knew. She wanted him to talk about everything.

"What else do you know about Stuart?"

"Pretty much what Matt told me, to be honest. I didn't live with them. He had a job, but I do think he spent a lot of time at home, and Nelly didn't know that. The days she went to work, I don't know what he did."

"You never followed Stuart around? Tried to find out what he was up to?"

Mark frowned, some colour returning to his face. "No, of course I didn't. I didn't care about him. I just wanted to know that Matt was okay. Nelly assured me that he was."

"Did you send Nelly and Stuart a ransom note, and sign it as 'the Keeper'?"

The change of subject seemed to throw Mark.

"What? I don't know anything about a ransom letter."

"Well, yesterday morning, a letter was sent to them with Matt's photo. It was from the abductor, and he signed his name as 'the Keeper.' He wants £100,000, left under a bench in North Cliff Park, opposite the bandstand."

The frown remained on Mark's face, and he shook his head slowly.

"I don't know anything about that." He glanced from Rizwan back to Rita. "Where is Matt? Please tell me he's okay."

Rita stared back at him. He seemed earnest enough, but she knew looks could be deceiving. However, her instincts told her Mark wasn't acting.

"If you've got Matt hidden somewhere, please tell us now." She raised a hand before Mark could speak. "And if you do, we will find out sooner or later. Later won't be good for you." Rita softened her voice. "I know that you care for Matt. You love your son, don't you?"

Mark seemed surprised by Rita's change in manner. He gulped once, his Adam's apple bobbing up and down. The regret remained in his eyes, weighing him down. His forehead creased as he stared at the table.

"Yes, I do. I love my son. I've done some wrong things, but never to him. I want him back in my life. I didn't get much custody when Nelly and I separated, and I never had the money to fight a legal custody battle. But I missed Matt a lot. After Nelly moved in with Stuart, I could see Matt wasn't happy. He didn't like Stuart, but I guess Nelly didn't listen."

Rita thought of the scribble on Matt’s wall: *I want to see my daddy.*

Again, her instincts told her Mark’s words were genuine. His earlier hostility had evaporated. He looked like the broken shell of a man, his thousand-yard stare directed at the floor.

"Where do you think Matt could be? Who could have taken him?" Rizwan asked.

Mark looked up at him, his frozen expression helpless, desperate. His cracked lips moved, his voice a whisper.

"I don’t know. I wish I could tell you."

CHAPTER 42

Eight-year-old Matthew lay shivering in his cot. The bed was big enough for two people, but the wooden slats were thin, and they creaked when he moved. His duvet was also thin, and the basement was cold. Damp gathered at the corners of the walls, and water left dark stains. Beams of light spilled in from a window high over his head, drilled up. Matthew didn't like this place. He felt sad and sick and missed his mother terribly. He kept hoping either his dad, or someone with money, would come and get him out of here. He had not lost hope.

He had learned to be careful of the man. Matt knew him, of course. He used to be nice, but now he was weird. Before, in the old days, he was happy and cheerful. But now he could be mean.

The man was always silent and watchful. He had done things to Matt that he found strange. Matt didn't understand what they meant, but he knew the man liked to get into bed with him. The man had told Matt not to tell anyone about those things, or he would never see his parents again. Matt believed him. The man had become strange and scary.

Matt heard footsteps coming down. They stopped at the door, and the handle turned. Matt faced the wall, clutching the bedsheet to his chin, pretending to be asleep. The man came in, and Matt trembled as he felt the man's presence behind him. Then he heard the clink of metal as a plate was put on the ground. His breakfast had arrived. But Matt didn't feel hungry. He had learned not to eat the food, as it made him very sleepy. The effects wore off as the day went on, but he didn't like feeling that way.

The man sat down at the edge of the bed, then moved closer. He shook Matt's shoulders, and then his hand roamed around Matt's body.

"Come on, get up. It's time for you to eat your food."

Matt didn't reply, so the man shook him harder, his voice becoming more insistent. He could get angry, and that scared Matt even more.

"You need to eat something. Now. Have you been to the toilet?"

There was a small toilet next to Matt's bedroom. A staircase led upstairs to the ground floor, but the door at the top was always locked, and the man had the key. Matt had gone up once and listened with his ear against the door.

Funnily enough, he had seen Stuart do that at Nelly's bedroom door when Nelly was on the phone. When Stuart saw Matt, he frowned and slipped away. Matt didn’t like Stuart. He wished his dad, Mark, would come back to live with them.

The man’s grip hardened on Matt's shoulder, then he grabbed his neck, lifting Matt like a ragdoll. Matt didn’t resist. He had done that before, and the result had been a slap to the back of his head, followed by another slap to his cheeks. The man had been remorseful afterward, but Matt had learned to be wary of him.

"If you don't eat, then you're going to be starving all day. We're going on a drive, and there won’t be any other food."

A small candle of hope flickered to life in Matt's sad heart. "Are we going to see Mum or Dad?"

"Maybe," the man said shortly. "Just eat your food. Have you been to the loo?"

Matt nodded silently. He swung his legs down from the bed. The basement floor was freezing when he stood up. He put on his socks and quickly got changed, feeling the man’s eyes on him. He could hear the man sighing as he watched.

"I need to go to the loo again before I eat."

Matt looked at the man, who stared back for a few seconds. His blonde hair was cut short, and his blue eyes glinted. A beam of sunlight fell across the man's face, lighting it up. He seemed like a hungry lion, about to bare his teeth. Matt shivered and looked down at his feet.

"Go on, then," the man said. "Hurry up. We don't have much time. We have to leave in the next half an hour."

As Matt padded to the toilet, he wondered what was happening. They had already moved once, from that big farmhouse. Stuart had been there too, which Matt found strange. But then again, it was Stuart who had picked him up, put him in the car, and taken him to the farmhouse. The man had also been there. Matt’s memory of that day was vague. He had been so sleepy, and he had dozed off during the drive. He heard Stuart and the man talking. They spoke in whispers, and Matt didn’t understand what they were saying.

Matt turned on the tap, then sat down on the loo. He needed time to think. Was the man taking him further away from his parents? He must be, hence the urgency. Matt had been sleepy when they left the farmhouse. He had hated that cage in the farmhouse, where the man made him sleep. At least Stuart had taken him out and given him a bike to ride. When the man came back and saw Matt on the bike, he got angry. There had been an argument between him and Stuart, and then the man took the bike away from Matt. The thought of that cage made Matt shudder. He never wanted to experience that again.

He got up, turned off the tap, and flushed the loo. He needed to think quickly. When they arrived at this house, Matt had been half-awake. It was another farmhouse, but much smaller. It was in good condition, and people lived here—he could tell. There was a car in the front yard, and he had heard voices upstairs. He knew someone else lived here apart from the man. It wasn't Stuart, because when the man had spoken with the upstairs door open, a woman's voice had answered back. Matt hadn't seen Stuart in days and wondered what had happened to him.

Above all else, he thought about his parents, and he desperately wanted to be back with them.

Which is why, he vowed silently, *I can't let this man take me further away*. He was convinced that's what the man wanted to do.

But how could he stop him?

The idea came to Matt as he finished in the toilet and flushed again. When he opened the door, the man was standing there, frowning. His face lowered to Matt's, and Matt shrank back.

"What were you doing in there?"

Matt held his tummy and pretended to be sick. "I need to poo all the time. It's smelly."

This was a half-truth. Matt had loose stools that morning, which he blamed on the food. It had tasted strange. He hated the food here and longed for his mother's cooking again.

"I need to poo," Matt repeated.

The man frowned, staring at Matt. Then he opened the bathroom door and stepped inside, waving his hand in front of his nose. He grimaced, then dragged Matt back outside.

"Get ready first."

"But my tummy hurts," Matt said, clutching his abdomen and kneeling on the floor. If he couldn't escape, he could at least delay them leaving.

The man made that impatient sound in his throat that adults make when they're annoyed. "Put your clothes on. And eat your food. We have to leave soon."

Matt stood, his lips downturned, looking like he wanted to cry. "My tummy hurts. I need to poo again."

He went to the loo, and the man didn't stop him. He cursed loudly and stomped up the staircase as Matt sat back down. He didn't need to go again, but he felt pleased as he heard the man's heavy footsteps clumping upstairs, followed by the slam of the door.

Matt smiled. Something was working. He crept out of the toilet and glanced at the upstairs door, which remained shut. But he knew the man would come back soon. Matt ran into the cold basement room and picked up his plate. It had porridge in it—a thin gruel that looked revolting. He took it into the bathroom and flushed it down the toilet. It didn't flush very well, but Matt thought he could tell the man it was his poo.

He didn't get ready. Instead, he lay down on the bed, facing the wall, and covered himself with the sheets. He hoped he had bought himself some time. He knew his parents were looking for him.

"Come on, hurry up," Matt prayed silently. A tear trickled down his cheek, and he brushed it away. *"Please help me."*

CHAPTER 43

Holbeck Hill was a respectable neighbourhood in Scarborough. It was on the southwestern side of town, and looking to her right, facing west, Rita could just make out a sliver of the sea in the distance.

She transferred her gaze back to the buzz of activity in the alley. She had walked up and down it, noting the lack of any lights or CCTV. The roads on either end were lined with rows of houses—this was a quiet residential area. The roads led down to the main avenue, where traffic flowed, and there was a bus stop.

A white forensic tent had been erected, and Rita watched as Shola, pristine in her white Michelin suit, lifted the flap of the tent and went inside. Lights had come on inside the tent, giving the white surface an ethereal yellow glow. Rita hadn't seen the body yet. She was trying to retrace Stuart's steps. He had come from the west, which would make sense if he had been running from her house.

She went to the end of the alley and looked at the streetlights in either direction. Her frustration mounted as she noted the lack of CCTV. She had to follow the bend of the road and walk out to the main avenue before she saw any cameras. That was useful—they would show Stuart coming down here, and whoever had followed him. Rizwan and Richard were already busy analysing as much of the camera footage as they could.

Again, Rita got the feeling that Stuart had cracked under pressure. He had been coerced into abducting Matt. The stress of urgency bubbled in Rita's veins. She felt it deep in her bones—the abductor would try to vanish with Matt now, if he hadn't done so already. She walked back to the crime scene and entered the white tent.

Shola was kneeling on the ground, focused on the pools of dark blood on the paving stones.

Rita crouched next to her.

"Found anything?"

"Blood, as you can see, and some flecks of saliva. There are boot prints here as well." Shola pointed to where her assistant, Henry, had made three white circles.

"They're man-sized, about 10 to 11. The prints are jumbled up, which means they stepped over each other—like in a struggle."

"And that's when Stuart was stabbed," Rita said. "Please keep me informed. I know I'm rushing you around, but did you manage to get down to the farmhouse?"

Shola pulled her mask down.

"Yes. My God, that was heartbreaking." Sorrow creased her face. "The poor child. We've got to find him."

Rita straightened, sighing. "Yes, I know."

"For this murder," Shola said, "you must have something on CCTV. I know there are no cameras outside, but someone followed him here. They might well have followed him from your house, and you should be able to spot that on CCTV."

"That's what the lads are busy doing now. But it's not easy. There was traffic, and Stuart was on foot. They have to trawl through hours of footage to find him getting on a bus."

"Good luck," Shola said. "I'll let you know as soon as I find anything. Hopefully, we get a DNA match with the attacker's blood this time."

Rita thanked her and went back to the station.

***

Rita walked through the sliding doors of the main entrance. The waiting room had the usual sprinkling of drunks and dishevelled petty criminals sitting on the stiff, green plastic seats. One of them was speaking in a low voice to a man in a suit. It was Jack.

He looked up, and when he saw Rita, he didn't acknowledge her. Rita appreciated that. He was with a client and didn't want to attract the client's attention to her. It was good to know that Jack was around. She could bounce ideas off him later.

The duty sergeant, a tall, handsome Afro-Caribbean man called Yemi, got her attention.

"The boss wants to see you in her office."

The slight curl in Yemi's lips made it clear that there was no love lost for Nicola Perkins. She was as curt with the rest of the staff as she was with Rita.

"Jolly good," Rita said dryly. "I can't wait."

Yemi grinned, showing his perfect white teeth.

"Better you than me, guv."

Rita thanked him and walked towards the double doors at the back. She pressed a fob key to the wall-mounted holder and glanced at Jack. He was facing Rita, while his client had his back to her. Jack nodded briefly, and Rita knew he would contact her soon. She went into the office and found it empty. Taking a moment to herself, she then took the stairs up to the third floor.

Detective Superintendent Nicola Perkins put down her pen and sat up straighter when Rita entered. Rita closed the door behind her. Nicola didn't ask her to sit down, as usual. Rita noticed that Nicola had done her hair; it was now cut straight to her shoulders with a fringe above her forehead. It suited her, giving her focused, pinched face a better frame.

Nicola was dressed in a burgundy suit. Rita couldn't see her legs, but assumed Nicola wore a skirt, as that was her preference. The woman looked small in the long armchair, and it didn't help when she leaned back and swivelled slightly to one side. She made a soft clucking sound with her tongue and shook her head.

"A murder now as well? And of the main suspect?" Nicola raised her eyebrows. Her face was expressionless, but Rita knew she was enjoying it. For the life of her, Rita didn't know what Nicola had against her. The woman had been on her back ever since she started working here.

"Yes, ma'am. The suspect actually came to my house last night. He was killed later on—silenced, in other words."

Nicola blinked a couple of times. Rita wondered if she would be concerned that the suspect had turned up at Rita's house. Nicola seemed to weigh her options before she spoke again.

"How did that happen?"

"He could have followed me. That's the working hypothesis right now, and the team are going through CCTV to verify it. He also knew my full name, so he could have looked me up," Rita shrugged. "Not difficult these days."

Nicola nodded. If they had a normal working relationship, Rita would have expected some concern, maybe a touch of sympathy. Instead, she got frosty indifference.

"Who got to Stuart? The killer, maybe?"

"That's what I think. Stuart lost his nerve and wanted to spill the beans. Hence, he was murdered. We'll find his killer on CCTV. He couldn't have followed Stuart on foot the entire time. Or maybe he did. Either way, we'll find him."

"The Chief Constable has heard the news. The media will be on this like vultures on a corpse. For now, we have to keep it quiet, but news will leak out very quickly. We don't want the extra attention, do we?"

Rita's jaw stiffened as she realised Nicola was putting her to the test.

"No, ma'am. I'm expecting to have some answers by the end of today. My priority, of course, remains finding Matt."

Nicola nodded.

“Any news from the search parties, or the media channels?” TV, radio, and online social media were ablaze with Matt’s disappearance. Every hour, new but contradictory sightings seemed to flow in.

“The media liaison office is struggling,” Rita sighed. “Too many scammers and an overload of fake news. No one’s seen Matt yet. But we know he was in that farmhouse.” Rita told Nicola where she suspected Matt had been.

“A child’s drawing was in that cage?” Nicola raised an eyebrow. Even her tight, pinched face showed signs of softening, and she looked troubled.

“Yes, ma’am. Matt was moved quickly from the farmhouse, and I think he’s going to be moved again today—unless that already happened last night. In either case, I think we should put checkpoints on the motorways leaving Scarborough.” Nicola went to speak, but Rita raised a hand to stop her. From the grim set of Nicola’s lips, she knew her boss was offended, but she didn’t care.

“I’m only talking about the A165 and A171. And also the A64, going down to York and Leeds. If we can set up checkpoints on those three main roads, there’s a chance we might be able to stop the abductor from escaping.”

“That’s a big ask,” Nicola retorted, “and you know it.”

“We need to find Matt,” Rita said simply, shrugging. “As you know, ma’am, time is not on our side. If the abductor escapes through one of the main roads, he could be long gone before we're even aware of his identity."

Nicola stared at the wall behind Rita's head, as if someone was standing there. It was a strange look, but Rita ignored it. Nicola was a strange person.

"Okay," Nicola said shortly. "I'll speak to the Chief Constable now, and he will order traffic control to liaise with the national highways police. I'll keep you informed."

"Thank you, ma'am." Rita turned to leave, but Nicola spoke again.

"You have a murder and a missing child on your hands. The Chief Constable has asked me again if you are up to the task. What do you want me to tell him?"

Slowly, Rita turned back. Her hands had clenched into fists, but she relaxed them. Anger jolted through her spine, but she didn't want to give Nicola the satisfaction.

"If you can find anyone to replace me now, ma'am, that's up to you." She stared at Nicola, whose eyes blazed back at her.

"Get the job done, DI Gupta. Don't let me down," Nicola said in a low whisper. It sounded like a warning. She picked up her pen and transferred her attention to the papers on her desk.

Rita knew she was dismissed, and she was glad. She shut the door quietly behind her and walked quickly to the staircase.

CHAPTER 44

Matt lay very still as he heard the man come down the stairs and into the basement room. He came closer and stood by the bed.

"What's the matter with you?" he demanded in a rough voice. "Get up. Didn't you hear what I said? We need to get moving."

In response, Matt remained facing the wall and didn't move. He had his back to the man and kept his head down, the covers pulled up to his ears. His breath was making his body warm.

"I said get up!" the man shouted, grabbing his shoulder and forcibly turning Matt around. This time, Matt was prepared. His mouth was full of water. He acted like he was vomiting, retching on the floor, and the water splashed onto the man's trousers. The man yelped, swore loudly, and jumped backwards. Matt noted with satisfaction that the water had landed on his crotch, creating a darker stain already.

"You swine!" the man thundered. He came closer and raised his hand to slap Matt. Matt crouched under the bed covers, and the blow landed on his shoulders. He was hit again, but he kept his face down, pressed into the bed.

"What the hell is wrong with you?"

Matt didn't say anything. He lay there, his heart beating wildly. Had he just done the right thing? He wanted to pretend he was sick. When he had a bad tummy, his mother kept him off school. He was hoping the same would happen now and they would stay here.

In a small voice, he said, "My tummy hurts, and I feel sick. I need to see a doctor."

Matt didn't know where the words came from, but he was suddenly very proud of himself. Yes, that's right. His mother had said she'd take him to a doctor, though Matt didn't like doctors. They poked around and gave him medicine that tasted awful.

But now, he wished desperately that the man would take him to a doctor. Matt hadn't seen another human being in the last three days. If he did, he'd definitely tell them what this man was doing to him.

Judging by the silence, broken only by the man's heavy breathing, Matt knew his words were having an effect. The man was considering his options. Then he turned around, and Matt heard him go into the bathroom.

He must have seen the porridge in the toilet because he swore again, loudly. The man came back, and Matt pretended to be asleep. He remembered that the man would expect him to be sleepy if he had eaten some of that porridge.

The man pulled on his shoulder and laid Matt on his back. Matt pretended to be floppy and kept his eyes closed. The man touched his tummy, and Matt winced in pain, then pretended to cry. He couldn't believe he was actually doing this, but he had seen Lucy, his friend from next door, do this sometimes when she wanted something from her mother. Matt hoped he could make this acting work for himself.

He was glad when the man moved his hand away. Matt curled himself up into a tight ball, clutching his tummy and moaning. "It really hurts," he mumbled drowsily. Then he pretended to sleep.

The man felt his forehead once, then swore again. He stood up and left the basement. Matt heard him go up the steps.

Matt's eyes blinked open. His room's door was open, and he could see the landing and the stairs. This time, he didn't hear the man shut the door upstairs. Was the door open? And if he could get up there, what would he find? Maybe the front door… Could he open the front door?

Matt crept out of bed. He scurried to the door and then out onto the landing. His heart was beating so fast he thought it might break his ribs. He tiptoed up a couple of steps. They didn't make any sound.

The door was open, and he could hear some faint sounds, but not the man's loud footsteps. He went up a couple more steps and managed to peek out the door. The floor had large cream tiles. It was a wide landing, and there was a mirror opposite, which reflected a framed photo of a river and mountains. Next to the mirror, there was a door to a room. The door was shut. Matt stretched his neck out.

He could see a staircase to his left after another door, opposite the room next to the mirror. He turned his head right, and his heart raced faster. There was a wide brown door that looked like the front door. It had wooden panels on each side, and the ceiling was made of the same wooden beams.

He made up his mind. He would try to get out of that front door.

Slowly, Matt stood up. He put his hand on the basement door and stepped onto the tiled floor. He was wearing his shoes now, but he had forgotten his jacket. Still, the sunlight was strong outside, and he'd be okay. Then he heard the man coming back. Loud footsteps, coming down the staircase to his left. The man was quick, and Matt knew he'd be here in seconds. He wanted to make a dash for it, but then he saw the door opposite starting to open.

Oh no, Matt thought. Double trouble.

He didn't have a choice anymore. He left the basement door open and ran down the stairs. He dashed into his room and had just thrown himself into bed, covering himself with the sheets, when he heard the man coming down the staircase.

"Here, drink this," the man said. "It's got medicine in it."

Matt didn't move. His forehead was caked with sweat, and he was breathing fast. The man touched his head again, and Matt knew he had felt the sweat. His heart constricted with fear. Could the man tell that he had gone up the stairs?

"You've got a fever," the man said.

A fever? Of course, he'd felt the sweat, and Matt felt hot. Maybe this had worked out in his favour.

"Drink the medicine," the man said shortly. Then he turned on his heels and strode out of the room.

CHAPTER 45

Keeper II paced his room. His thoughts were scattered, anxiety poking around his skull. An open suitcase lay on his bed. He had thrown clothes into it, and his toiletries. Beneath it, in a secret compartment, he had his collection of small knives. They fit easily into his sock, or the palm of his hand. They were switchblade knives, and he could disguise them as harmless objects easily. He wanted to hide them in the boot of his car, but he didn't have the time. He needed to get out of here.

Dixon had told him so. He needed to heed that advice. Dixon had gone too hard for revenge, and ended up in prison. As Keeper II, he had to keep the flame alive. That meant being different. McFarlane had stayed in Scarborough for too long. He had grown complacent. That's why that Inspector Rita Gupta found him.

That bloody Inspector.

Rage ignited in his spine, and he flung a tee shirt into the suitcase. His hands curled into fists. He wanted to get her. Finish her off, once and for all. Ever since she had arrived here, everything was going wrong. One by one, all their groups were getting shut down. Dixon had tried something new. Maybe he made his name too quickly. His group, The Gathering, had become famous. Keeper II smiled. It was good that Dixon was now mentoring him. Guiding him in new directions.

He packed the rest of his clothes, then sat down to think. He planned ahead, and knew where he was going. His mother lived with him, but he had already paid a carer to come in once a day to look after her. He couldn't tell his mother where he was going, of course. She would have to live with the uncertainly of not knowing. That lack of knowledge would protect her. He felt no remorse. She had borne him when he was a child, but had always been distant. He couldn't kill his mother. She acted like she cared for him, but he knew better.

He was closer to his uncle, who had now died. His uncle paid the mortgage, and had moved in with them. He also came into his room at night. He had done despicable things to Keeper II. Things that made him ashamed, even now. He tried to tell his mother, and did she listen?

No.

Regardless, he had carried on. He was now left with these violent, uncontrollable urges. It was his way of controlling the world. People deserved to die. He wanted to coerce and abuse them before they took their last breath, staring at him in the eye. He thought of the girl he had killed. Then he thought of Matt. Lying in that bed downstairs, shivering and pitiful. He had been like that once, when his uncle used to come into his room.

He could see Matt's eyes, getting wide with horror as his hands tightened around his throat. He had done that to the boy, but released his hand. It was just a trial, to see how scared he would get. It made him feel good to see the sheer panic in Matt's bulging eyes. Now, he knew it was time to let Matt go. The boy was holding him back. He had planned to have more fun with him, but there would be other boys and girls. He was headed to a city, and there would be plenty of schools there, and children ripe for the picking.

Keeper II smiled. He got up, and picked one of the knives from the bottom of his suitcase. It had a grey, polished steel handle. He pressed the switch and the blade flicked out. It was five inches long, and the sharp tip gleamed in the daylight. He hadn't used this knife before. Matt would be the first to feel its sharpness. First, but not the last.

"Blood begets blood", he whispered to himself.

CHAPTER 46

“Come and have a look at this, guv,” Rizwan said. Rita got up from her desk and walked over to his.

Rizwan's screen was playing CCTV footage. It showed a man hurrying down a street. He crossed the road, and the camera picked him up again before he went down a side alley.

"That was Stuart, last night at 12:10. He had just left your house."

Rizwan played the CCTV again. Rita and Richard stared intently at the screen. In a few seconds, another man appeared. He was slightly shorter and wore a black hoodie pulled low over his head. His hands were thrust inside his pockets, and he walked quickly.

"No visible signs of identification," Rizwan said. "He knows where the cameras are."

Rita nodded, noticing how the man kept his eyes on the ground, his hoodie pulled low over his face. The skin on his hands wasn't visible, hidden inside his pockets. Rizwan stopped, pressed fast forward, and played the footage again, fifteen minutes later. The man hurried out of the alley, but there was no sign of Stuart. The man crossed the road, but instead of heading out into the main avenue with traffic, he ducked inside another alley and disappeared from view.

"He knows the CCTV dark spots," Rizwan said. "Either that, or he keeps getting lucky."

"Luck has nothing to do with it," Richard murmured, voicing what was on everyone's mind. "We are dealing with a very dangerous individual here, one who plans his moves in advance. I think he might well have left Scarborough already."

Rita said, "I spoke to the boss. She's agreed to ask the Chief Constable to put roadblocks on the main dual carriageways."

Richard and Rizwan looked surprised.

"Will they get mobilised now?" Richard asked.

As if in response, Rita's phone buzzed. It was a text from Nicola.

Rita read from the screen. "The Chief Constable has granted permission, but only for the next 12 hours. It's going to cause massive traffic disruption. But it's our best chance of stopping any suspicious cars."

Rita put the phone back in her pocket. "Speaking of which," she indicated the screen, "any news of the cars leaving Osgodby Lane the day of Matt's abduction?"

"Maggie was dealing with that, upstairs with traffic. But I went up to catch up with them," Richard said.

He moved to his desk and got his laptop. "Not much here that's suspicious. Traffic checked all the cars that left Osgodby Lane that day. We checked the details with the DVLA and rang them, one by one."

He cleared his throat. "There were two couples, two solitary men, and three solitary women. The two men live locally and have families. One had dropped by to pick up his daughter from a playdate, and the other had his elderly mother living in the neighbourhood."

"The two couples had children in the back seat. They live nearby and were en route to a concert. Of the three solitary women, two were housewives going out to do some late evening shopping. The final woman was elderly, and she couldn't remember driving that day. We couldn't get hold of her at first."

Richard looked up at Rita. "The second, or third time, her son answered. He says his mother can be forgetful sometimes. She's got friends there that she sometimes goes to visit. She went out with the car that evening."

"Who spoke to the elderly woman?"

"One of the Traffic sergeants."

Rita frowned. “If she was forgetful, then why would she be driving a car?”

The others shrugged. “Call that number again,” Rita said. “I want to speak to the woman, and her son. Something doesn’t add up here.”

Rizwan did so. Rita watched him as the number rang out on his phone. He tried twice, but there was no answer.

An odd anxiety was nibbling away at the corner of Rita's mind. "Did we see that car driving into Osgodby Lane that day?"

"Yes, in the afternoon, around 11.30am. It leaves the area about 2:30."

Right on time for Matt’s abduction, Rita thought. An ominous feeling was spreading inside her. "Show me the footage," she said.

Richard got the images up on the screen. They saw an old navy-blue Ford Focus trundling slowly down the road. Two and a half hours later, they saw the same car going slowly back out. It seemed like an old woman was driving. Her face was not visible, just the hands.

"Zoom in," Rita said.

Richard did so, and all they could see were the woman's hands.

"Big hands for a woman, aren't they?" Rita said.

Richard grinned. "My ex-wife has large hands. Much bigger than mine. I don't think we can draw any conclusions from that, guv."

"What's the son's name?"

"I don't know," Richard said. "One of the traffic sergeants spoke to him."

"Where is that car registered to?"

Rizwan looked at the address on the DVLA. "Hutton Buscel. Near the North Ridings Forest Park. It's in one of the small villages there."

He pulled up a map on his screen, then cocked his head to the left. “Well, fancy that. It’s the next village along from East Ayton. That’s where our kid Maggie lives.”

“Maggie lives in East Ayton?” Richard said. “Never knew that. My mum comes from Sawdon, not far from there.”

Rita paced the room, hands behind her back, a cloud of concern moving in her mind. This was important—her instincts were screaming at her. Again, she got that odd sensation that something big was just within her reach, but somehow still evading her.

She stopped and looked at the two men, who were staring at her. "The two families who drove out were doing normal children's duties. The two solitary men were fathers, whose alibis are sound. As for the two housewives, they came back to their homes in Osgoodby Lane that night, didn't they?"

Richard nodded.

Rita said, "What about the two men who drove in and out that day?"

"We checked with their families and spoke to them. Their stories check out."

"But we haven't spoken to the old woman, have we? We only have her son's statement."

"That's right," Richard said.

"Try her on the phone again. I want to speak to her now."

CHAPTER 47

After the man had gone, Matt got up quickly. He took the cup with the liquid medicine. He stopped by the door, making sure the man wasn't outside on the landing. When he opened the door, the landing was dark and empty. The door at the top of the stairs was shut. Matt chucked the medicine down the sink, then went back to his room.

Had he bought himself some time?

He hoped so, but he knew that wasn't enough. The man had no intention of letting him go. Matt knew he had to try and escape, but how?

In desperation, he looked at the grilled window far above his head. Daylight streamed in, but he had no hope of reaching that. A thought struck him. Every house had two doors; he had learned that in school. He had also seen it in his own house—the rear door opened out into the garden. It should be the same here. If he could get out on the ground floor and the front door was shut, could he get out into the back garden?

But he didn't know what to do once he was outside. If there was a fence in the back garden, he wouldn't be able to climb it. And what if they had a dog? The animal would start barking as soon as it saw Matt, because it wouldn't know him.

That made Matt think of Pike, his own dog. Pike barked when he saw strangers. Pike was a lovely cocker spaniel, and Matt missed him. Apart from Nelly, Pike was his best friend. Matt knew Pike would be missing him as well.

If there was a dog here, why had Matt never heard it bark? It made him wonder if there was a dog here at all.

But one thing he knew for certain—someone else lived here too. The door opposite the basement entrance had started to open when he had peeked outside. He didn't wait to see who it was, but it wasn't the man, because the man came down from upstairs.

Could Matt speak to the other person in the house? It could be a woman. Maybe it was the man's wife. Matt shook his head. He frowned, his nails digging into his hands as he thought of a way out. No, even if it was a woman, he couldn't speak to her.

She'd probably just listen to her husband. And he might be wrong about it being his wife. Maybe he lived with another man. What if it was Stuart? Matt didn't trust Stuart anymore. He might be guarding the place, for all he knew. But he didn’t hear Stuart’s voice anymore.

Then he had an idea.

When the man came down to see him, did he always lock the door upstairs?

Maybe he didn't. Matt couldn't go to the front door, so there was no reason for the man to lock it always. Maybe… Matt thought hard, and a plan began to form in his mind.

He got dressed and put his shoes on. There was still water left in the glass, and he picked it up. He went outside his room, then poured the water just inside the doorway. He shut the door. Now, if anyone came into the room, they would slip and fall.

Matt hid under the staircase. If the man came down, he could see him. But it was dark and scary underneath the staircase. Matt could hear some distant sounds, and something was scraping in the corners. Was it a mouse? Or was it a rat?

His heart thudded painfully, and his eyes bulged with fear. No, he couldn't do this. He came out from under the staircase and flattened himself against the wall. He breathed fast, sweat pouring down his forehead.

He closed his eyes and thought of something comforting. He loved Manchester United football club. He thought of his favourite players. He imagined them kicking the ball really hard and scoring a goal. That made him happy. Couldn't he be strong like the football players?

Yes, he could. At least, he had to try.

He was drumming up courage when he heard footsteps above. He knew it was the man. Matt didn't waste any time. He hid under the staircase quickly. Above his head, the door opened. Then the door shut, but the key didn't turn in the lock. Thank God for that, Matt thought.

Blood pounded in his ears as he watched the man's big shoes appear. They went down the stairway and onto the landing. Then the man opened the door. There was a crashing sound, and the man cursed. He had slipped on the water and fallen.

This was his moment.

Matt ran out from under the staircase. The man was picking himself up slowly, cursing in a loud voice.

Matt ran up the staircase, and the man heard him. He got up, then crashed to his knees again.

Matt got to the top of the staircase, adrenaline pumping through every fibre of his body.

The door was not locked. He opened it and got out.

CHAPTER 48

Matt shut the basement door and ran towards the front door. He hadn't run for a while, and his legs felt weak. He pulled at the front door, but it was locked. There was a chain, and he tried to reach it, but it was too high.

He could hear the man coming up the stairs quickly. Matt looked around, his chest heaving, panic bursting in his head. He was trapped.

He ran back and went to the door opposite the basement. It was open. He slipped inside, just as the man appeared on the landing. Matt heard the man run to the front door and then go upstairs.

Then Matt realised he wasn't alone in the room. He turned around slowly, fearfully.

To his surprise, an elderly woman was sitting in a chair, gaping at him. She was dressed in a long black gown, and she had a pink and purple cardigan on her shoulders. She had a walking stick in her right hand, which she used to lean forward. She looked as astonished as Matt was.

"Who are you?" the woman asked.

Matt went forward to the woman. Maybe she could help him. He remembered the way his mother had taught him to speak to strangers.

"My name is Matthew Crosby. I go to St. Bede's School. There's a man outside who brought me here. I want to go back to my mummy. Will you please help me?"

The older woman had glasses on, and deep lines crisscrossed her face. But her eyes were kind, and they hung on to every word Matt had said. She stared at him for a while, unblinking.

"Please help me," Matt repeated. Behind him, a fearful sound grew in volume. It was the man's footsteps, rushing down the stairs. Matt got closer to the woman and pulled on her sleeve.

"Please help me. Please call my mummy. Her name is Nelly Crosby." Then he started to cry.

"Oh, you poor child." Matt felt the woman's arm go around his thin shoulders, and she pulled him into a hug. She smelled of lavender soap and nice, clean clothes. It was a comforting, homely smell.

The door behind them opened, and Matthew startled. He looked behind and saw the man standing there. He was frozen, mouth open, shocked and disbelieving eyes staring at the scene in front of him. Matthew all but jumped into the older woman's lap. He clung to her as she planted the walking stick on the ground and stood. Mathew stood behind her, clutching the hem of her gown.

"Son," she said in a low but harsh voice, "how did this boy get here?"

The man stood there, seemingly incapable of speech. He blinked a few times, and his mouth opened and closed. "He… he was lost. I found him on the lane this morning when I was driving back. I brought him here."

"No," Matt said, "that's not true."

The woman looked down at Matt. Her arm went around his shoulders again, and she pulled him into her. She was a solid, comforting presence, and Matt clung onto her.

"What's going on?" the woman demanded. "Who is this boy?"

"Like I said, I found him on the road. I'll take him back to his parents now." The man came forward, and Matt shrunk back, hiding behind the woman's legs. He peered from behind her. The woman raised her stick and stopped the man in his tracks.

"Now, wait a minute. The little one's scared. He says his mother is called Nelly. I don't know how he got here, but we need to get him back to his mother. What's your last name?" she asked Matt.

When he told her, the woman turned back to the man. It was her son, Matt thought. Fancy that.

The woman spoke to the man. "Look up Nelly Crosby in the directory. There must be a number for her. Call her and say—"

The man wasn't listening anymore. His head turned to the left, as if he had heard something. Then he went out the door. Matt heard the front door open and shut. Then the house was quiet. Matt's knuckles were white from holding the woman's gown.

When he looked at the woman's face, he saw sadness there. She sat down heavily, as if a weight was pressing down on her.

"Help me find my mummy. Please."

Without responding, the woman's eyes flickered down to the floor. When she looked up, her eyes were heavy and red-rimmed, full of grief. She shook her head once, then took off her glasses, and wiped her eyes. "I… I… let's do that. Come with me, little one."

Matt stayed behind the woman as they went out into the hallway. There was a phone under the mirror on a small table. The woman picked it up, and Matt heard her speak.

"Oh, hello, could you please get the police for me? Yes, it's important." Then the woman gave Matt the phone. “Here, you tell them your name, and your parents’ details.”

Matt grabbed the phone. “Hello?”

“Hi, what’s your name?” A woman’s voice asked. Matt gave his name, his parents, and his address. Then in a rush, he told the woman what had happened.

CHAPTER 49

Rizwan pressed the phone to his ear, then grimaced. He looked up at Rita, who had stopped pacing and was staring at him intently.

"No response, guv," Rizwan said. "The line's engaged. I've tried three times now."

A swarm of bees was knocking against the inside of Rita's skull. She sat down at a desk and pulled up the police database.

"What's the old woman's name again?"

"Edna Warren," Richard said, looking at the notes on his screen. "She's lived in Hutton Buscel most of her life, it seems. Her husband died many years ago. She's 78 years old."

Rita nodded. "She doesn't have a criminal record. That car is definitely registered to her, but she doesn't have an active driving licence anymore. So how could she be driving that car?"

"Her son said she forgot... Do you think he was lying?" Understanding dawned on Richard's face.

Rizwan had caught on and was busy typing on his keyboard.

"I'm looking for alternative numbers and checking who else is registered at her property."

"If she doesn't have a driving licence," Rita said, "then she wouldn't be driving the car. Her son claims she gets forgetful, but if she has even mild dementia, she wouldn't be driving. Her licence might simply have lapsed, and she didn't renew it. Can we pull up her medical records?"

Before Richard could answer, Rizwan looked up.

"There's another person registered at her home address—86 Foothills Lane, Hutton Buscel. A man called Edward Warren. He's 40 years old. That must be her son."

The name was familiar to Rita. "Edward… Ed Warren."

The two words hit her like bullets, smashing through her mind. If she hadn't been sitting down, she might have fallen over. Synapses fired in her brain, lighting up parts that had remained dormant for so long. Suddenly, everything was clear. Her heart constricted, and her lungs expelled air in a tight gasp. Her jaw dropped as she slowly got to her feet.

"The school psychologist," she breathed. The two men stared at her, slowly realising the gravity of her words.

"He knew Matt. He also knew Nelly and had access to the house. Oh my God."

Rita's fingers were numb with shock. They trembled as she opened her drawer and gripped her baton. She picked up her radio and was about to leave the room when the phone on her desk rang loudly. Richard and Rizwan were also getting ready. Rita snatched up the phone.

"DI Gupta. I don't have time to talk. Who is this?"

It was the woman from switchboard. "Sorry to bother you, guv. This might be a hoax call, but a woman called Edna Warren just rang. She says she has an eight-year-old boy called Matthew Crosby in her house. She doesn't know how the boy got there but is concerned about him. She thinks it's the boy who was abducted."

Rita could barely breathe. Finally, she gasped, and the words tumbled out.

"Send a uniforms unit there right now. This is a Category One emergency. We're on our way."

"Matt's at Edna Warren's house. Let's go."

She slammed the phone down and spoke as she opened the door. Richard and Rizwan piled in behind her.

The three of them ran down the hallway and out into the rear car park. They got into Richard's car, and he turned on the siren. The car screamed onto the dual carriageway of the A64. Cars scattered as Richard gripped the steering wheel tight and pressed the accelerator all the way down. They sliced through the traffic like a hot knife through butter. Soon, they were on the A170, flashing past the smaller villages that dotted the North Riding Forest.

Hutton Buscle was a picturesque little village on relatively flat land. The car blazed down Foothills Lane and arrived at number 86. The uniforms car wasn't visible yet. The property was a medium-sized farmhouse, with open farmland next to it. The borders of the house had cattle gates protecting the side and rear gardens.

Rita jumped out and rushed through the front yard. On the gravel drive, she noted drops of oil and the grooves of a car's tyres, but no vehicle was visible. She saw a garage and a shed and asked Rizwan to check them. She rang the doorbell, then hammered on it. But there was no answer. She joined Richard in looking through the bay windows on either side.

"No car in the garage," Rizwan called out. He dived into the shed and reappeared seconds later.

"Nowt in here either. I'm going down the side."

"There might be a dog," Richard called out, but Rizwan had already gone, running down the path to the rear garden. Rita heard a sound at the front door and quickly went up the steps again. The door slowly opened, and an elderly woman peeked out.

She was wearing a pink and blue cardigan and a black gown that covered her to the ankles. Her thick black walking stick had ornate carvings and an ivory white handle.

"Are you the police?" she asked.

"Yes," Rita said, holding up her warrant card. Then her eyes fell on the little face peeking out from behind the woman's gown.

"Is that Matt?" Rita asked breathlessly. "Matt Crosby?"

The woman didn't answer. She examined Rita's warrant card carefully, still not opening the door or letting her in.

Finally, she seemed satisfied with the identification and handed it back to Rita.

"Yes, this is Matt. The boy who disappeared. I heard about him on the news."

She opened the door wider, allowing Richard and Rita to enter. Rita knelt on one knee and stared at Matt. He had big brown eyes and dark hair that fell over his forehead. He was a beautiful little boy, but she could see the sadness in his face, the shadows under his eyes.

"Are you Matt?" she whispered. A lump pressed against her throat, and her heart felt it was being squeezed by iron hands.

Matt observed her carefully, not letting go of Edna's gown. Edna kept her arm firmly around Matt's shoulders, as if no force could take him from her. Matt nodded silently.

"What's your mother's name?"

"Nelly. Crosby," he added after a few seconds.

"And your father's name?"

"Mark Aldridge."

"Where does your father live?"

"In York. But he comes to see me every two weeks." Matt swallowed and blinked. "Do you know my parents?"

Rita's nose twitched, and she dabbed at her eyes. She needed to get a grip on herself but couldn't stop the surge of relief and sadness cascading in her heart.

"Yes," she whispered. "I've been looking for you, Matt." She put a hand on the boy's frail shoulder. He stiffened, then relaxed.

"I'm so glad you're safe."

"Will you take me back to my mummy?" Matt asked.

Rita gave the boy a hug, and he didn't seem to mind.

"Yes," she whispered. She managed a smile. "Yes, of course, I will."

Richard had walked through the hallway and returned. "There's a basement." His face was set in stone, his eyes dark. Rita nodded. She didn't need any further explanation. Rizwan came in through the front door.

"Nothing around the back. There's another shed, but it's just got gardening and farming stuff." His eyes fell on Matt. His face lit up like the morning sun rising over the hills.

"Are you Matt?"

Matt nodded, looking a little uncertain. He was holding Rita's hand, while his other hand still clutched Edna's gown.

Rita looked at the older woman.

"Where is your son?" Rita asked.

A shadow passed over Edna's face. Her eyes were dull, the lines on her face deep.

"I don't know," she said. "He left. I don't know where he's gone."

"Is his name Edward Warren?"

"Yes."

"He was the psychologist at Matt's school," Rita said. "We suspect him of abducting Matt."

The corners of Edna's eyes drooped, and it seemed to Rita that if she didn't have a walking stick, the woman would have slowly lowered herself to the floor. Rita took her arm.

"Would you like to sit down?"

With surprising strength, Edna brushed off Rita's hand.

"Don't touch me," she said brusquely. In slow, measured steps, she walked to the chair next to the telephone in the hallway. Matt followed her. She sat down and stared forward, her eyes focused on an invisible point on the wall.

Rita watched her. "Are you sure you don't know where you son might have gone?"

"I don't know where he is," she said eventually. She tore her eyes from the wall and glanced at Rita. "So don't be asking me again."

"When did you find Matt?" Rita asked. Edna told her how Matt had appeared in her room and how shocked she had been.

"I do read the papers, and look at social media. I knew about the missing boy. I couldn't believe it at first.But then it started to make sense. I put two and two together, as shocking as it was." Edna gripped her cane tightly, and her eyes dropped to the floor.

Sirens sounded from outside, and seconds later, two uniformed officers came in through the front door.

"Secure the perimeter," Rita said. "We found the boy, but the abductor isn't far. Put out an APB for Edward Warren."

The uniformed officers nodded and set off. Rita looked at Matt. She pointed at the basement door.

"Is that where you lived?"

Matt nodded in silence. With Richard, Rita went down the steps. The room was bare, apart from a bed with a mattress and a thin duvet. There was also a chair and a cup and plate on the floor next to the bed. She looked up at the open grill window, the only source of light and air in the room. Her body felt cold, frozen, her heart withered and shrunk as she looked around the dank, horrible space.

Richard muttered a curse under his breath. "We need to find him, guv."

Rita's jaws were set tight as she nodded. With gloved hands, she opened the bathroom door. It was empty. Then she went back upstairs and pulled out her radio. She called traffic control and spoke to the duty officer.

"Block exits in both directions on the A170. The suspect's name is Edward Warren, and he's driving a black Honda." She gave the radio to Rizwan, who had the car's registration number.

There was no time to waste, she thought. They needed to catch Ed Warren before he could travel another mile.

CHAPTER 50

Maggie had thought long and hard about her options. She stared down at her nails and at the sunlight streaming in through the back windows, pooling at her feet and warming her legs. Her mother, Susan, sat opposite her.

"You have to tell him," Susan said.

"Yes, I know," Maggie replied in a small voice. "I'm just not sure if this is what he wants. He doesn't seem too keen on a long-term relationship, and I doubt he'll want to have children."

"But have you asked him? How do you know?"

Maggie sighed. "He's a good person. Polite and courteous. But he was scarred from the divorce. He said he lost a lot of money and doesn't want something that will lead in that direction."

Maggie looked at her mother and didn't like the frown on her face. Susan's expression softened, and the gentle tone returned to her voice. She was trying to be non-judgemental.

"And what do *you* want?"

Maggie closed her eyes, and her head dropped into her palms.

Susan gave her some time, but Maggie heard the soft, long sigh of frustration. She felt it too. Initially, she didn't want to discuss it with her mother, but deep down, she knew it was the right thing to do.

"I wish I knew," Maggie mumbled. "I don't want to let it go. I want to have a child."

Susan came and sat next to her, putting an arm around her shoulders.

"Then do what you think is right. You know me and your father will support you."

Maggie raised her head and looked at her mother. "Have you told Dad?"

"Not yet. But I know he won't mind. He's always wanted grandchildren. True, if Kyle isn't going to be around, that's going to take some getting used to. But he won't let you do this alone," Susan pressed Maggie's hand. "Neither of us will."

Maggie rested her head on her mother's shoulder. They stayed like that for a while. Then Maggie's phone beeped. She had a text from Kyle. She had told him this morning there was something important she needed to share.

"I'm coming over. See you in 10 minutes."

Maggie told her mother, then stood. She was already dressed and got ready quickly. She stood outside, and before long, Kyle pulled up. She got into the passenger side. He looked at her quizzically. She noticed the sweat on his forehead and a strange look in his eyes.

"Are you okay?" she asked.

"Yes," he smiled and nodded. "Are you?" Concern clouded his eyes. "What's happened?"

Maggie looked down at her hands.

"Let's drive somewhere," he suggested.

He indicated and pulled out onto the empty road. He picked up speed, then turned into a narrow farm lane that snaked up into the North Riding Forest.

"Where are we going?" Maggie asked.

"I know a place up here," he said. He turned onto a dirt track road, and the car bobbed up and down. Small stones flew under the wheels, and dust rose around them in a cloud. Kyle didn't slow down. Maggie looked at him, frowning. His hands were tight on the steering wheel, knuckles white.

"Why are you driving so fast?"

"Oh, sorry." He took his foot off the accelerator, and the car slowed. "I'm just in a rush to get back, that's all." He pulled over to the side of the road and turned the engine off.

"What did you want to talk about?" he asked, turning to her.

There was no delaying it, Maggie thought.

"I'm pregnant," she said, searching his eyes for a response. His face remained blank, devoid of expression. His eyes were cold and hard, his lips set in a tight line. Maggie's heart sank like a stone. She had been afraid of this. A black wave of disappointment swept across her soul. She shook her head slightly and stared out the window.

"What do you think?" she asked in the end, not looking at him.

When he didn't answer, she glanced at him. His head was moving, like he was checking the road. He was jittery, restless. Maggie felt uneasy.

"What's going on? You seem stressed."

He forced himself to relax and sat back in his seat. A forced smile appeared on his lips, before slowly fading.

"Nothing, I'm fine." He passed a hand over his face. She noticed the sheen of sweat on his forehead. His hand shook as he passed a hand through his hair.

"Yes, I didn't expect that. What do you want to do?"

"I asked you," Maggie cried out, unable to hide her frustration. "I want to hear it from your lips. Tell me, please."

His eyes closed, his head drooping forward. "It's not what I want," he whispered. "I told you I wasn't interested in starting a family. Not so soon, anyway."

Maggie felt bitter tears prickle her eyes, and she wiped them away. She had been foolish. What was she thinking? She had to do this on her own. Luckily, she had her parents. As hard as this would be, she would have to make it without Kyle.

"Just take me back home," she said.

Kyle glanced at her, then nodded. He started the car and began driving down the dirt track. Maggie couldn't see anything but dense woods on either side, and the car wobbled on the track.

She knew they had to go in the opposite direction to hit the main road. "Where are we going?"

"There's a shortcut up ahead," Kyle said. His eyes were fixed on the road, and there was something different about him—a wild look in his eyes, and a hardness in the angle of his jaw. Maggie hadn't seen it before, and it scared her.

She pulled out her phone and saw she had a message. It was from Rizwan.

"We've got Matt," Rizwan had written. "There's an APB out for Edward Warren, the school psychologist. He abducted him. He's driving a black Honda, and he might be on the A170. We've blocked the road in both directions. If you see a black Honda, let us know. How are you?"

Maggie put the phone down slowly, panic suddenly swelling in her chest. She gasped, trying to force air into her lungs.

Edward Warren… Edward was Kyle's middle name. That's what he told her. He had told her he liked to be called Kyle.

When she visited his house, his mother called him Ed. That's when she knew his real name. but she had kept calling him Kyle, and the name stuck. And Warren was definitely his last name. She remembered seeing a bill on the table in the hallway. It was for Edna Warren, his mother.

She had never seen his ID. Never seen his driving licence or passport.

Could it be... No, surely there was a mistake.

Breath shaking, heart pounding painfully, she looked at Kyle. "Take me back home, now. Turn the car around."

He didn't answer. Instead, he increased the speed slightly.

Maggie gasped, nausea pulling at her belly, rising up her throat. "What are you doing? Kyle?"

He remained silent, face set in stone. Maggie stared at him, aghast. “Or are you Edward Warren? The psychologist at St Bede’s school.”

She saw his jaws harden, and his nostrils flared. His hands gripped the steering wheel harder.

A wave of cold ice was claiming Maggie’s body, turning it numb.

She gasped. "It was you? You abducted that boy?"

Kyle’s face went rigid, and his whole body started to shake. He turned to look at Maggie, and she shrank back, scared by the ferocious look on his face.

"Shut up," he snarled. He floored the accelerator, and her head banged against the window as the car shot down the dirt track.

Want to read more? Book 4. **The Broken Souls** - *is out soon!*

Printed in Great Britain
by Amazon

61180040R00201